1. 1 7. 9

ALSO BY MARK SIMON SMITH

Sir Nathan and the Quest
for Queen Gobbledeegook

Sir Nathan and the
Troublesome Task

# SIR NATHAN

## and the

# CLAMMY

## CALAMITY

### by

## Mark Simon Smith

Sir Nathan and the Clammy Calamity
by Mark Simon Smith

Published by Mark Simon Smith
Cover art and Interior Illustrations by
Derek K. Gebler

ISBN 978-1483978031

author website: SomewhatSillyStory.com
author contact: Mark@SomewhatSillyStory.com

Available as an E-book on Amazon.com,
BarnesAndNoble.com, and Smashwords.com.

For Mariska,
the Hero's
very own
guardian angel

## ACKNOWLEDGMENTS

There are a lot of people cheering
me on as I continue on this
nutty writing adventure.

A big Mariskatanian thank-you to
Deb, Michael, Rose and Catherine
for their editing work.
And the biggest thank you
to all my family and friends –
your encouragement has
gone a long way.

# PART I

The land of Mariskatania was a beautiful place. A wonderful place. Sometimes it was even a magical place. And, on this day, it also happened to be a quiet place.

That was unusual.

For a change, no one was missing. No one had been kidnapped. There were absolutely zero giants stomping around the place, snatching people up and using them as dolls. There wasn't a single dragon sneaking past the Royal Palace, hoping to avoid notice as it snuck over to the candy shop for a treat.

It was just nice and quiet.

The Jubb Jubb Trees filled the land with brightness, the bark of each tree different from the next, indicating the color of the wood underneath. Their cotton-puff tops swayed gently in the comfortable summer breeze. In the open spaces amongst the trees, the people of Mariskatania flew kites and ate picnics with kite-shaped sandwiches and played games (most of which involved kite-flying, kite-building, or answering kite-themed trivia questions). In the nearby fields, the Licorice Sheep stood placidly in the afternoon sun, chewing on lush, green grass and working very hard to grow their delicious coats of licorice.

It was simply a peaceful, quiet, wonderful day in which it seemed nothing could possibly go wrong.

"This sure is a quiet and wonderful day," said a farmer to his field hand as he took a break from his chores to take a drink of water.

"Yep," answered the field hand, "peaceful, too."

"Yep."

The farmer leaned on his pitchfork and took a long, slow look at the world around him. To his left, a young Licorice Lamb pranced and kicked in the sweet grass while her mother stared at nothing, concentrating on chewing her cud. To his right, beyond a fence built from the colorful boards that were so easily harvested from any Jubb Jubb Tree, he could see a large gathering of people from the nearby town engaged in a kite-flying contest. Dozens of colorful kites danced in the bright, blue sky.

"Yep," he said again. "On a day like this, it just seems as if there's absolutely nothing that could possibly go wrong."

"Yep," agreed the field hand, taking his own long look around. "Except for that."

The farmer looked to where the hired farmhand was pointing and saw the baby lamb had tipped over and was lying on her back, looking sad and confused.

"Well," said the farmer, chuckling softly. "I don't think we need to worry too much about that. She's just a young lamb, after all, and still learning to walk."

"Just wait," said the farmhand.

The farmer looked back and forth, between his employee and the young sheep. He didn't see what all the fuss was about. *All* young critters were prone to occasionally tipping over every now and then. It happened when they were still growing into their wobbly legs and knobby knees. There wasn't anything unusual about that. Certainly it wasn't anything the farmer would categorize as "going wrong."

The lamb climbed clumsily to her feet and looked cautiously around. Her mother stood there, silently, unmoving except for her lower jaw as it chewed another mouthful of grass. The lamb took a cautious step, then another, and finally decided everything was okay and started to scamper around again.

Seven steps later, she suddenly popped up into the air like the last seed of Sodapopcorn flying out of a hot pan. The farmer's eyebrows shot up in surprise.

"Now, what do you reckon caused her to do a thing like that?"

The field hand simply shrugged. "I don't know, but it's the fourth time she's done it."

About this, the hired worker was wrong. It was actually the *fifth* time, with each unexpected pop bouncing the lamb higher than the last. The farmhand went back to raking up the Licorice Sheep droppings, which were just as disgusting as they sounded, while the farmer kept watching the lamb.

Every time the little thing would convince herself everything was okay, she'd get to her feet and take a few careful steps only to unexpectedly bounce up into the air again. Three feet, four feet, five. She kept bouncing higher and higher. After a bit, the farmer wondered if maybe he wasn't bouncing, too.

"Hey, Herkimer," he called out to his farmhand as the lamb popped up in the air behind him, "does it look to you like I'm bouncing?"

"Nope," said the farmhand slowly, not even pausing to look up at his boss. Bouncing sheep were one thing, but the piles of doo-doo weren't going to pick themselves up.

"There!" cried the farmer, pointing at nothing in particular. "It happened again!"

"Right," agreed the field hand in a tone that clearly meant he didn't.

The farmer spun slowly in a circle, gazing all around him. He held his pitchfork in front of his chest with both hands as if to use it as a shield against bouncing sheep. Off to the side, the lamb had given up on trying to walk at all and simply lay where she had fallen, giant tears rolling down her cheeks and soaking into her licorice fur. Her mother rolled her eyes, thinking about all the cud chewing she had to get done and wondering where she was going to get the time if she kept getting interrupted over every little thing.

"Freeze!" hissed the farmer. "It happened again!"

Despite thinking his boss had become completely goofy in the brain, the farmhand froze. The farmer was still his boss, after all, and let the field hand eat all the licorice he could stomach as a treat. However, he had just stepped into a particularly large pile of fresh, steaming sheep droppings – freezing in place was the last thing he wanted to do.

A lot of people thought Licorice Sheep droppings were where jelly beans came from, but they were wrong. Jelly beans came from a source *way* more disgusting, which is why the jelly bean farmers always pointed to something off in the distance with a fake, surprised look on their face whenever the subject came up and then ran away. They knew if the truth were ever found out, jelly bean sales would plummet.

Looking about suspiciously, the farmer whispered, "Yep, I'm pretty sure I just bounced again. That's odd ... I don't remember eating anything that would cause me to bounce like that. What do you suppose would cause such a thing?"

Still frozen in place, his boot becoming unspeakably soiled from the pile of used sheep food, the field hand considered the question for a few long, quiet moments. In the time it took him to answer, both he and the farmer bounced off the ground a total of three times, each one higher than the last.

"Well," the field hand said at last, "I reckon it

could be several things. It could be a ground quake. You see, way far down in the ground, way beneath our feet at least ... oh ... ten or maybe even twenty feet, there's these great big plates. But I don't mean nuthin' like no dinner plates. No sir, these are giant plates of rock and they sorts of rubs together like a Grasspopper rubbin' its hind legs together like they do to make that poppin' sound and then —"

"I know what a ground quake is, you dolt!" snapped the farmer. He bounced again, noticing that now just about every animal on the farm was bouncing along with him. "If it were a ground quake, we wouldn't be bouncing, we'd be shaking!"

"Oh. All right then," said the field hand, scratching his head. "Well, perhaps it's because of that Hero fellow they've got over there, what works in the Royal Palace. You know how big and powerful he is. Perhaps he's out, smashing some enemies with that there magical sword of his. I reckon that would make a particularly large, loud thump that could be bouncing us all up in the air."

The farmer (and everyone else) bounced again while he thought this over. It was getting to be that he rose so far in the air with each new bounce, pretty soon he'd have to get a ladder to get back down.

"You know, you're right about that Hero and his mighty sword. But we'd have heard the bells ringing in the Palace Tower if there was some evil enemy that needed dealing with. That's how they always call the Hero whenever there's trouble afoot, but them bells haven't dinged a single dong."

They were both quiet as they thought about it

some more.

*Bounce ... bounce ... bounce ...*

The mother Licorice Sheep had gotten so fed up with how the bouncing interrupted her cud chewing that she finally just tied herself to a Produce Tree so she could get on with her work.

"Well, then, if it's not any of that stuff," said the field hand, "then I reckon it's that there massive whale walking up the road what's causing all the fuss."

The farmer was about to yell at his field hand for such a ridiculous suggestion when he, too, saw the whale. It was a monster of a creature, so big the farmer would have a difficult time fitting it into his largest barn. And as sure as Snapperjack Corn, the creature was walking up the road, its massive footsteps shaking the ground beneath their feet and flinging everyone (everyone not tied down, that is) high into the air with each heavy footstep.

Most people would tell you whales can't walk, and they'd be right. They can't. But, there was at least one whale in the land who was smart enough to have invented and built a heavy, massive walking apparatus. The device looked like a spider's legs crossed with a heavy wagon, but much, much bigger, and the whale rode atop it as comfortably as the farmer road his wagon into town every Higgledee Piggledee Eve.

The combined weight of the huge contraption and the whale's enormous body caused each and every footstep to shake the ground hard enough to bounce every nearby thing high into the air.

At this rate, it was really going to be difficult for

the farmer to get the day's chores finished.

"Pardon me," said the whale, stomping to a halt alongside the farmer and his worker. The creature's voice was deep, deeper than the biggest bell in the Palace Tower. The heavy vibrations from it caused one of the farmer's teeth, the one way in back he could never brush very well, to ache. "Would you be so kind as to point me in the direction of the Royal Palace."

The farmer simply pointed down the road in the direction the whale was headed. He was too thankful the heavy bouncing had come to a stop to even think about how absurd it was that a talking whale was walking past his fields.

"Thank you very much," said the whale, a relieved look crossing his enormous face. "I've been wandering for hours and was starting to think I had gone and gotten *really* lost. Already wasted half the day and I've got so much to do, what with taking over the entire world and everything. You just wouldn't believe how much work it is, being an evil villain and all."

The farmer and the field hand just stared at the whale, blank looks on their faces. Their minds were used to simple things, like how often to water the Wobble Melon patch and knowing just how to not accidentally step in a steaming pile of Licorice Sheep doo-doo. The sight of the whale walking by had so clogged up their thinking that words like "taking over the entire world" and "evil villain" went by completely unnoticed.

Starting to feel uncomfortable from all the stares their eyes were giving him, and all the silence their

tongues were giving him, the whale cleared his throat and mumbled his good-byes. Slowly and steadily, he marched off in the direction the farmer had pointed and, bit by bit, the bouncing of the farmer, the field hand, and all the farm critters subsided.

A long time went by with the farmer and his worker just staring at where the whale had disappeared down the dusty road. They could just barely hear the distant thump, thump, thump of his footsteps.

"Say," said the farmer slowly, "did anything about that seem particularly odd to you?"

"What ... the fact that a whale, out of water, stomping around the land on a mechanical contraption, came by asking us for directions to the Royal Palace?" asked the field hand, leaning on his pitchfork and wiping his forehead with a hanky he pulled from a back pocket.

"Yeah, that."

The field hand thought about it for a moment.

"Well ... yes, now that you mention it, there was something odd."

"Oh, yeah? What?"

"It was that you told him to keep on going the way he was headed, when everyone knows that it's faster to get to the Royal Palace by taking the path behind Old Man Hornbacher's farm."

\* \* \* \* \*

The Royal Palace was smack dab in the middle of the capital city of Mariskatania. It was a good building, not too big and not too small, built from a combination of stone and the colorful wood of the land's plentiful Jubb Jubb Trees.

The Mariskatanian countryside was filled to overflowing with the wondrous trees, which grew straight and tall, with no branches whatsoever, and their tops were covered in a giant, cottony puff instead of leaves. They grew quickly and were easy to harvest for materials. All one had to do was pull a golden ring located at the bottom of every tree and it would fall right over. The smooth, colorful bark was easily removed in one enormous piece, yielding a giant pile of waterproof fabric. The puffy tops were rolled away and used for mattress padding and other comfy things, leaving only the smooth, cylindrical trunk behind.

Kick a fallen Jubb Jubb Tree in the exact right spot and it fell apart into an easy-to-sort pile of lumber, ready for construction. The boards were straight and true and brightly colored the same as their bark. That made it easy for people building a blue house to get more blue boards, if they so desired. Nothing ruined the mood of a Mariskatanian faster then accidentally nailing a red board to a blue house.

The palace was the home of Queen Gobbledeegook, the fair and wise ruler of Mariskatania. From her comfy throne in the Big Comfy Chair Room, she met with the citizens of the land and made the big, important decisions that kept Mariskatania the wonderful place that it was.

She made important decisions about taxes. She made important decisions about laws. She made important decisions about what to serve for dessert at the Higgledee Piggledee Eve Ball (the fanciest and most special event of the year during which everyone dressed up as their favorite kite-maker and went around talking like a pirate).

The Queen's daughter, Princess Abbey, also lived in the palace, along with the Queen's adopted twin sons (who used to be giants, but that was a long time ago and no one really held it against them anymore). Everyone found the young twins to be a delightful addition to the royal family.

Everyone, that is, except the Hero.

Sir Nathan, knight and appointed Hero of Mariskatania, was known for his honor and braveness and for protecting Mariskatania against countless dangers. Back when the twins were still giants, they had kidnapped the Queen and Sir Nathan had fearlessly rescued her despite the fact the giants had stepped on him a time or two.

And, once the giants had been magically converted into a more normal size and adopted by the Queen, they too had gone missing and Sir Nathan had gone through great peril to bring them home after they had been kidnapped by a giant crab.

There was even the time Sir Nathan had been swallowed alive by the Zero-Headed Meeko Monster while helping Princess Abbey with her homework.

So it was obvious Sir Nathan was very noble and kind since he'd go through so much trouble to help so many people. But when it came to the Royal Twins, he was often surprised at how much he disliked them.

Perhaps it was because his honor wouldn't let him forget they were once marauding giants, stomping through the land and causing mischief. Or, more likely, it was because the twins were constantly pulling pranks on the Hero without ever getting caught.

When Sir Nathan had complained to the Queen about how they had switched all of his left socks with his right ones, the Queen hadn't believed him.

When he had informed her that the twins had glued him to the ceiling of the Breaking Fast room just before it was unbolted from the palace and moved to the storage sheds to make room for the Whining and Dining room, the Queen had told him he was being ridiculous.

When the Hero had thrown a very large tantrum because the twins had snuck a sleeping potion into his Smooshelberry milkshake and then, after he had fallen into a deep slumber, nailed him inside a crate and shipped him off to the distant country of New New Fubwubble (the old New Fubwubble had accidentally been built on the back of a massive dragon and had never been seen again after the beast had flown south for the winter), Queen Gobbledeegook had yelled at him for telling lies and sent him to his room for missing a month of work without an excuse.

So when the Hobnobber Squirrel crept into Sir Nathan's room while he was taking his afternoon nap, the Hero barely stirred, figuring it was just the twins trying to pull yet another prank.

"If you two don't get out of my room right now," he mumbled tiredly from his bed without even opening his eyes, "I'm going to smite you into the middle of next week!"

The Hobnobber Squirrel just stopped where it stood. It clearly wasn't expecting this sort of reaction if it was caught. Normally, Hobnobber Squirrels weren't known for sneaking around palaces. They were typically found scampering through the branches of Huckle Nut Trees, looking for nuts to eat, which was a very odd thing since Huckle Nuts were extremely poisonous to them. Maybe that was why there were so very few of the fuzzy, blue creatures to be found.

However, this wasn't a typical Hobnobber Squirrel.

Perched on its tiny, cute skull was a very odd-looking thing. It was a helmet, but not like one ever seen before, especially one worn by a squirrel. It was oddly shaped and so big it should have just fallen off from its own massive weight. It was covered in tiny, little gears and pulleys, with a blinking light here and there, and tiny puffs of steam coming out of the top.

If the squirrel thought there was anything odd about the fact that it was wearing a massive helmet, it showed no sign.

Seeing the Hero had fallen back to sleep, the fuzzy creature carefully moved further into the room, pulling a large, cloth sack behind it. Checking once more to be sure Sir Nathan was asleep, it tip-toed over to where the Hero kept all of his hero supplies when not in use. From inside the cloth sack the rodent pulled a helmet very similar to its own, but big enough for a human. Quietly, the squirrel replaced Sir Nathan's regular helmet with the strange new one. It then stuffed the stolen helm into the sack and snuck quietly back out of the room.

Had the Hero been awake and paying attention, he would have been very surprised to see the squirrel walk right past a bowl of Huckle Nuts kept on hand for when his horse, Tupolev, was around. Ever since Sir Nathan's steed had been temporarily changed into a Hobnobber Squirrel (a story the horse angrily denied), Tupolev had an insatiable craving for the nuts. However, the squirrel walked right past them without so much as a twitch of its whiskers.

The squirrel simply had no desire for the nuts. There was no room in its tiny mind for anything other than seeing to it that every wish of its master was carried out. The helmet on its head saw to that. It was an impressive contraption that accomplished with mechanical bits and pieces what others could only do using magic. For powerful spell-casters, such as the Warlock Christofer or the Prestidigitator Porter (magicians that ran Mariskatania's Royal Institute of Hocus Pocus), controlling the mind of a simple creature like a Hobnobber Squirrel would have been easy. Most any student at the Institute should have been capable of such a trick by their second year of schooling.

Without magic, however, about the only way you could get a Hobnobber Squirrel to ignore a Huckle Nut was to threaten it with a stick. If the stick happened to have an angry dragon at one end, that worked even better. But even then, odds are the squirrel would just scamper up the stick, bite you (and the dragon) on the nose and scamper off with the nut.

The odd helmet on its head was a mechanical masterpiece, the likes of which had never before been seen in the land of Mariskatania. It completely drained all of the squirrel's own thoughts and replaced them with the wishes of its master. Powered by strange energies derived from sea water, the helmet's control over the squirrel was unbreakable. Whenever a stray hankering for Huckle Nuts would appear, like a barely seen shape in the fog, the normal, calm rotation of the helmet's gears and cogs and pulleys would be replaced by spinning and whirring fast enough to be a blur. In a flash, the stray, unwanted thought would be washed away like a Smooshelberry stain and replaced with happy, warm thoughts about carrying out its master's commands.

With a satisfied twitch of its tail at the thought of a job well done, the squirrel scampered unnoticed down the hallway, dragging Sir Nathan's helmet with it.

\* \* \* \* \*

Queen Gobbledeegook sat on the floor next to the Big Comfy Chair that was really the only piece of furniture in the Big Comfy Chair Room. This room was exactly what it sounded like; a room with a large, comfortable chair in it. The ceiling rose high above her head, held aloft by flowing spans of Jubb Jubb wood. Stained glass windows, set in both the walls and ceiling, flooded the room in a rainbow of colored shafts and small particles of dust danced like tiny jewels in the air.

The Big Comfy Chair Room was the biggest in the palace, almost as long as the palace itself. The Big Comfy Chair sat at one end of the room on a small raised platform. It was a tall seat, and wide, like a small couch, and it was what Queen Gobbledeegook used for a throne. The room used to be called the This Ugly Chair Is Making My Butt Fall Asleep Room until the queen realized, as ruler of the land, she could have whatever throne she wanted.

The old throne was quietly chopped into tiny bits and dumped into the furnace.

The Big Comfy Chair was covered in a soft fabric knit from the finest Jubb Jubb fluff, all dyed emerald green. The wall behind the Chair was covered in draped, red, velvety fabric and a giant $M$ for Mariskatania, carved from the rarest Jubb Jubb wood, emblazoned the middle. While most Jubb Jubb wood was red, blue, yellow, green and all those standard assorted colors, a few rare trees were very different. They grew wood that shone like the brightest gold and silver and copper. The giant $M$, carved to look like a winged dragon, was made of all three of these rare woods and shone in the streaming sunlight.

Curiously enough, the hills of Mariskatania were filled almost to overflowing with rich pockets of gold and silver and copper, but since no one had ever invented a shovel, it all remained hidden away underground.

It had been a long day for the Queen, listening to the questions, concerns, and complaints of the citizens of Mariskatania and she was tired. It hadn't helped matters any that over half of the people coming to see her that day were only there to complain about a whale stomping through their gardens, lost and asking for directions.

"Do you realize how difficult it is to keep a straight face when you're listening to the thirteenth complaint in a row about a whale squishing an entire patch of Punkolanterns?" she asked the Chief Butler.

Standing at attention near the Queen, the Chief Butler nodded in understanding. He was dressed in his red and white striped uniform, with his ceremonial blue and yellow checkered hat perched on his bald head. It was his duty to take care of the small things in the Royal Palace in order to free up the Queen's time for the important stuff (like choosing the official candy flavor of the week). He had stood solemnly by while citizen after citizen had come before the Queen and complained about the whale. Not once had he smiled or snickered or chuckled at the absurdity of the very idea of a whale somehow walking through the land. However, more than once, he had to remind the Junior Butlers in the room to keep quiet. Usually, a stern glance from the Chief Butler was more than enough to get the job done.

There was a rumor in the palace about a Junior Butler who had continued to have loud, distracting hiccups during one of the Queen's speeches, even after the Chief Butler had given him two glances, a glare, and a meaningful throat-clearing. According to the rumor, the Chief Butler had punished the hiccuping Junior Butler by having the Prestidigitator Porter turn him into a cockroach, which the Chief Butler kept in a small cage and fed garbage. It was either that, or the Junior Butler was sent to bed without dessert. No one was really sure, but both stories sounded too terrible to think about.

At least the Chief Butler hadn't had to deal with Sir Nathan lately and all the problems the Hero seemed to cause. The knight was known for acting on impulse, without really thinking things through very carefully. He'd charge through the castle, waving his massive Sword of Power in the air and yelling loudly about how naughty evil was, just because the Queen had mentioned a slight chill in the air or had pointed out she had a slight headache.

The Hero's magical sword was a mighty weapon, awarded to Sir Nathan when he had been appointed Hero of the land. But the problem was the sword was a little too long for Sir Nathan. Or, maybe Sir Nathan was a little too short for the sword. Oddly enough, no one had really noticed it before. Because he ran around shouting about giving evil a good kick in the teeth all the time, he appeared to be filled with all sorts of tall-ness. But in reality, Sir Nathan was no taller than Princess Abbey and Princess Abbey was no taller than any princess ever needed to be, which wasn't very tall at all.

This meant when the Hero carried the long sword in its special sheath on his back, its magically sharpened tip dragged on the floor, carving a deep furrow wherever he went. No material was impervious to the impossibly sharp weapon. Wood, stone, metal – all were cut as easily as if they were made of marshmallow fluff. The problem had become so bad, the Chief Butler had formed a group of repair specialists whose only job was to go around fixing the deep grooves the Hero carved into the floor.

One trick the Chief Butler had learned to use whenever the Hero was walking by, his dragging sword leaving a gouged trail behind him, was to point behind Sir Nathan and shout, "Look! Evil!"

Sir Nathan couldn't resist whirling about, whipping the sword out of its sheath and charging away, screaming about smiting. That worked most of the time and actually prevented quite a bit of damage to the floors. Unfortunately, it had the unintended affect of a dramatic increase in the number of gouged walls, chopped doorways, and hacked-apart lanterns that had been doing nothing more evil than being in the wrong place at the wrong time as the Hero came charging down the hallway, slicing at anything that got in his way.

As the Queen leaned back against the Big Comfy Chair, closing her eyes for a momentary rest, the Chief Butler couldn't resist looking down at the most recent fix to the room's floor. The floor repair specialists were getting quite good at their job and he could barely see the spot where the Hero had chopped a deep hole one day when he had mistaken a dropped bit of crumpled paper for the white, fluffy tail of a Blabbity Rabbit.

"Tell me, Sir Nathan," the Queen had asked the

Hero in a tired voice after the incident, "why would you think it necessary to attack a rabbit?"

The Hero had still been standing over the hole in the floor as if he still wasn't completely convinced it wasn't a Blabbity Rabbit he had seen. "Well, Your Highness, since the Big Comfy Chair room is where you take care of all your important, official queen-stuff, that rabbit would have heard all sorts of secret, hush-hush, important queen-secrets. *Everyone* knows that a Blabbity Rabbit can't keep a secret. The pest would have hopped out of here and straight to our enemies and blabbed to them about everything it had heard. I *had* to smite it!"

"You had to smite ... the rabbit that wasn't there in the first place?"

The Hero looked unsure of himself. He poked at the hole with the tip of his sword. "Well ... I had to smite the rabbit that *might* have been there. You can never be too safe."

Though the memory of that day still pained him, the Chief Butler nodded with approval at the repair job. He also allowed himself a tiny sigh of satisfaction since it had been almost two whole weeks since the Hero had done anything foolish. The Chief Butler felt strongly that things were finally going to be quiet for a good long time. Maybe now he could take that vacation he had been thinking of.

His peaceful thoughts were interrupted by a massive boom coming from down the hall. The Chief Butler could feel the powerful shockwaves of the thuds vibrating through the floor. *Boom! Boom!* The sound grew louder and louder.

Again and again, the deafening bangs echoed through the palace. Small cracks appeared in the stone walls and a fine dust drifted down from the ceiling. The Chief Butler rushed to the Queen and was pulling her to her feet, ready to rush her to safety when a Junior Butler ran into the room. He was out of breath and his eyes were wide with the shock of what he had seen.

"There's a ... there's a ...," gasped the Junior Butler, panting heavily. "Sir, there's a whale at the door!"

"A what?!"

"A whale! He's banging on the front gate, demanding to see the Queen!"

The Chief Butler turned to Queen Gobbledeegook and grabbed her by the arm, something he never would have dared to do unless he felt she was in terrible danger. "Your Majesty, we have to get you out of here at once! We must get you to safety before this intruder gets into the palace and —"

But before he could finish, there was a deafening crash of breaking wood and stone. A thick, choking cloud of dust rolled down the hallway from the direction of the front gate and poured into the Big Comfy Chair Room. The shafts of sunlight pouring in through the stained glass windows cast waves of color over the spreading cloud.

"Too late," whispered the Junior Butler.

His eyes watering, his throat burning from the dust, the Chief Butler pulled the Queen up onto the low stage and pushed her down behind the Big

Comfy Chair. He motioned for the Junior Butlers to form a protective ring around her and then did the bravest thing he had ever done in his life by walking slowly towards the doorway.

It was as if the dust cloud had muffled all the sound in the world. After the deafening booms, the silence seemed to be filled with unseen threats. The Chief Butler could barely hear his own footsteps over the sound of his heart pounding in his ears. His eyes watering from the irritation of the dust, he reached the open doorway and cautiously stuck his head out into the hallway. The grey cloud prevented him from seeing anything at all. The entire Foul-Tempered Army of Mungsquat could have been hiding in the hall and he wouldn't have been able to tell.

He felt, more than heard, the thud that suddenly broke the silence. It was so deep and low, it travelled through the stone of the palace floors and into his body through his feet. There was another, then another. The thuds were different than the booms at the front gate. They had a slow, deliberate pace to them. *Thud, thud, thud.* The Chief Butler could feel the source of the sound growing closer, as well as hear it growing louder.

Something was walking down the hallway towards the Big Comfy Chair Room. Something big.

"Where is that dratted Hero when we need him?" spat the Chief Butler before he could stop himself. He never thought he'd hear those words coming out of his mouth.

The thuds were footsteps and they were coming

closer. The Chief Butler found himself retreating from the doorway without thinking about it. He stopped when his heels bumped up against the low stage upon which sat the Big Comfy Chair.

The dust was finally settling somewhat, leaving everything and everyone covered with a fine layer of white grit. The Chief Butler plucked a polka-dot handkerchief from his back pocket and quickly wiped his eyes. Just then, he saw a shadow move in the hallway. The shadow was big, big enough to account for the loud footsteps.

Then he heard a voice. It was a deep voice, made by a mouth and tongue and vocal chords so big, so massive, the words had a bigness of their own. Had the words said something like, "Prepare to meet your doom," the Chief Butler was pretty sure he would have fainted with fear, right then and there.

But the words didn't say anything nearly so terrifying. What they did say was, "Did those guards say fourth door on the left, or fifth? Oh, poop, I hope I'm not lost."

What the Chief Butler saw next was something terribly odd. Walking down the hallway, as calmly as if on one of the daily guided tours of the palace, was a whale. A genuine, normally-swimming-in-water whale. It was so big, it barely fit in the palace hallway even though the passageway was quite large. The Chief Butler wasn't quite sure which was more odd – the fact that the whale was in the palace or the bizarre contraption it was walking around on.

The device was a massive frame, built from thick timbers and metal girders, large enough and strong enough to hold the whale's enormous weight. His tail was held up by parts that looked cobbled together from the modified bits of a wagon. Underneath the whale's belly, the frame sprouted three sets of legs that reminded the Chief Butler of a spider's. The front pair of legs ended in a set of enormous, metal hands the whale seemed able to control and the rest of the legs ended in solid clawed feet, like those of a bird.

The doorway filled with the great, grey side of the whale, blocking the exit as effectively as any gate. In the middle of it all was a single, large eye, peering unblinkingly into the room.

"Oh!" said the whale, sounding relieved. "There you are! I was starting to worry that I was completely turned around and mixed up. Just give me one second to get organized here, won't you?"

As the Chief Butler and the Queen and all the Junior Butlers looked on in stunned silence, the whale used one of the metal hands to reach up and tear the doorway apart as easily as a child knocked down a tower of toy blocks. Stone and wood ripped apart effortlessly and soon there was a hole large enough for the whale to walk through. Its mechanical feet thudded across the floor as it walked into the room, chipping and cracking the stone. The Chief Butler couldn't help thinking about how busy the floor repair specialists were going to be afterwards.

Staring at the stunned humans, the whale stopped in front of the Big Comfy Chair. His massive body filled most of the room and the Chief Butler was pretty sure there was still a bit of tail out in the hallway yet. The sheer size of the creature was intimidating enough without the addition of the strange metal limbs that could easily rip apart stone walls.

For a long while, the whale did nothing but stare at the group of dust-covered humans. Eventually he looked at the Chief Butler and said in a somewhat puzzled voice, "You know, for a queen, you kind of look like a man."

The Chief Butler seethed and spluttered with rage. How dare the whale say the Queen was manly? The Junior Butlers sucked in their breath at the insult. Whale or not, they were pretty sure the Chief Butler wouldn't stand for anyone or anything calling their Queen names.

Just as the Chief Butler was about to tell the whale a thing or two, Queen Gobbledeegook stepped out from behind the Big Comfy Chair. Though covered with dust and more than a little shocked at the presence of such a large beast in her throne room, there was no mistaking her nobility and honor.

"He is not the Queen," she said in an icy tone, gesturing at the Chief Butler. "I am. I am Queen Gobbledeegook, ruler of all Mariskatania."

"Oh. Well, that makes more sense then. I was going to say, it didn't seem very queen-like to be in bad need of a shave."

The Queen stared at the whale, her hands on her hips. The Chief Butler recognized the look on her face. She normally looked like that just before she was about to yell at the Hero for doing something stupid.

The anger was audible in her voice as she said in barely controlled tones, "Is there something you wanted or were you just going to smash your way into my palace and then stare at me?"

"What?" The whale was caught a little bit off guard. No one, not even a villain, could stand in front of a true queen without being thrown off at least a little bit, especially when she was mad. "Oh, right."

He cleared his throat. The deep noise vibrated the Chief Butler's skull, causing his vision to temporarily blur.

"Hear me now, oh wretched humans!" said the whale, starting what was clearly a well-practiced speech. "Your kind has made a real mess of things, they most surely have! For too long, your pollution has fouled the waters of the creeks. The polluted creeks flow into the streams, the streams flow into the rivers and eventually, all rivers flow into the sea!"

He paused to make sure he had the Queen's attention. The glare on her face was almost enough to get him to stop, right then and there, and turn around and leave.

He cleared his throat once more. He had been planning this day for a long time and couldn't turn back now.

"So ... what I'm saying is, all the pollution that you dump into the creeks eventually ends up in the sea."

"Yes, I do believe we all got that," said the Queen impatiently. "Is there more?"

"What? Yes, of course there's more! Much

more! Much, much more!"

There was a long, uncomfortable pause.

"Well, unless you want us to guess what the rest of your speech is, I suggest you get on with it then."

"Yes! Right!" The whale was finding this much more difficult than he had thought it would be. Perhaps he should have practiced on a farmer or kite-maker before marching off and confronting a genuine queen. "So, we've established that all the pollution is making its way to the sea, then, have we?"

The Queen motioned impatiently for him to continue.

"Seeing as how there is no way for the inhabitants of the sea to get their garbage to flow to the land ... since, you know, there aren't any rivers flowing backwards out of the sea and all that ... I, Kale the Whale, have decided to declare war! No more shall humans create a mess of the world! No more shall their laziness threaten the health of the waters! No more .... uh ... no more ... oh blast!"

Obviously frustrated, the whale used one of his mechanical hands to reach back and fish around on the back-end of his mechanical transportation. His enormous tongue stuck out of one side of his mouth in concentration as he rummaged around, looking for something.

"A-ha!" Pinched precariously in the massive, metal hand, the whale pulled out a stack of note cards. He delicately flipped through them until he found the one he was looking for.

"I knew it would be a good idea to write this down," he muttered to himself. Then, continuing on in his loud, speech voice, he said, "No more will humans do a really good job of messing things up, which is to say, they're doing a really *bad* job of keeping things clean! Those days are over! From now on I, Kale the Whale, claim *all* the lands as belonging to the Empire of the Waters! From this day forth, your land shall be mine, submerged forever, so that the fishes and whales and sharks and guppies and octopusesses and other creatures of the waters may come and go as they like and humans shall pollute the sea no more!"

Through his whole speech, the Queen's anger grew and grew. She wasn't about to let anyone threaten her citizens and get away with it. She definitely wasn't about to let anyone threaten *all* the lands *everywhere* with being submerged. And she most definitely wasn't about to let anyone smash their way into her home and leave without cleaning up their mess first.

It was clear to her this whale hadn't done his homework, for if he had, he would have known all about Sir Nathan, the Hero of Mariskatania. Sir Nathan had protected the land from the Invisible Shoe-Eating Monster of Podiatruss. He had easily fought off the Drooling Seven-Tailed Serpent of Zert. And he'd had no problem at all disposing of the Flatulent Bean Gobbler of Flapdoodle. Taking care of a single whale on a weird walking contraption wasn't going to be any problem at all.

"Mr. Kale the Whale, there are a few things you ought to know," said the Queen quietly and calmly, but with a menacing undertone to her voice, like a dangerous school of Nipper Fish swimming just beneath the surface of a calm pond. "We here in Mariskatania are very thorough at cleaning up and recycling after ourselves. We have won the Tillie J. Blummer Award for Cleanest Lakes, Rivers, and Bathrooms three years in a row! Also, I will not stand for anyone ... *anyone* ... tearing a hole through the walls of my home and standing there lecturing me! I will not tolerate rude behavior! And lastly, you didn't take into account that the citizens and land of Mariskatania are protected by Sir Nathan, a great and true hero. I'm sure he will have no problem knocking your whale-sized ego down a size or two!"

The Queen found herself disappointed to see the whale didn't seem concerned in the slightest when she brought up the Hero. In fact, he even seemed to smile a little bit at the mention of Sir Nathan's name. Was there something she was missing?

Shrugging off her growing doubt, the Queen forced herself to be calm and unworried. For all his faults, the Hero was truly heroic. That was why he got to be called the Hero. Otherwise he would have been called That Guy With The Really Long Sword. He had yet to fail the people of Mariskatania in any way, other than in how he was slowly hacking the palace apart. He had always come to their aid in the past and there was no reason to think he should fail today, when his Queen and country once again needed him.

In a quiet, yet carrying voice, she said, "Summon the Hero."

Instantly, as if they had been waiting to be called upon, the giant bells in the Palace Tower rang out loud and clear. Their peal spread across the land, signaling that danger had once again reared its ugly head and the Hero was needed.

The Chief Butler couldn't stifle the groan that escaped from his lips. In the past, summoning the Hero had meant gouged floors and mass confusion. But now, with the massive whale not three feet away and staring at them all with an odd, smug look on his face, the Chief Butler quickly changed his mind and decided having the Hero around might not be such a bad thing after all.

\* \* \* \* \*

Not far away, in his own room in the Royal Palace, Sir Nathan lay sleeping in a tangle of bedsheets. His pillow had been knocked to the floor along with his stuffed animal, Blunk. Blunk was a knit PigWiggle, so amazingly crafted he was almost lifelike.

Sir Nathan had been given Blunk as a gift from Mitzy, who was just a little something the Warlock Christofer had whipped together one night when he had been feeling overwhelmed with work and felt he could use an assistant. Instead of making the long trip to the nearest village to see if there was someone he could hire, the Warlock had rummage around in his castle and dug up some unused, mismatched parts lying around and hastily threw them together. Perhaps he would have taken a bit more time had it been a more important project, but really all he needed was someone to help keep the castle clean and run an errand or two.

Once Mitzy started stomping around the place, a very disturbing look on her face, the Warlock wondered if maybe some of the pieces he used to build her were a bit ... not quite fresh. As a result, his new assistant was a bit upsetting to the stomach to behold. She had the sweet face of a little girl, but everything else about her was enough to put a dragon off its lunch.

Despite her oddities, Mitzy was extremely sweet and tender, in her own creepy way. Needless to say, it was best to avoid her hugs, her home-cooked meals, and her offers to clean your room. They all could end in needless bloodshed.

On the other hand, her knitting was second to none and she regularly took home the first place trophy at the Happyfest Hullabaloo Summer Fair. Mitzy could knit a cute little something like Blunk in half an hour, and have enough yarn left over to whip up a scarf or two.

Blunk's button eyes watched as the Hero snored on. Un-hero-like drool ran out of his mouth and down his cheek. When the tower bells rang out, he sat upright with a sudden jolt, the sheets wound around him like an ugly dress.

"The bells!" he cried groggily, his eyes not even open. "I must go! The Queen needs me!"

But, instead of leaping out of bed and flying down the hallway, he merely sat there, groggy and confused. As if to urge him along, the ringing of the bells grew louder and faster. One problem the Hero frequently encountered was his thoughts sometimes got crammed together in his head if they came whizzing along too fast. This was because of the many thumps his head had received in Basic Knight Sword Practice. His brain was having a difficult time handling all the complex things involved in both waking up *and* responding to the tower bells.

"The bells!" he cried again through a massive yawn. Finally, getting all his mental bits and pieces sorted out, he jumped from his bed and immediately crashed to the floor, his feet entangled in the twisted sheets.

"Unhand me you agents of evil!" he cried out, a hand grasping for the Sword of Power standing next to the bed. Thrashing about, he kicked the sheets off and jumped to his feet. For good measure, he grabbed the sword and gave the bedclothes a few solid whacks. The crew in the Royal Laundry had stopped being surprised a long time ago at the condition of Sir Nathan's sheets and blankets.

Once, every single one of the Hero's socks had arrived in the laundry room filled with rocks, which Sir Nathan had claimed were there to keep them from crawling off during the night while he slept.

Faster than seemed possible, he threw on his suit of armor. He had learned from past experience that a Hero that ran around in his underwear all the time wasn't much use to anybody.

"That's funny, I don't remember my helmet being this big," he said as he lifted the device the Hobnobber Squirrel had left behind. "I also don't remember it being covered in gears and pulleys and twirling doodads. But I am a Hero and this is the Hero's room and this helmet is in the Hero's room so therefore it is my helmet!"

Convinced all was as it should be, he plopped

the enormous helmet onto his head and dashed out of the door, swinging his sword and screaming at the top of his lungs about evil and treachery and interrupted naps.

* * * * *

In the Big Comfy Chair Room, the Queen stared unblinkingly at Kale the Whale. The evil villain simply stared back as if expecting something.

"You would have been wise to stay in your waters, Mr. Whale," said the Queen with a scowl. "I think you will find that your rampage here is nearing an end."

"Oh, we shall see about that," said the whale with a deep chuckle. The Queen thought this was the normal thing for a villain to say and so didn't hear the dangerous threat in his words.

At that moment, the Hero charged into the room, running as fast as his little legs could carry him. He charged through the shattered doorway, leaping nimbly over the giant chunks of rubble covering the floor.

"Excuse me," he said politely to the whale, edging around the large villain (who took up most of the room) and rushing to kneel before the Queen. "Your Highness! I have heard the summoning of the bells and come immediately to your aid! Fear not! Evil shall tremble and naughtiness will run and hide, for I shall let nothing threaten the peace of Mariskatania! Just tell me where the evil is and I shall ride forth and smite it immediately!"

Behind the Queen, the Chief Butler heaved a

heavy sigh. As good as he was at protecting the land and its citizens, the Hero wasn't always so good at seeing the nose on his own face, as it were. Or, in this case, at seeing the massive whale on a mechanical walking-gadget filling up most of the Big Comfy Chair Room.

"Sir Nathan," said the Queen with as much patience as she could muster, "the trouble is *behind* you."

"Behind me?! If it is all behind me, then my work here is done! I am glad I could once again save the day!" He swung his sword up in a sharp salute and turned on his heel to leave. If there hadn't been a massive sea creature in his way, he would have run out of the door and it would have taken wasted hours to get him back.

"Wait!" called the Queen, while Sir Nathan squeezed past the whale on the way out. Sir Nathan came running back, dropping to a knee once more, head bowed. "The trouble is *behind you* as in it is *actually* behind you, as in *behind your back*, right this moment!"

The Hero took a moment to puzzle this out. A look of realization blinked onto his face. "Oh! You should have said so! Very well! I shall take care of this evil once and for all, keeping the citizens of Mariskatania safe! Fear not! Nothing shall escape my all-seeing gaze! No creature of evil shall escape my wrath! Not even the tiniest speck of naughtiness will be free of my smiting!"

Again he saluted and turned sharply, then excused himself once more as he stepped politely around the massive, blocking bulk of the villain.

Kale the Whale chuckled again, the deep voice loosening some dust from the cracked ceiling.

It was the Queen's turn to heave a heavy sigh.

"Wait!" the Queen called again, extreme frustration showing in her tired-sounding voice. Again, the Hero turned and rushed back to kneel before the Queen.

"Lsten to me very carefully. I want you to stand up," she said.

Sir Nathan stood up.

"Now, slowly, turn around so that you're facing away from me."

Sir Nathan pivoted sharply on his heel, snapping to attention with his back to the Queen.

"Now ... tell me what you see," the Queen commanded, already pretty sure she wasn't going to like the Hero's answer, whatever it was.

"I see nothing," said Sir Nathan, staring directly at the massive front end of Kale the Whale. The Chief Butler almost choked on his own tongue at the Hero's ridiculous answer. The Queen motioned for him to keep his frustrated spluttering to himself.

"Nothing at all? Before you answer, be sure to look *very* carefully."

Sir Nathan looked very carefully at the wall of whale filling up every inch of his vision. "Nope! Nothing!"

The Chief Butler gave the Queen a look that said he very much wanted to bonk the Hero over the head with the Sword of Power. Queen Gobbledeegook was very close to letting him.

The normally very-controlled and very-calm Queen was quickly losing her temper. She was having second-thoughts about ever having made Sir Nathan the Hero. Surely it would have been less frustrating to just let the Apocalyptic Goose of Destruction destroy most of their country when it had come rampaging through the land the previous summer. Rebuilding all of Mariskatania had to be easier than dealing with the Hero's infuriating ways.

Through clenched teeth, her hands uncontrollably balled into fists, the Queen asked, "Sir Nathan, how is it even remotely possible that you see absolutely nothing?!"

"Well," said the Hero, oblivious to the Queen's frustration, "it's really hard with this massive whale in my way. Can't you see how big he is? He takes up the *whole* room! What's the matter .... don't you see him?"

A savage scream tore from the Queen's throat, fueled by feelings of anger she didn't even know she had for the Hero. She leaped for Sir Nathan like a wild jungle cat pouncing on an unsuspecting baby Gobble Goat. Time seemed to slow to a crawl as the Chief Butler stared on in horror at his Queen acting in such an un-queenly way. His mouth hanging open in shock and terror, he watched as Her Majesty's leap carried her through the air. Her fingers were curled into claws, her teeth were bared, her eyes filled with fury and fire.

And then, without even turning around, the Hero plucked her out of the air as easily as catching a drifting snowflake. With a single, gauntlet-covered hand, he simply reached behind him and caught the Queen around the waist as she came down. The Queen thrashed and fought and clawed with every bit of her strength, but the Hero simply held her in a vice-like grip. All of the Queen's fighting and struggling was useless. She simply could not shift the Hero's hold on her by even a fraction of an inch.

Without ever taking his eyes off the whale, Sir Nathan set the Queen carefully on the ground. "Be careful, Your Highness. That's a nasty trip and fall you were having there. It's a good thing I was here to catch you."

If the Hero's painfully frustrating behavior was enough to cause the most dignified person in all the land of Mariskatania to lose her cool and attack him like a wild animal, his amazing reactions and strength and sheer awesomeness were enough to remind the Queen and the Chief Butler just why he was the Hero in the first place. No one could do what he did. After all, not only did he prevent the Apocalyptic Goose of Destruction from destroying a single blade of grass on the day it had come to attack, he had also convinced it to stick around for the summer, laying enormous eggs for some of the most delicious meals ever prepared in the kitchens of the Royal Palace.

Huggo, the Head Royal Baker and Cake-Maker, had wept massive tears of happiness upon seeing the eggs. "At long last!" he cheerfully cried through tears the size of Huckle Nuts. "I can finally use my *One Million and One Scrambled Egg Recipes* cookbook me Auntie Broadbottom gave ter me for me birthday!"

Sir Nathan had met Huggo at the Downside-Up Lake of Most-Terrible Screams during a previous adventure. Though Huggo was massive, and looked like he was carved from a solid block of stone, he had one of the most gentle souls the Hero had ever met. The hulking beast loved cooking as much as Mitzy loved knitting and the two were often spotted sitting under a tree, talking about their passions.

"There's nothing I loves more then 'ter be workin' in me kitchens, whipping up one of me Auntie Broadbottom's delicious recipes for fish and fig stew," Huggo would say, wiggling his masive toes in the afternoon breeze.

Mitzy would just sit there, her mismatched hands knitting faster than the eye could follow. She was so talented, she didn't even need to watch what she was doing, but would often just stare straight ahead, her unfocused eyes going whole hours without blinking.

"Me give friendsh lotsh of kishes," she would say on occasion, which was usually a good sign it was time to be somewhere else, fast.

With an embarrassed look on her face, the Queen quickly composed herself. She straightened the crown on her head, which had gone terribly askew in her temporary lack of control.

Kale the Whale watched the whole scene with a large, amused look on his large, aquatic face.

"Yes. The whale. That is *exactly* what I had wanted to talk to you about. *He* is the trouble I was telling you about. He is a threat, to *all* of Mariskatania, and he must be stopped!"

"Oh," said the Hero simply. "Okay."

Turning to face Kale the Whale, the Queen shook a menacing finger in the villain's massive face. "Now you're going to be sorry you ever barged into my palace and threatened to flood the whole land! Now you will forever regret the day you decided to swim ... er, step ... one inch into the land of Mariskatania! When the Hero is done with you, you'll wish you were just someone's pet goldfish, living out a quiet, peaceful life in a quiet, peaceful pond!"

Behind her, the Hero's face started to take on the grim look it got whenever Sir Nathan was thinking heroic thoughts about how goodness always wins out over evil. He started to swish the Sword of Power around like a cat angrily twitching its tail. Impressive looking in most of his armor (he did get dressed in a hurry after all and was missing a few pieces) he was an intimidating sight to behold, even with the odd device on his head instead of his normal helmet.

The Hero was very eager to get on with all the smiting he was going to do to the whale, but knew better than to interrupt his queen. He fidgeted from foot to foot, grinding his teeth in heroic anger, a low growl emanating from deep in his throat.

"Sir Nathan has defeated villains much more awful and much more evil and much more bigger than you!" continued the Queen. She had been going on and on for so long, the Chief Butler started to wonder if she'd ever stop and actually let the Hero do any smiting. "How dare you stomp in here and make demands of us! How dare you smash your way through my Royal Palace! How dare you think you can even *begin* to threaten me and our lands and our peoples!"

The Queen was about to launch into a whole other bunch of angry screams she had been saving for a good occasion, when the whale interrupted her with a deafening shout.

"SILENCE!"

His yell was so loud, it snuffed out several burning torches in the room. A Junior Butler fainted in terror.

"I've listened to enough of this babbling nonsense!" bellowed the whale, his voice so deep they could feel it vibrating in their teeth. "I think you'll find you're quite mistaken! The world *will* flood and all the land *will* be underwater and soon I *will* be ruler of the entire planet!"

Angered beyond belief that anyone would dare talk to his queen this way, especially when he was standing right there, sword in hand and everything, the Hero did some shouting of his own.

"Quiet, creature of evil! Know you now that your days of evilness and awfulness and badness and yucky behavior are over! I, Sir Nathan, Hero of Mariskatania, will smite you so hard, you'll be picking bits of my anger out of your teeth for a month!"

Sir Nathan gathered himself for the attack, filled with more heroic courage than he had ever felt before. Not since the Royal Twins had kidnapped the Queen back when they were still marauding giants had anyone directly threatened her to her face. And even then, the twins just wanted her for a doll to play with. They weren't trying to hurt her. The Hero raised his sword over his head and prepared to leap at the foul creature before him.

"Prepare to get smote!" snarled Sir Nathan.

But the whale merely said, "I don't think so."

With one mechanical arm, he reached for a set of levers built into the side of his walking apparatus. He quickly pulled three of them, one after the other, and a small panel popped open, revealing a dangerous-looking black button. Painted on the button's front was a smiley face.

Just as Sir Nathan jumped at the villain, Kale the Whale pushed the black button.

Instantly, a change came over the Hero.

He stopped where he was, frozen in place, as the helmet-shaped contraption on his head came to life. The gears and cogs started spinning, driving little belts and pulleys and chains. Small puffs of steam squirted out of the tiny brass pipes criss-crossing the helm's surface. A single, dull, orange light blinked on, flickering as if lit from within by a single, tiny candle.

A noise grew from the odd apparatus, like the combination of a teapot building up to a steaming whistle and the clunking of the giant, mechanical clock adorning the Palace Tower. The whole time, the Hero stood as if frozen in ice, his body rigid. The sneer of rage on his face faded and was slowly replaced with first a look of surprise, then one of fear.

The sound from the gizmo on his head grew and grew, drowning out the Queen's confused questions as she shouted orders to the Chief Butler. Around them, the Junior Butlers plugged their ears and dropped to the floor, trying to escape the terrifying noise. The whole time, the whale merely stood there and his wicked smile filled the room with the promise of danger.

Suddenly, like the angry scream of a dragon, the bizarre helmet on Sir Nathan's head screeched in a fury of steam. A gush of vapor filled the room, shooting out of a small pipe and blinding everyone in a thick, hot fog. Then, just as quickly, the sound cut off and was followed by a noise that sounded like a collapsing pile of pots and pans.

The whale's deep voice cut through the fog, though the mist was so thick even a creature as big as he was couldn't be seen. "How are you going to stop me," he asked slowly and dangerously, "without your precious Hero and his precious courage?"

They heard the whale's deep chuckle slowly fading as he turned and left the room, the sound of his mechanical footsteps shaking the floor.

"Get him!" yelled the Chief Butler, but in the thick fog, no one could be sure who he was giving orders to. The few Junior Butlers who had recovered their wits enough to move tried to chase after the whale, but unable to see, they merely ran into the stone walls at full speed. The Chief Butler shook his head in disappointment at the sound of them repeatedly smashing into the walls and each other.

"Your Majesty!" he cried. "Are you safe?! Where are you?!"

Though just a few feet away, the Queen's voice sounded dwarfed with distance in the thick mist filling the room.

"I am fine. However, I believe something is

wrong with the Hero!"

The Chief Butler followed her voice as best he could, stumbling across the floor until he found the Queen kneeling next to the fallen form of Sir Nathan. The knight wasn't moving.

"What is that thing?" asked the Chief Butler. In the thinning fog, he could just make out the odd shape of the contraption on the Hero's head. "That isn't his normal helmet. Is it some sort of experimental device from the Royal Blacksmith?"

"No," answered the Queen as she gently rolled Sir Nathan over onto his back. The device on his head was quiet, the gears and cogs unmoving. Though the Hero's eyes were closed, his mouth was frozen in a silent scream of fear. "I told the Hero that he and the Royal Blacksmith weren't supposed to conduct any more of their special armor experiments without first checking with me. I don't want a repeat of what happened after their disastrous experiment with jellyfish armor."

"Well, in his defense, the Hero did think jellyfish were actually made out of jelly."

The Chief Butler leaned down to get a closer look at the odd device on Sir Nathan's head. He had never seen anything like it.

"I've never seen anything like it," he whispered. "All those little spinning and twirling bits – they all came to life right when that terrible whale pushed that black button on his odd walking contraption. Do you suppose that's what caused the Hero to collapse like this?"

"If it is, we must get it off of him immediately!" The Queen reached out to pluck the odd doohickey from Sir Nathan's head, only to be stopped by the Chief Butler grabbing her hands.

"Don't touch it! If it knocked out someone as strong and formidable as the Hero, who knows what it could do to you!"

The Chief Butler decided that, if it wasn't safe to remove the device from the Hero, they would remove the Hero from the device. He moved to Sir Nathan's feet and grabbed him by the ankles. It didn't take long for him to realize that a job that consisted mostly of bossing the Junior Butlers around didn't keep him in any sort of physical condition strong enough to move the Hero, especially when Sir Nathan was clad in the additional weight of his suit of armor.

With the Queen's help, each of them tugging on one of Sir Nathan's ankles, they could just slightly budge the Hero.

"One ... two ... three ... pull!" They each yanked on the Hero's legs, hard. Sir Nathan barely moved.

"Again! One, two, three ... pull!" They yanked and pulled and tugged as hard as they could, each time dragging the Hero a small distance across the stone floor. The odd device seemed stuck to his head and refused to pop loose.

Finally, after one particularly vigorous pull, the contraption came off. It happened after the Queen tripped backwards, ripping Sir Nathan's entire armored boot off his foot. The metal footwear flipped up into the air, spinning end over end. The Chief Butler watched as the incredibly heavy boot headed straight for a rough landing on the Hero's face. For many days after, the Chief Butler secretly wondered if the Queen had planned it that way all along. The Hero was quite frustrating much of the time, after all, and the Chief Butler found he couldn't really blame the Queen if little bursts of anger slipped out of her every now and then.

The Chief Butler's doubts were doubled when the Queen pumped her fist and gave a triumphant, little cheer as the boot crashed into Sir Nathan's unprotected nose, armored-toe first.

Either way, the boot succeeded where all their pulling and dragging and tugging had failed. After bouncing off the Hero's nose, the armored footwear rolled once, then slammed into the contraption and kicked it free of his head.

After that, three very odd things happened.

The first was that the Hero suddenly awoke. Ignoring the blood streaming from his nose, he curled himself into a tight ball and started to sob uncontrollably. Rocking back and forth while hugging his knees to his chest, Sir Nathan cried like a small child afraid of monsters hiding in the closet.

The second thing that happened was the helmet apparatus, once free of Sir Nathan's head, rolled slowly across the floor, making a sound like an empty tin can bouncing down the street. Both the Chief Butler and the Queen would later say it seemed like an odd thing had happened as it rolled over and bumped into Sir Nathan's dropped Sword of Power, which lay on the floor nearby. As the strange helmet came in contact with the magical sword, they thought they saw a tiny flash, like the light of a firefly winking in the night. Though they weren't positive exactly what had happened, they both were pretty sure they also heard a tiny noise. It was a kind of high-pitched buzzing sound, like the drone of a disgruntled Grumble Bee, and lasted just for a moment.

The third thing to happen was perhaps the oddest of all. As the thick mist filling the room started to fade, they noticed a strange object sitting in the middle of the floor that hadn't been there before. It was a large, bulky crate, perhaps three or four feet on a side. It was made of metal, riveted and bolted together. A small light flickered on its side, as if there was a tiny candle burning inside the box and shining its dim light out through a small, glass-covered hole. The whole thing looked as if it had been sitting submerged at the bottom of the ocean for a long time. Its metal sides were pitted with rust and corrosion. Small colonies of barnacles dotted the sides, like a terrible outbreak of bumpy pimples. Sea weed and algae grew on the crate, hanging limply and dripping water.

One of the Junior Butlers had run into the box full speed when chasing blindly after the whale in the thick fog. He lay on the floor, rubbing at a bump the size of a Huckle Nut rising from his forehead, red and sore. He propped himself up on one elbow, then reached tentatively for the crate's textured side.

"Don't touch that!" commanded the Queen. The Junior Butler pulled away from the crate as quickly as if he was withdrawing his hand from a hot fire and scrambled backwards across the floor.

He was very fortunate, for at that very moment they heard the whale's voice echoing down the hallway to them as he charged out of the palace.

"Soon, the Empire of the Waters will rule over *everything*! Say hello to my delightful invention, the Cataclysm Crate! Say goodbye to all the trees and the bushes and the rocks you love! I think you'll find your spirits are about to be ... dampened!"

At the exact same moment, the sides of the crate split open. The heavy metal panels fell to the ground, revealing an interior as bizarre as the device the Hero had worn on his head. Had the Junior Butler not moved, he would have been crushed. Gears and cog and pulleys filled every available inch of the crate's interior, along with a twisted tangle of pipes and hoses. With a loud, rusty screech, the device came to life. Its innards started to spin and whirl with a heavy, grinding sound.

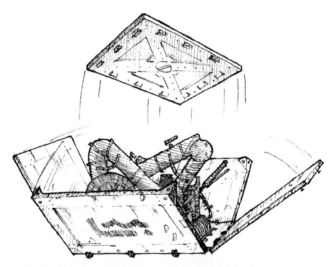

The inside of the crate was covered with just as much algae and seaweed as the outside. A few tiny crabs could be seen scuttling for cover when exposed to the light of the room. Like a devious, mechanical flower unfurling its pedals in the morning sunlight, the moving pieces of the crate unfolded, expanding outwards into the room.

The top of the crate popped off as if it were kicked by some strong creature hiding inside. It flew across the room and crashed into a wall. Then a pipe slowly telescoped upwards out of the crate. It was thick and heavy and somehow curved and twisted as it rose like a metallic vine growing with unnatural speed.

Looking on in fascination, the Queen and Chief Butler watched as a tiny trickle of water dribbled out of the open end of the pipe. It dropped from the dark opening and splattered on the floor.

"Correct me if I'm wrong," said the Chief Butler, "but if it's the whale's plan to flood us with this odd device, I think it's going to be a while before we have to worry about the Big Comfy Chair floating away."

The Queen wasn't so sure. A feeling of dread filled her stomach. The whale's machine looked too sinister, its inner workings too complex, to do nothing more than drop a few cupfuls of water onto the floor. The palace Cleaning and Preening Crew would hardly notice such a tiny mess as they went about their daily work of tidying up the palace. The Hero made more of a mess any time he visited the palace kitchens for one of his so-called *Midnight Snacks of Goodness and Honor*.

The Queen was pretty sure there was more to the whale's plan than just a few dribbles of water.

She was right. Moments later, a gurgling noise came echoing out of the wide mouth of the pipe and a gush of foaming water followed, spewing into the room. The Queen watched for a few moments more, waiting for the crate to run out of water, until she realized there was no way all of the water she was seeing could have been held in some hidden reservoir inside the crate. The metal box wasn't big enough! The water poured and poured out of the pipe and showed no sign of stopping. The whale had been right! With just this one device, it wouldn't be long before the Preening and Cleaning Crew had used up their monthly allotment of absorbent towels! If they couldn't find a way to turn the machine off, they would all be swimming to breakfast in no time at all.

And ... what if there was more than one device?

Already, a large pool of water was spreading out from the gushing pipe, threatening to cover the entire floor and flow out of the room's smashed doorway.

She rushed to kneel next to Sir Nathan. The Hero still cried and wailed, as if trapped in a frightening dream. The Queen shook him by the shoulders. "Sir Nathan! We need you! Evil is afoot! Rise up, oh Hero, and fight the naughtiness of Kale the Whale! Rise up and put an end to his evil ways! Rise up and defeat this machine of evil, which threatens to drown us all!"

The Queen knew that if a rousing speech about fighting evil didn't get the Hero off the floor and swinging his massive sword around, nothing would. She turned to the Chief Butler, her own royal courage taking over in the time of trouble. "First, send someone to bring the Warlock Christofer and the Prestidigitator Porter here, immediately! Second, get the Hero off the floor so he doesn't drown!"

Turning, she saw Sir Nathan was already sucking in occasional mouthfuls of the rapidly rising water with every sobbing cry. She added, "Uh ... I guess you'd better make getting the Hero off the floor the first thing, *then* get the Prestidigitator Porter and Warlock Christofer."

The Chief Butler turned and relayed the Queen's orders. Immediately, the Junior Butlers hopped to do as he commanded. Some ran out of the room to bring back the nation's most powerful sorcerers, the Warlock Christofer and the Prestidigitator Porter, from where they taught young magicians at the Royal Institute of Hocus Pocus. It took the rest of them to lift Sir Nathan off the floor, as heavy as he was in his suit of thick plate mail.

By the time the two spell-casters had been summoned from their nearby school of magic, the Queen had received reports of more mysterious crates scattered about. There was one more at the palace gates, pumping water as quickly as the one in the Big Comfy Chair Room and at least one more between the palace and the Royal Institute of Hocus Pocus. The water pouring out of each of the devices showed no sign of slowing down.

As the magicians entered the room, the Chief Butler gave up on figuring out a way to stop the mechanical crate from flooding the palace on his own. Everything he had ordered the Junior Butlers to try had failed. Jamming broom handles and mop heads and anything else they could think of into the gears of the crate did nothing but create a large collection of broken broom handles and mop heads. Trying to smash the crate with the broken bits of stone lying around from the whale's forced entrance into the room only resulted in a lot of Junior Butlers collapsed in the rising water, exhausted from the effort.

Even the Chief Butler's brilliant idea of plugging up the pipe with all of Sir Nathan's dirty laundry didn't work. He figured, and with good reason, that the filth and stink of the Hero's dirty socks and worn underwear would help to disable the device's inner workings. They had tried the same thing once against an infestation of Grab Crabs that had threatened to take over the palace kitchens after the tiny critters had gotten a taste for Huggo's Pigwiggle Pot Pies and it had worked like a charm. Those crabs that didn't die immediately from the stench were driven out of the palace in just a few minutes. The survivors fled to a faraway land and formed their own crabby country. The first law the newly elected crab king made was to forever ban socks and underwear, which really made it awkward whenever tourists came to visit.

As the Prestidigitator Porter and Warlock Christofer entered the room, the water was already up to their shins and starting to overflow the low stage on which sat the Big Comfy Chair.

The Hero, still crying uncontrollably, was floating around on the room's wooden door, which had been knocked off its hinges when the whale had shoved his way inside. His Sword of Power and the odd, mechanical device he had mistaken for his helmet floated nearby on a small, overturned wooden table.

The Warlock and the Prestidigitator were the most powerful spell casters in all the land. No one could rival their amazing magical skills. After all, who else could have so easily cured Princess Abbey after she had been stricken with the dreaded Burpso-Fartso disease. Until cured, she hadn't been able to leave her room for a week out of fear of suffering a sudden gas attack.

The spell-casters were wise.

They were cunning.

The were like kids in a kite shop once they saw the mysterious crate and its endless supply of water.

"Holy Hobnobber Squirrel!" cried the Warlock. "Look at that!"

"Cool!" cried the Prestidigitator. "Why, that's even better than my spell for watering crops using nothing but the juice from a single Wobble Melon!"

The two magicians knelt down next to the device, not caring how soaked they got from the splashing water. They stuck their fingers into every nook and cranny in an effort to understand how the contraption worked. The Prestidigitator even got a bit carried away and managed to get two of his fingers chopped cleanly off by the whirling gears and cogs deep inside the machine, but a quick spell later and the fingers were replaced. Of course, in the excitement of the moment, he accidentally replaced his fingers with vegetables, but it wasn't anything he couldn't fix later.

"See this?" he called to the Warlock as he pointed out a particular gizmo with a carrot finger.

"It's got an interlocking twirling-differential driving the whole systematic power-coupling! There's a whole subsystem here with nothing but reduction gears converting capacitor resistance into forward synergy!"

"Wow! Neat!" cried the Warlock, shoving the Prestidigitator over so he could get a better look.

"If you gentlemen don't mind, that's not why you're here!" snapped the Queen. She was standing on the Big Comfy Chair so as to keep out of the rising waters. Queen or not, no one likes standing around in wet shoes.

The spell-casters jumped in surprise, having forgotten anyone else was even in the room. They got to their feet and hurriedly bowed to the Queen.

"Nine-hundred and ninety-nine apologies, Your Highness," said the Prestidigitator. "Our curiosity got the better of us."

"Indeed," said the Queen, giving them both a sour look. "I summoned you here, not to play with that odd device, but to tell me what's wrong with the Hero."

She gestured to the floating door on which Sir Nathan lie, still sobbing quietly and sucking his thumb. The Queen explained to the spell-casters all that had happened as best and as quickly as she could, with the Chief Butler interrupting with the bits he thought important.

If the magicians thought a crate that could produce an endless stream of water was neat, they were absolutely crazy about the odd helmet and its tragic affect on the Hero. They poked and prodded Sir Nathan and carefully studied the helmet while being careful not to touch it. They even cast a few, hastily prepared spells to try and restore the Hero to normal, but the only thing that changed was Sir Nathan's sobs grew a bit louder as they did their work.

For a long moment, the two simply stood, their heads together, quietly discussing the situation. There was much pointing and gesturing, back and forth between the crate and the helmet.

After a bit, the Warlock looked at the Queen, who was still standing on the Big Comfy Chair, a dark look on her face as the waters threatened to crest over the top of its seat. "Your Highness, you say the Hero was normal when he first entered the room?"

"Well ... normal for Sir Nathan, yes."

"And the whale didn't touch the Hero or seem to be casting any sort of spell when Sir Nathan was afflicted?"

"No, nothing of the sort. He simply pushed a black button on his odd walking-contraption and the Hero fell, instantly."

"And the crate?" asked the Prestidigitator, gesturing at the still gurgling device. "You say the whale wasn't even in the same room when it started to spew forth the endless flow of waters?"

The Queen nodded.

"Fascinating. Absolutely genius. We've never heard of anything so brilliant, so wonderful, so amazing! How incredible that —"

"If you're quite done complimenting the villain that smashed his way into my palace, threatened to take over the world, incapacitated my Hero *and* is quite actively flooding Mariskatania, I'd like to know just what is going on! Just how did he accomplish all of this?!"

"Another apology, Your Majesty," said the Warlock, his clear excitement showing through even after the Queen's scolding. "It's just this whale has managed to do something we would have thought impossible!"

"Yes, yes!" interrupted the Prestidigitator. "You see, he has somehow managed to achieve magical results ... without using magic! Somehow, using nothing but mechanical devices, he's accomplishing things even a strong magician would have a difficult time with. Reducing the Hero to a heap of crying tears wouldn't be so tough. I write spells to do the same thing all of the time, you know ... just for practice."

The Queen's scowl deepened.

"Well, it's not like I ever used one of them! I just like to be prepared in case he ever tried to smite my magical Punkolantern again." Punkolanterns were a type of pumpkin that grew, already carved, and were often used for celebrating Higgledee Piggledee Eve. The Prestidigitator had enchanted one to keep him company in his laboratory of magic and it had sung the most beautiful ballads ... until Sir Nathan had overheard it one day. "Just because it was singing about the Hero's stinky feet didn't mean he had to chop it to pieces!"

"Anyhow," continued the Warlock, calming his companion with a pat on the arm, "if we were to create a spell that could produce a non-stop flow of water, the work would take us the better part of two or three years! It would require all of the resources of the Royal Institute of Hocus Pocus and would take quite a few magical ingredients. For the whale to have done so using only a mechanical device is absolutely astounding! And, for there to be more than one of these contraptions – it really is quite genius. It will be interesting to see if they really do keep producing water until the world is flooded."

"I hope you won't be disappointed," said the Queen in the voice she used when she was controlling her anger, like the time she talked to Sir Nathan about not cleaning the palace windows with his Sword of Power, "but I'd rather *not* wait to see if they are able to pour out enough water to flood the land, if that's okay with you? We need to be able to stop these devices! Is this something you can do or isn't it?!"

The look on the spell-casters' faces was all the answer the Queen needed.

"We apologize, Your Highness. We wouldn't even know where to start. If the machines can't be jammed or broken, as the Junior Butlers tried, it would take us long days of studying them to understood how they work. Someone like the Royal Blacksmith might have an easier time, with all his knowledge of metals."

The Queen nodded at the Chief Butler, who immediately sent one of the Junior Butlers to fetch the blacksmith. "We will try everything that we can. However, in the mean time, we cannot assume that *any* of us will be able to stop the device. Therefore, we need someone who *can*. Since the Hero's second-in-command, Amazing Grace, is away on assignment, what can you two do to get Sir Nathan on his feet and smiting things once again? I'm sure that contraption wouldn't stand one second of the Hero's wrath."

"The Hero's wrath is exactly the problem, Your Highness. Uh ... it's gone."

"What?!"

"You see," said the Prestidigitator, "in much the same way the whale has been able to create a contraption capable of spewing a seeming endless supply of water, using only a mechanical device, he's also created a helmet-shaped gizmo that used the same mechanical means to suck all of the courage out of Sir Nathan."

As if to emphasize this point, the Hero let loose with a particularly pitiful whimper.

"That's impossible!" the Queen gasped. "Uh ... isn't it?"

"I'm afraid my colleague is correct." The Warlock's voice was filled with a deep regret. "Our spells clearly indicate to us that all of the Hero's courage is gone, sucked away like a Smooshelberry milkshake through a straw."

"Gone?! But where? Where did it go?! Is it lost forever?!"

"Your Majesty, the answer to that is almost more puzzling than the fact that his courage has been removed in the first place. You see, the Prestidigitator and I could use magical means to accomplish this very same thing. It's kind of like the time you had us drain away all of Sir Nathan's cravings for Smooshelberries after he kept raiding the Princess' garden. But, if you recall, we couldn't simply eliminate his hunger for the berries. The laws of magic make that impossible. You can't just unmake something. That desire for the fruit had to go somewhere and so we placed it into my assistant, Mitzy, for safe keeping until you decided whether or not to restore it to the Hero."

"Yes. I remember," said the Queen, a scowl crossing her already troubled face. Removing Sir Nathan's insatiable appetite for Smooshelberries had indeed protected Princess Abbey's prize-winning berry patch. However, inserting it into the hulking (and always hungry) Mitzy had been a poor choice. The massive creature had roamed the land for days, eating every Smooshelberry in sight. She had stripped entire farms clean of the fruit, gobbling down every last berry along with a couple of slow Cuddle Cows that hadn't moved out of the way fast enough.

The Prestidigitator and the Warlock looked at each other nervously. It had taken them the better part of a week to track down the perpetually-hungry Mitzy and remove the cravings for Smooshelberries from her. It had taken three dozen of Sir Nathan's knights just to hold her down long enough for the magicians to cast their spell. After that, the Hero's cravings had been sealed in a metal pot for safe keeping and kept in a dark, cool place until the Queen said it was okay to give them back.

"So, answer my original question! Is Sir Nathan's courage lost forever?!"

"My Queen, the courage has to be somewhere. We've checked and we're quite certain the courage is *not* trapped inside the odd helmet. However, until we can find where it went, I'm afraid the Hero will be ... well ... a little bit unhelpful."

They all looked over to where Sir Nathan drifted about on the door, pushed around the room by water currents. His face was as wet with tears as if he had held his head beneath the flow of water from the crate's pipe.

"This is *awful*, my Queen," said the Chief Butler in a sad, quiet whisper. "Without the Hero ... we may be ... doomed."

The Queen turned to the Chief Butler, a hurt look on her face. How could he dare to say such things about Mariskatania! The country had prospered under her rule, as it had for countless generations under the kings and queens (and a few accidentally-elected Licorice Sheep) before her. But now they were facing a threat unlike anything they had ever encountered before and the Hero couldn't help them. Perhaps the Chief Butler was right.

Perhaps it was indeed the end of Mariskatania, forever.

Before she became completely overwhelmed by her grief, however, her thoughts were interrupted by a loud splashing and a screaming voice coming from the hallway.

"Stand aside! Stand aside!" It was Princess Abbey, shouting at some guards who had positioned themselves at the room's ruined doorway. The Queen's daughter elbowed her way into the room, shoving one guard so hard he fell over backwards into the deepening water. Held beneath the water's surface by his heavy coat of chain mail armor, it took another guard and two Junior Butlers to get him back on his feet.

"Mother!" yelled the Princess, her face nearly as red with anger as the flowing dress she wore. "This is a tragedy!"

"Calm yourself, my darling," said the Queen. Her feet already wet from the water flowing onto the seat of the Big Comfy Chair, she stepped down onto the low stage and took her daughter into her arms. "Shouting angrily and drowning the guards isn't going to solve anything."

But the Princess wasn't about to be so easily calmed.

"This can not be allowed, Mother! Do you hear me?! This can not be allowed!" She stamped her foot in anger, the motion invisible under the rising flood. "I received a report from one of the guards, about a whale smashing his way in here and throwing down that ... that ... that odd doohickey!"

She pointed a finger shaking with rage at the crate and its endless flow of water.

"The guard told me there are even *more* of these, all of them flooding the lands and that it's his intention to flood *all* of Mariskatania! This can not be allowed!"

The Queen was impressed. Though Abbey was a hard worker and excelled in school, she usually didn't take much of an interest in anything around her. If it didn't involve her homework from her *Advanced Princessing Class*, or tending to her award-winning patch of Smooshelberry bushes, or what seemed to be an ever-increasing amount of flirting with Prince Thomas the Brave, Princess Abbey tended to not get involved. The Queen had started to worry maybe her daughter wouldn't follow in her footsteps and wasn't interested in ruling the land after her.

But now Queen Gobbledeegook was pleasantly surprised, despite the dire situation, to find her daughter was angered by the attack on their lands. It showed that maybe the Princess *was* capable of caring about other things, too, beyond school projects and mushy love letters. If Abbey was this upset about the whale's attack, it showed she cared for the land and the people around her and how the flooding waters would affect the country.

A small smile crept onto the Queen's face as her daughter continued to rant and rave about the whale's attack. The Princess *did* care about the citizens who could lose their homes in the flood. She *did* care about the farmers and how the waters could destroy their farms. She *did* care about the blacksmiths and the ranchers and the bakers and the kite makers, all of whom would be affected by the rising waters.

"Mother, are you listening to me?!" screamed the Princess, mistaking the Queen's slight smile as the look of someone not paying attention.

"Yes, dear, I'm listening. And I just want you to know that, despite all the troubles we're now facing, I'm just so proud of —"

"Well?! What about my shoes?!" The Princess screamed in frustration and stamped her foot again. The motion caused a burst of bubbles to rise up from her foot.

"Uh ... what?" said the Queen in a confused tone.

"My shoes! All this water is going to ruin my shoes! I won't be able to go anywhere! What will Prince Thomas think of me if all my shoes are water-damaged?! He'll decide he likes that stupid Princess Derba from Prettyville! She thinks she's *so* special, just because her father gave her a dragon for a pet! Ha! She won't think she's special after it accidentally sets her hair on fire!"

"Your ... uh ... your shoes?"

"Yes, my shoes! What did you think I was talking about?! I'm a princess! I can't be expected to walk around bare-footed, can I?! And I'm certainly not going to walk around wearing nothing but galoshes! So you tell that stupid Hero to quit goofing off and get to work putting a stop to all of this, or I'll hold my breath for a week!"

With this, the Princess sucked in a big gulp of air and crossed her arms angrily. Her puffed-out cheeks definitely made her look like someone who wouldn't be moved until she got her way.

She was only able to hold her breath for as long as it took the Queen to say, "Well, the Hero *can't* put a stop to this because he's been cursed in some way we can't understand."

Princess Abbey, her face bright red, exhaled loudly and struggled to catch her breath. The Queen pointed to where Sir Nathan lie huddled on the floating door. The overturned table holding his Sword of Power and the odd helmet floated next to him. The Princess looked at the Hero for a long moment. He cried almost silently, the tears streaming down his cheeks.

The Queen quickly explained to the Princess

what had happened to the Hero and how the Warlock and Prestidigitator had discovered his courage had been stolen. She expected her daughter to explode in another fit of screaming, but the Princess just stood there calmly.

After another long moment, she said in a quiet voice, "Well, that's just great. It's just like I've always said ... if you want something to get done, you've got to do it yourself."

Hiking up her dress to keep it from dragging through the water, the Princess strode across the room. Her legs kicked up splashes as she walked over to the floating door holding the sobbing Hero. Seeing Princess Abbey march towards him, a grim look on her face, Sir Nathan let loose with another fit of loud sobbing, his body wracked with heavy sobs. He acted as if he was a naughty child getting punished by the meanest parent in the world, just for sneaking a cookie.

"Oh, be quiet!" snapped the Princess. "You're either stealing all of my Smooshelberries or you're going and getting all of your courage stolen! Why can't you be normal!"

And before anyone could stop her, the Princess reached for the Hero's sword, saying, "I'll smat or smoot this whale myself, or whatever it's called!"

Neither the Queen nor the Chief Butler tried to stop her. Firstly, the Princess usually did what she wanted and nothing they could say or do would have any effect. But mostly they didn't bother to try to stop her because they knew it took a heroic effort to lift the Hero's magical weapon. No ordinary knight could carry the immense blade, no average soldier could manage to pick it up, no run-of-the-mill warrior could even hope to budge the sword from where it sat. It was a special weapon and it took a special sort of person to carry it.

The Chief Butler and the Queen simply watched as the Princess reached for the pommel of the weapon, waiting for the silly girl to realize her mistake. As her fingers moved to within just a fraction of an inch of the sword, a tiny flash of bluish-white light arced to her fingertips from the metal of the weapon. A sharp, crackling buzz filled the room and there was a charged, tingling smell like the air gets after a vicious lightning storm has rumbled past.

Princess Abbey froze. An odd look filled her face as if she had just learned the biggest secret in the whole world. Without uttering a sound, she toppled over backwards into the water and sank beneath the surface.

"My Princess!" yelled the Chief Butler at the same time as the Queen yelled out her name. They both thrashed through the water, rushing over to where she had disappeared. The waves they made pushed the Hero's floating door around like a tiny boat bobbing on the stormy waves of the ocean. They reached down and tried to locate the girl, but couldn't find her. Where could she have gone! They had seen right where she had fallen and they hadn't been very far away when she had disappeared beneath the water, but it was if she had been pulled off by some hidden sea creature lurking underneath the surface.

In the darkness of the dimly lit room, it was

difficult to see into the frothy, churned-up water. Splash around as they might, they could find no trace of the Princess.

The Junior Butlers rushed to help, spreading out from where they had seen her disappear, but they could also find no sign of her. Forgotten, the Hero lay sobbing on the door, having floated to the other end of the room, the small table floating after him. The waves kicked up by everyone frantically splashing around, searching for the Princess, rocked the door and table violently. The Hero's sword slid off the wildly tilting table and fell into the water with a plop.

"Where is she!" screamed the Queen, dropping to her knees. Her dress and hair were soaked from the effort of looking for her daughter. Her crown hung crookedly on her head. "Where is she! Where could she have gone! She can't be missing!"

The Chief Butler screamed orders at the Junior Butlers to search faster, search harder, search better, but it was no use. It was if the Princess had never been there. He yelled at a guard standing in the doorway, the soldier terrified and confused by the situation in front of him. "You! Spread the word immediately! Tell *everyone* in the palace to search the rising waters, from end to end! We *must* find the missing Princess!"

"Did you say the Princess is missing?!" came a booming, heroic voice from the other end of the room. The Hero! He was finally okay! The Queen's relief was immediate, the stress and worry draining from her face and shoulders. With the Chief Butler's help, she climbed to her feet and turned towards the far end of the room.

"Sir Nathan, I am *most* relieved you have recovered from —" Her voice trailed off, dying in a quiet gurgle in the back of her throat. Her eyes grew wide, wider even than when Kale the Whale had smashed his way into the Big Comfy Chair Room. Still holding the Queen's arm, the Chief Butler's look was even more puzzled. Could he really be seeing what he saw?

At the other end of the room, Sir Nathan still lay on the door, still curled in a ball, still crying and whimpering. However, standing next to the door as if the room weren't filling with water, as if the water couldn't touch her at all, was Princess Abbey. Her soaking dress was plastered to her body. Her drenched hair was a wild tangle, half covering her face. Her shoes were most likely ruined.

But none of this seemed to be of concern to the young lady. In days past, the Chief Butler had known the Princess to refuse to leave her room if she thought so much as a single hair was out of place on her delicately styled head. He had seen her throw a tantrum when the one specific dress (out of the thousands she owned) wasn't clean when she wanted to wear it. He had seen her send a Junior Butler to be imprisoned in the dungeons for the rest of his life for accidentally spilling a single drop of Smooshelberry Juice on the floor next to her easily stained shoes. But the fact that the Princess suddenly seemed unconcerned for the way she looked wasn't what had stunned the Chief Butler more than even the time he awoke to find Mitzy had disassembled the entire Royal Palace, stone by stone, in order to move it a few feet to the right.

"Palash wash crooked," the Warlock's assistant had mumbled in explanation.

No, what had the Chief Butler so perplexed was the fact that Princess Abbey was standing there with the Sword of Power held lightly in one hand as if it were no heavier than a butter knife.

"I ask again, did you say the Princess is missing?!"

The voice, deep and bold and heroic, came *not* from Sir Nathan, but from Princess Abbey herself.

"Uh ..." was all the Queen managed to say. She was more surprised than she had been the time Mitzy had disassembled the entire Royal Palace, stone by stone, in order to move it back a few feet to the left.

"Palash wash shtill crooked," she had explained.

Without waiting further for an answer, the Princess marched across the room, kicking through the water as if it didn't exist. "This will not stand! This abduction of the Princess is clearly an act of evil and treachery and I say it will not stand! Goodness will always overcome evil! You'd think evil would know that by now!"

Princess Abbey marched over and knelt deeply before the astonished Queen, not noticing that doing so almost submerged her own face in the water as she bowed her head low. "Your Majesty, I pledge to you that I, the Hero of all Mariskatania, shall ride forth on my trusted steed and I shall not rest until the villain responsible for this attack is brought to justice! Fear not!"

The Princess stood and saluted smartly with the

sword, apparently unaware of the fact that she shouldn't be able to lift it, then turned on her heel and strode out of the room.

"Tupolev!" the Princess yelled, calling out the name of the Hero's horse. "To me, Tupolev! We ride at once to find the Princess!"

Long after the splashes of her determined march had faded away to silence, long after the roiled waters in the room had calmed once more, long after a fainting Junior Butler had been pulled from the waters before he could drown, the Queen managed to say just one, single word.

"... but ..."

* * * * *

# PART II

The McSkooble Family had been farming in Mariskatania for just as long as anyone could remember. As a matter of fact, the Royal Register of Everything (a set of 10,000 hand-written ledgers that recorded every little tidbit of information known to the people of Mariskatania) listed the McSkooble Family as the first farmers to ever grow the delicious Smooshelberry fruit in the land.

The McSkoobles were also listed as being the first farmers to ever grow the not-so-loved Gasplort fruit which, while just as delicious as Smooshelberries, also had the tendency to use their clinging vines to grab unsuspecting farmers and pull them deep underground. Several members of the McSkooble family had disappeared before they decided to grow something a little less dangerous.

Like Exploding Death Plumbs.

It was not so long ago that most of the McSkooble family farm had been destroyed in an epic battle between a giant Grab Crab responsible for kidnapping the Queen's children, the Royal Twins, and the heroic pair of Sir Nathan and Amazing Grace. Originally part of the palace's

72

Cleaning and Preening Crew, Grace was one of the newest knights to be sworn in by the Queen. She had wanted to be a knight more than anything, but unfortunately her parents wouldn't allow her to attend the required two-hour Basic Knight Training Class and she had had to resort to sneaking off and trying to solve the mystery of the Queen's missing twins on her own.

After much bickering and arguing, Sir Nathan had finally seen how truly brave and heroic Grace was and, after they had rescued the twins, she had joined the knights sworn to protect Mariskatania.

Grab Crabs normally found their meals by hiding in someone's house, then dashing out and stealing a bit of food when the owner's back was turned. Grab Crabs would also take more than food and were responsible for all types of missing things. They would take keys and coins and important notes you had left reminding your children to clean their room. The more frustrated people became looking for the the thing they had just set down a second ago, the happier the crabs were.

They earned special crab bonus-points if they could get someone to say a naughty word in frustration.

You could tell where there was a particularly bad Grab Crab infestation by looking for a particularly thick swarm of PigWiggles. These creatures were pigs of a sort, but nothing like those normally found on farms. They were small creatures, a little bit smaller than a Hobnobber Squirrel even, but very round like a ball. Bright green in color, the PigWiggles moved around by rapidly spinning their tails fast enough to lift themselves into the air.

They were definitely cute and made a high-pitched squeaking sound when excited. They livened up any landscape as they drifted here and there on the wind like little, pink-tongued balloons.

Unfortunately, PigWiggles didn't feed on roots and nuts and grass like their regular pig cousins. Instead they fed on frustration. If a PigWiggle happened to be nearby when you were feeling particularly annoyed, it would home in on you like a bee to a flower and hover around your head, squeaking in happiness. Its cry would attract other PigWiggles and pretty soon, unless you could calm yourself down, you'd be smothered in a swarm of the creatures flying around your head. They simply *thrived* on frustration.

The more a Grab Crab could get you to shout and scream about the slice of Huckle Nut cake it snuck away with while you were out in the kitchen getting a fork, the happier the Pigwiggles were and their excited honks and squeaks would fill the air.

One particularly clever crab had learned that PigWiggles were much more delicious, much more nutritious, and much more easy to come by than random bits of food stolen here and there. The crab had grown incredibly huge on the easily-caught critters and was soon roaming the land, unstoppable, eating whatever it could find and taking whatever it wanted, which had included the Royal Twins.

When Sir Nathan and Amazing Grace had finally caught up to the crab, they had smote it good and hard, so hard in fact that crab meat had rained down upon the countryside for miles in every direction. Unfortunately, the battle had taken place smack dab in the middle of the McSkooble farm. Fences and sheds and fields and barns had all been wrecked. Hardly anything had been left intact.

Never one to complain much ("Complaining don't milk the Cuddle Cows," Farmer McSkooble was fond of saying), the farm had been rebuilt. Farmer McSkooble had even used the Grab Crab's massive, fifty-foot-wide shell as a roof for a new barn to replace one that had burned to the ground in the battle. He admired the way the greenish-white shell gleamed in the morning sunlight ... at least on those mornings when the sun decided to rise. In Mariskatania, one could never really be sure what the sun was going to do day to day and most people learned to just get along with a lantern or two until the silly thing decided to show up.

Once, the sun had hidden in the land's deepest and darkest cave for a whole week, just to see how people would react.

It was while Farmer McSkooble was high up on a ladder, nailing the very last green board (harvested fresh from a bright green Jubb Jubb Tree) onto his very new green barn, that he noticed an odd thing.

Looking down, he saw that the bottom rung of his ladder was under water.

"That's peculiar," he mumbled to himself around a mouthful of nails. "I don't remember setting my ladder down in the creek."

Looking around a bit more, he added, "As a matter of fact, I don't remember building this barn in the middle of the creek neither. Nor do I remember building any of my barns and sheds and fences in the middle of the creek. Why, if I couldn't see it for myself, I'd say I didn't set up any of the new fields and orchards and gardens in the middle of the creek either. How odd."

Now, Farmer McSkooble was a patient man, as all McSkoobles were. If he had thrown a fit every time a Cuddle Cow had gone missing or the Wobble Melon crops had run away again or the Produce Trees had decided to grow nothing but left-handed can openers, he'd be too busy to get any actual farming done.

Hanging his hammer from his tool belt, he climbed up on to the roof of his new barn and sat down to puzzle things through. The noon-day sun was high in the sky (for a change) and warmed his skin pleasantly. He pulled a Mango Mackerel Munchy-Munch Bam-Bam Bar from his pocket and slowly savored the candy treat as he pondered his situation.

It seemed pretty obvious that something strange was happening. Though Farmer McSkooble was a busy man, with a lot on his mind, he was smart enough to know better than to have rebuilt his devastated farm in the middle of what appeared to be a spreading flood.

What could have caused such a disturbance?

A pair of Cuddle Cows slowly floated by, riding a hastily-assembled raft of hay bales. There was an old saying in the McSkooble family. It went, "If the cows are afloat, sit up and take note."

The McSkoobles *loved* their old sayings.

Equally important was the one that went, "If a massive crab is killed on your property, don't waste time making up silly rhymes about it. Get out there and build yourself a new barn out of its shell."

As the cows drifted by, Farmer McSkooble saw there was indeed water spreading across the land just about as far as he could see. All the low-lying areas were covered and only the higher hills and ridges were still dry.

"Now, none of that there water was in place when I first started doing my chores this morning," he said to himself. "For the water to have covered all that it has, in such a short span of time, why it must be rising at an almost magical rate. I sure hope them fellers down there at that Royal Institute of Humbo Jumbo or whatever it's called haven't gone and goofed things up with all their magical hullaballoo."

Taking another bite of his candy bar, Farmer McSkooble watched as a Licorice Sheep went floating by, its fluffy coat keeping it afloat in the rising waters. He had just made up his mind to climb back down the ladder (after he finished his candy bar, of course) and start rounding up all his livestock before they floated away, when a curious thing happened.

A booming noise came echoing across the land, so low and deep, that it could more easily be felt in his bones than heard with his ears. A tiny tremor vibrated through the hard shell of the barn's roof.

It grew quiet for many long seconds and then there was another boom, slightly louder than the first. By the tenth deep rumble, Farmer McSkooble could hear the sound clearly.

*Boom, boom, boom.*

Finally, the farmer could see the source of the sound. It was the second most peculiar thing he had seen that day (the first being his prize Gobble Goat, Sir Edmund von Grilled Cheese, trying to fly south for the winter after carefully watching some ducks do the same all morning). Right about where the road that wound through the farm should have been, a whale came wandering through. Normally, he would have expected the whale to be swimming, what with all the water everywhere. But this whale was walking. That only made sense, the farmer thought, seeing as how the flood wasn't deep enough for a sea creature as large as a whale. At least not yet.

The creature came stomping and splashing through the water, riding on a curious device made out of metal and wood that made it look like he was riding on the back of a monstrous spider. A giant pair of metal hands stuck out of the front of the contraption. Each footstep, despite having to splash through a foot or two of water, still hit hard enough to send a shockwave rippling through the ground.

*Boom, boom, boom.*

If it wasn't weird enough that the whale was there in the first place, and if it wasn't weird enough that the whale was riding an incredibly bizarre walking contraption, it was totally weird enough the whale seemed to be talking to itself as it went.

"Oh, ho, I'll show them! I'll show the *lot* of them! They'll all be sorry once I'm done, yes they will! Pretty soon all of this will be flooded and then everything will belong to the Empire of the Waters! No more of their garbage flowing into my home. No more rotten vegetables clogging up the waters. No more lost kites getting stuck on every outcropping of rock, tangling all the sea plants with that infernal kite string. No more dirty socks plugging up my blow hole when I least expect it, making it impossible to breathe. Do they understand how difficult it is to get the stench of dirty socks out of your nose?! Just because my nose is on the top of my head – oh, hello!" The whale paused momentarily in his ranting to wave a mechanical hand at Farmer McSkooble, who was still perched up on the roof of his barn. The farmer hesitantly waved back. "Where was I? Oh, yeah ... rotten socks! Well, it's over, I tell you! Over and done with! I won't stand for it! Or ... float for it! Or, whatever it is that whales do! Those days are over and they'll *all* pay!"

The whale stopped in his tracks. He reached to the back of his walking contraption with both mechanically operated hands. After a moment, he found what he was looking for and lifted two similar items into the air. A massive, sinister smile slowly crept across the whale's face, partially because the whale liked how evil it looked when he smiled like that, and partially because with a face so big, slowly was the only way any whale's smile could creep.

Kale the Whale knew one of his relatives that had tried to smile quickly, only to have her lips shoot right off her head due to the speed they had reached trying to make such a long trip in such a short time. That was the day Kale had first started to tinker with mechanical devices. It was clumsy going at first, what with the fact that he had no hands nor fingers with which to grip the tools. But, practice makes perfect as they say, and soon he had gotten the hang of things. In very little time, he had crafted a set of mechanical lips for his female cousin and, other than the fact that they tended to rust quickly in the salt water, she was quite pleased with them.

After that, Kale was hooked. He loved inventing new things! He set about building countless gadgets and gizmos and whatchamacallits. One of the first things he built was a set of tools that could easily be used by a whale. He saw no sense in drafting the perfect design for a mechanical blow-hole sock-guard if you didn't have the right tools for the job. There was nothing more frustrating than not being able to complete a project, just because you couldn't hold the capacitor screwdriver in your fin.

The rest of the whales and fishes and other aquatic creatures were amused by Kale's fascination with mechanical devices, but they saw no real need for his work. They mostly felt it was just a passing hobby, something he would soon outgrow. Kale had tried, again and again, to show them how his inventions could help, but they usually just smiled kindly and patted him on the head in the way grownups always do when they don't understand what their kids are really talking about.

It was after Kale the Whale had invented his most-prized contraption that a master plan had started to form in his brain. He had just finished a device that could be used to help the forgetful creatures of the sea remember the things they were always forgetting to remember. There was nothing more embarrassing than a clam going out for the day without his shell. Or a sea turtle that swims into school, also without his shell. Or a snail, out for nothing more than a lovely stroll in the evening surf, without his shell. Actually, the more Kale had thought about it, the more he realized a lot of sea creatures were often strolling about naked. And he had invented something that could help!

But when he revealed his wonderful inventions they just smiled in a way that showed they didn't truly understand what he was trying to show them and swam away, many of them naked.

Frustrated beyond belief, Kale had hidden for days in a hollow, rocky hill at the bottom of the sea that no one knew about. It was where he kept his work shop. Alone in the darkness, he swam back and forth, back and forth, muttering to himself in anger. If only there was something he could do to show all his friends and family how important his work was! If only there was some way he could prove how clever he was! Then he'd show them and they'd be sorry they had ever ignored him!

That's when the idea struck him. He realized that, with just a few adjustments, his memory-reminding device could be used in a much more brilliant, much more fantastic, much more devious way.

Now, as he thought back to that day long ago, a chuckle echoed up from the depths of Kale's throat, sounding like an avalanche of crashing boulders.

Looking at the two objects he held in his

mechanical hands, the whale chuckled again. Though not his best work, the devices were still among some of his most impressive inventions. In one mechanical hand, he held an exact copy of the Cataclysm Crate he had left behind in the Big Comfy Chair Room. In the other was another metallic box that might at first have been mistaken for the same thing, but upon closer inspection was slightly different.

Though it was the same size, with the same rusted and algae-covered sides, this one was just slightly different in how it was put together. Also, on its side the whale had painted a simple design of what looked liked a thick claw.

Kale the Whale carelessly tossed the first crate off to the side. Farmer McSkooble watched as it splashed through the water, rolling end over end and coming to a stop below him. He saw the crate land on its side and wondered if maybe the whale was just discarding it in favor of the other one. But then it vibrated, just a little bit and, as Farmer McSkooble watched, a small mechanical arm very similar to the ones built into the whale's walking device reached out of a hatch on the side of the crate and pushed the box upright.

The Cataclysm Crate flopped over onto its base, throwing up a wave of water as it landed. The mechanical arm slowly retracted back into the side panel, but not before first giving the farmer a friendly little wave.

Next, the crate unfolded exactly like the one in the Big Comfy Chair Room had and the same sort of wide pipe rose out of its innards. Farmer

McSkooble watched in stunned amazement as a rapid flow of water started to gush out of the pipe, with no sign of stopping. He now understood where the rising flood was coming from. He looked over to where the whale was carefully studying the second crate in his mechanical hand and could see there were many, many more of the boxes tied to the back of his walking contraption. The whale was clearly seeding them all across Mariskatania and the water gushing out of each one was combining to quickly flood the world.

Showing much more care than he had with the first crate, the whale set the second down very gently. Unfortunately, it just so happened that he set it on top of a new shed Farmer McSkooble had just finished building the day before, in which he stored all of the sugar cubes he fed to the Licorice Sheep to make sure they grew a nice, sweet coat of licorice.

The massive bulk of the crate easily crushed the shed flat and the surrounding waters washed through the splintered pile of wood and quickly dissolved the sugar stored inside.

"Oh, the Licorice Sheep aren't going to like that one bit when they find out, I can guarantee you that," said Farmer McSkooble sadly. It was difficult enough dealing with the stubborn animals on the best of days and he didn't want to be the one to tell them their sugar cubes were gone. The last time he had tried to feed them regular sheep food, they had locked themselves in his house and made him sleep in the barn until he could get more treats.

The whale stood back and admired the crate,

pausing to pluck off a tiny shrimp clinging to a bit of seaweed. He carelessly flicked the shrimp aside.

"Yes, I think they'll find my wonderfully evil Critter Crate a particularly nasty surprise," mused the whale quietly, seemingly having forgotten all about Farmer McSkooble. "Yes, I think they'll find it quite ... *pinchy*."

The whale laughed loud and hard, as if he had just said the most funny thing ever said in the history of all said things. Actually, the most funny thing ever said in the history of all said things, as recorded in the Royal Register of Everything, was a joke the Royal Blacksmith had made to the Chief Butler, but since it made fun of Sir Nathan's height and contained two and a half naughty words, it wasn't repeated in polite company.

Farmer McSkooble watched as the whale strode off, the booms of his footsteps fading as Kale followed the winding road to the South.

Looking down at the water, now rising very rapidly with yet another crate adding to the flood, Farmer McSkooble shook his head sadly. Adjusting his broad-brimmed hat, he sighed deeply and moved to climb down the ladder.

"Well, I guess there's no point in putting off telling the sheep about their sugar cubes," he said to himself as he climbed down. "Boy, I hope I can find a dry place to sleep in the barn tonight."

\* \* \* \* \*

Thanks to the dozens of Cataclysm Crates scattered here and there across the countryside, a lot of Mariskatania was underwater and things were only getting worse. In most places, the water was knee-high on a man of normal height, which meant it was much higher on the somewhat-not-tall Sir Nathan.

Fortunately that wasn't a problem for the Hero at the moment. He was curled up into a ball, crying his eyes out while tied to the back of a horse. However, for the horse, it meant carrying around not one, but two humans, both of whom were acting unusual.

Tupolev the horse was used to at least one bizarre human on his back, for he was Sir Nathan's steed. He was as fine a stallion as ever walked the land, with a soft coat like powdered sugar and a flowing mane like pouring cream. Most people who saw him suddenly craved a powdered donut and some milk, but never quite understood why.

It was Tupolev's job to carry the Hero from place to place as Sir Nathan smote evil wherever it appeared and he took this responsibility seriously. The steed had been *so* helpful, Queen Gobbledeegook had even knighted him and now most everyone referred to him as *Sir Tupolev*. Most everyone, that is, except for the Hero. Sir Nathan would be the first person to tell you what a wonderful horse Tupolev was. He would go to great lengths to explain to anyone who would listen about how fast and strong and smart his steed was. He'd even talk about the time Tupolev had been turned into a Hobnobber Squirrel in a way that didn't make fun of the horse at all.

But Sir Nathan still couldn't quite get over his

horse being knighted. *He* was the leader of the knights of Mariskatania and he didn't need any silly stallion getting any strange ideas in his head about just who was the Hero and who was the horse. Sir Nathan was worried it would all go a bit too far and then one day, his horse would be carrying around the Sword of Power while Sir Nathan stood by helplessly.

Besides, several years past, horses had lost a bet with humans in which the losers had to carry the winners around on their backs for a million years. Sir Nathan was bound and determined to see to it that horses kept their end of the bargain.

"Onwards, my fine steed!" yelled someone in a commanding voice from atop Tupolev's back. It wasn't the Hero. "We must travel quickly before that evil creature makes good his escape! We will smite that whale with our mighty Sword of Power and teach it that evil shall never win so long as there is a good and honorable Hero around to save the day!"

Tupolev sighed. It was a heavy sigh, the kind that comes from a horse completely fed up with getting orders shouted at him all day when he was the one doing all the work. To make matters worse, he wasn't just carrying Sir Nathan, but Princess Abbey as well.

For reasons he hadn't quite figured out yet, both the Hero and the Princess were acting oddly. But the horse knew his duty and so, when summoned, he did his job and carried both of them out of the Royal Palace and swiftly down the flooding road.

"At least when the Hero rides me, he isn't constantly jabbing my sides with his high heels," muttered the horse to himself.

"What's that, my fine steed?" yelled Princess Abbey from the saddle. She had been waving the Sword of Power in circles around her head ever since they left the palace and showed no sign of stopping. She reminded Tupolev of a windmill. "Speak up! Goodness and honor can never mumble, for it's not our way! We speak clearly and loudly, so all evil villains everywhere know we are here to protect the land!"

At the moment, they were standing on a slight rise where the roadway they were traveling rose up out of the rising waters for a few dozen feet before plunging back into the flood. Despite the fact they were just standing there, Abbey continued swinging the Hero's borrowed sword around and around in whooshing arcs and kicking at Tupolev's sides with her high-heeled shoes.

Tupolev sighed again. Sir Nathan had always left the steering and galloping and other fine horse details to him, leaving the Hero free to concentrate on more heroic things.

"If you'd stop doing that for a second —" started Tupolev.

"Onwards! We must travel ever onwards if ever we're going to —"

"I said, if you'd STOP DOING THAT FOR A SECOND!" the horse bellowed at the top of his lungs. The sheer volume of his voice finally got Princess Abbey's attention. The sword dropped to her side, her high-heels fell still. "If you'd stop doing that for a second, then we can talk about what it is exactly we're doing."

"I should think it obvious! We are smiting evil, righting wrongs, and bravely protecting the realm!"

As if to ruin all the heroic fun, Sir Nathan sobbed loudly from where he was tied like a bundle of dirty laundry to Tupolev's back. If it weren't for the fact that the horse's flanks were already soaked with water, his short fur would have been sopping wet from the Hero's constant tears.

"Sure, right, I got all that," said Tupolev, in a voice that said he clearly didn't. "But ... I mean ... what I *really* want to know is what is the ... uh ... the *Hero's* plan?"

"Why, the plan is whatever I say it is, for I am the Hero and the Hero is me! We shall ride forward, smiting evil and all that courageous stuff!"

They had been down this conversational path before, always ending up at the same destination – a sad, little place Tupolev called *Frustration Town*. No matter how he tackled the subject, no matter which way he asked his questions, he couldn't quite figure out exactly why both the Princess and the Hero were acting the way they were – which was pretty much exactly how you'd expect them *not* to act.

The horse had never seen Sir Nathan afraid in his entire life, even when he had fought the Face-Eating Blob Monster of Nasty Tempers. If ever there had been a time to be afraid, that was it. The Blob Monster had this horrible way of pinning its victims down with its slimy tentacles and then dissolving their face right off. What was worse, the creature would then wear the face around like a Higgledee Piggledee Eve mask, pretending to be a lost tourist asking for directions and generally being a nuisance. Tupolev, brave though he was, had hung well back and let Sir Nathan handle things on that day. He was a handsome horse and couldn't contemplate going through life without a face. What would his friends think?

But now, with nothing more dangerous threatening him than a case of wet feet, the Hero was curled up in a ball, crying like a child who had lost his favorite toy. Or, like a horse that had lost his face.

And the Princess ... what was she doing? When she was acting normally, she certainly wasn't any sort of frail, timid person who was afraid of her own shadow. But the only reason she would ever willingly get wet and dirty would be for one of her many school projects, and only then after donning one of her waterproof rain-gowns, made from the finest Jubb Jubb fluff and waterproofed with dragon spit. Dragon spit was wonderful stuff, with many uses, so long as you were careful about how you went about getting your hands on some.

Now, she sat astride Tupolev's back, her fancy gown wet, muddy, and ripped, her carefully styled hair a sloppy mess, her expensive shoes a complete wreck. Odder yet, she was swinging Sir Nathan's Sword of Power around as easily as she wielded her fork at dinner time. Tupolev knew not just anyone could lift the sword, let alone use it as a weapon. It took a true hero to hold the magical blade. As nice as Princess Abbey was (at least to Tupolev, to whom she snuck juicy Smooshelberries from her garden every day) she was no hero. Or, at least Tupolev wouldn't have thought so.

However, unless his eyes were fooling him, she was carrying the sword quite easily. There was something going on he couldn't quite understand.

Every time the horse tried to ask Sir Nathan what was going on, the Hero would just moan and cry louder. If it hadn't been for Princess Abbey tying him to Tupolev's back, the horse would have been tempted to just dump Sir Nathan in the nearest puddle until he started acting more like himself.

"Pretend for a second that I have absolutely no idea what is going on," the horse said wearily to the oddly-behaving Princess. "Explain to me, just one more time, what it is we're trying to do."

"Why, I should think it clear, my fine steed!" boomed the Princess. "We're out to defeat evil!"

"Yes, I got all that. I mean, more specifically, just what sort of evil are we out to defeat?"

"Ah, excellent question! Always be prepared, yes? Good! We seek to follow and find the nasty, evil, terrible villain, Kale the Whale! The creature of evil is guilty of smashing his way into the Royal Palace and taunting the Queen! I was just about to smite the whale and put a stop to his shenanigans once and for all when ... when ... well, I admit, that part is a little fuzzy. But I can tell you with certainty, that the whale is responsible for all this unwanted water that's flooding our beloved country and this atrocity will not stand!"

"A whale?" asked Tupolev, confused.

"Indeed! A whale! We will track down this whale and put a stop to his evil ways! I will smite him so soundly, I'll knock the nostrils off his face and onto the back of his head!"

"Uh, I think whales already have —"

"No one shall stand against my might and honor and courage! Ride, my valiant steed! Ride forward for glory!"

Normally, when Sir Nathan gave a rousing speech about honor and glory, Tupolev found himself very caught up in the moment. This time, however, there was just something not right about Princess Abbey and the way her own speech came out. To Tupolev, it felt as if he could sense that everything she was saying and doing wasn't quite what it seemed to be. He was very puzzled about the whole situation. But he knew, if indeed there were a villain roaming the land, he needed to do something. If the Princess was willing to help when the Hero's cheese had slipped off his cracker, mentally speaking, then who was Tupolev to stand in her way?

He knew the whale villain had to be caught and forced to turn off the mysterious crates. Their never ending water supply was surely going to flood the land if they weren't stopped. Even with the Sword of Power and her new-found courage, Princess Abbey hadn't been able to deactivate any of the crates they had come across on their journey so far. The whale had scattered several of the devices across the countryside and each and every one somehow proved invulnerable to the magically sharpened blade. Try as she might, the most the Princess had accomplished were a few shallow scratches on the crates' surfaces, along with a few disgruntled barnacles jolted out of a peaceful morning nap. Tupolev couldn't help but think the true Hero, Sir Nathan, would have been able to do better.

It seemed as if their only hope was to catch the whale and force him to deactivate the contraptions.

Thinking about it, Tupolev still wasn't sure the Princess had all her facts straight. Perhaps she was behaving so oddly because she had suffered some sort of nasty bonk to the head, confusing her brain. The horse knew Sir Nathan suffered from the exact same thing sometimes because he often chose to not wear the padded helmet that was so highly recommended during *Bashing People Over The Head With A Club* practice.

The way Tupolev saw it, the whale would have to first flood the land and then he could swim up to the Royal Palace and smash his way in, not the other way around.

Besides ... how exactly were they supposed to track a whale? By looking for flipper-prints?

With yet another heavy sigh and a sad shake of his head, the horse trotted off down the road, kicking up a splash as he plunged back into the water.

If the flooding got any deeper, Tupolev was going to have to see if he could remember any of those swimming lessons he had taken a few hundred years ago.

\* \* \* \* \*

Somewhere between the Royal Palace and Farmer McSkooble's farm, there was a quiet, peaceful pond. It was truly a beautiful place and its calm waters were a soothing sight to behold. It was a place where one could unwind and forget about all the stresses of life, be they keeping up with the demanding standards of the new Head Royal Baker and Cake-Maker or keeping a supply of Mango Mackerel Munchy-Munch Bam-Bam Bars in stock at the Vandy Zandy Candy Company or even staying ahead of the constant demand for new kites at any of the hundreds of kite shops scattered across Mariskatania.

Anyone feeling the stress could simply sit down, dangle their toes in the pond, and look out over the calm, still waters as their cares melted away.

However, no one had ever done such a thing, probably because the pond hadn't existed up until very recently. Had someone showed up, intent on all the toe-dangling and care-melting, just the day before, they would have been disappointed to see nothing but a bit of rocky ground, some weedy grass, and a lone Hootentoot Tree.

Hootentoot Trees were beautiful, especially in the autumn when their leaves changed color with the onset of cooler weather. A forest of Hootentoot Trees in the fall was an amazing place to be as all of their leaves would change from green to white with pink polka-dots. If the wind started to blow, the leaves would gently fall from the trees and rain down in an endless cascade of color, swirling and wafting and, interestingly enough, screaming all the way to the ground. It turned out nothing had a greater fear of falling than the leaves of a

Hootentoot Tree.

Anyone planning on going for a walk through a Hootentoot Forest during the autumn, on a particularly windy day, would be smart to bring along some ear plugs.

For now, the tree simply sat under the midday sun, its leaves shiny and green. Autumn was a ways off and the tree had bigger thoughts on its mind at the moment, such as "I wonder where all this water came from?" and "Is it just me or is the water rising really quickly?" and "If the water gets deep enough to completely cover me, will I have to hold my breath? Do I even know how to hold my breath? My mother was right ... I should have taken that job in the Swamp Forest of Misery working for my cousin."

A solitary Hobnobber Squirrel perched on one of its branches, trapped by the quickly rising floodwaters. Its only thought was "Huckle Nuts!"

Flitting about in the waters beneath the tree was a family of FlibbertyJibbits. The white-furred creatures cavorted in the water playfully, chattering to each other endlessly in their high-pitched voices. Their pink, fuzzy bellies practically glowed in the sunlight whenever they floated along on their backs, as they often liked to do. They were a close relative of the North Mariskatanian River Otter and had somehow learned to talk like humans. They spoke endlessly, about everything and anything, and only stopped long enough to shove a paw-full of fish into their mouths for a quick meal.

Unfortunately, whatever odd thing had taught the FlibbertyJibbits to speak had completely failed to teach them what any of the words meant. None of the fuzzy creatures could understand a single thing any of them said. If this bothered the animals, they showed no sign. Instead they all just chattered, on and on. One FlibbertyJibbit could be endlessly talking about the weather while its neighbor was going on about its concern that their species was getting hunted by trappers for their beautiful fur (and by regular folks who were just plain sick and tired of all the talking).

The peaceful pond (or what would have been a peaceful pond if it weren't for the deafening noise of all the talking FlibbertyJibbits) was disturbed by the loud splashes of a horse riding near.

Tupolev trotted along the edges of the pond, keeping to the shallow parts as best he could. On his back, Princess Abbey seemed intent on filling every passing second with as much useless conversation as a FlibbertyJibbit. Over and over again, she yelled about smiting and goodness and honor and courage. As glad as he was the Princess seemed willing to step in for the Hero until he was feeling better, Tupolev found himself wishing she would act more like herself and yell about getting her homework done on time, or about how the Hero had eaten of all her prize-winning Smooshelberries again, or about how her dress had been in the same general vicinity as some dirt and so she needed to go change it for a new, clean one.

Today, however, the Princess didn't seem to care one bit about dirt. In fact, she seemed to be incredibly happy to be incredibly filthy. Every time she was splashed with water or spattered with mud, she just whooped and hollered and yelled even louder about courage.

It was all very odd.

At one point she looked back at Sir Nathan and said, "It is such a grand day to be on such an important adventure! My fine fellow, why do you carry on so?"

The knight's sobbing stopped for the first time since he had been tied to Tupolev's back. He peered at the Princess with bloodshot eyes, red from crying. It seemed as if he were trying to recall some faint memory.

"I ... I cry because I'm afraid," he mumbled softly.

"Afraid?! Why, there is nothing to be afraid of!" the Princess bellowed in a voice ten times louder than it needed to be. "You are accompanied by the bravest, most courageous knight in all the land and nothing evil shall happen to you as long as I, the Hero of Mariskatania, am by your side! There ... that should make you no longer afraid. All is well!"

However, her bold speech did nothing to cheer Sir Nathan up. Instead he looked frantically about for a few seconds, as if he heard the footsteps of some terrible fiend sneaking up on them. He kept muttering to himself. "Where is it?! I know it's here, I *just* know it is! Where is it? Where could it be?!"

Princess Abbey looked back at him, a genuine look of confusion on her face. She leaned down to ask a quiet question in Tupolev's ear (which meant talking only *five* times louder than she needed to). "My fine and gallant steed, I don't understand. The strapping young man looks healthy enough, if not a little on the short side. What could possibly drive him to tears? The only one who should ever be afraid is a small child who has lost their toy, or perhaps a puppy, lost in the woods without its mother, or maybe even someone meeting Mitzy for the first time, especially when she's in a hugging mood. Beyond that, who would ever be afraid, especially if I am around?"

The horse had no answer. Sir Nathan's crying was as much a mystery to him as was the Princess acting like she was the Hero.

On and on the horse ran, following the scattered trail of the villain. Just like Sir Nathan, Tupolev was an excellent tracker, but his skills weren't needed today. Between the occasional Cataclysm Crates and the massive tracks the whale's odd walking contraption left in the few dry spots of land, the creature was proving easy to follow.

Soon they entered lands Tupolev remembered very well. Rising up a slight hill, they looked out over the fields of Farmer McSkooble's farm. The horse vividly remembered the hard-fought battle with a massive Grab Crab that had taken its toll on all of them that day. It was certainly one time when the horse hadn't been so sure they would survive. Most of the farm had been damaged or destroyed in the fierce fighting.

In the flooded valley below, he could see the repaired buildings and fields, all slowly getting ruined again by the rising flood waters. The largest building on the farm was a big barn using the vanquished Grab Crab's shell for a roof. Tupolev's keen eyes could see a figure on the roof, most likely the farmer himself. At first the horse thought Farmer McSkooble had climbed onto the roof to get away from the flood, but then he realized the farmer had climbed up there to get away from an angry mob surrounding the barn on all sides.

Princess Abbey had seen it, too. "Come, my find steed! That gentleman is in trouble! Ride forth so we can save him from danger and evil!"

Tupolev quickly galloped down the back side of the hill, though not so much to save Farmer McSkooble as to just avoid getting kicked in the sides again with the Princess' sharp high heels. They were worse than spurs! Besides, he didn't think the farmer really had anything to worry about since the angry mob surrounding the barn was only his flock of Licorice Sheep, and not a gang of evil monsters.

As they splashed their way closer to the barn, they could hear the farmer as he called down to the sheep. From the tone in his voice and the angry look the herd was giving him, it was probably a good thing Licorice Sheep couldn't climb ladders.

"Look, I told you," Farmer McSkooble was calling down to a particularly large Licorice Sheep ewe who seemed to be the leader of the flock, "*I* wasn't the one that ruined your sugar cube supply! It was this whale! He came walking through here and *he* was the one that crushed the sugar shed!"

The look the flock gave him at the ridiculous suggestion that a whale could walk made it obvious they had been through all this more than once before. Clearly, not a single Licorice Sheep, not even their youngest lamb, was going to believe any story about a walking whale.

From where she sat, tall and proud in the saddle, Princess Abbey called up to the trapped farmer. "I say, good day to you, sir! It seems you are in a bit of trouble! It is a good thing that I, the Hero of *all* Mariskatania, just happened to be passing by while on an urgent quest to save the land. Fear not! I shall smite your enemy and have you safe and sound and off that barn in no time!"

"Oh, Sir Nathan, I'm glad you're here," the farmer started to say. But then his voice stuck in his throat as he shielded his eyes from the sun and got a better look at who was talking to him. "I ... uh ... oh! Your Highness! I didn't see that it was you."

Farmer McSkooble bowed awkwardly from atop the barn while casting a nervous look at the angry sheep below. The flock didn't seem to care one bit about the newcomers and were intent only on getting revenge for their ruined sugar.

At first, the farmer thought he had been addressed by Sir Nathan. He knew both the Hero and his horse, as did pretty much everyone in Mariskatania, especially since the day they had fought the Grab Crab that had destroyed his land. In thanks, the farmer promised the Hero and Tupolev as much food as they ever wanted from his grove of Produce Trees. This was the best kind of reward as far as Tupolev was concerned since Produce Trees could indeed produce just about any type of produce, depending on what mood they were in. All the fresh fruits and vegetables (and occasional roasted ham) he could eat! Sir Nathan, on the other hand, would have been happier with a bit of armor polish or perhaps a pair of woolen socks. Other than

Smooshelberries (which he got plenty of by stealing them from Princess Abbey's garden), the Hero wasn't too keen on fresh produce. The thought of a radish as a reward made him wrinkle his nose in disgust.

Farmer McSkooble then realized, though the Hero was indeed there on his horse, the only thing he really seemed to be contributing to the conversation was a low, pitiful sobbing sound. It was Princess Abbey's voice he had heard, though she spoke in a tone the farmer had never heard her use before.

"*Your Highness*?" Princess Abbey asked. "Why do you call me that? Oh, you must have me confused with someone royal. No, good sir, it is I, the Hero of Mariskatania, and I am here to save you!"

"You say you're the what now exactly?" asked the farmer, pushing his hat back to scratch behind one ear in confusion.

Tupolev caught the farmer's eye and shook his head slightly in a sort of "Ask me about all this later" sort of way.

"Surely you recognize me! I am the Hero and I'm here to save you! I shall smite this fuzzy flock of villains in a flash and have you off your roof in no time!" The Princess made to climb down from the saddle, brandishing the Sword of Power with an intense gleam in her eye.

"No! Nope ... no, no, no, no, no! Not necessary!" yelled the farmer once he realized what the Princess intended to do. As grumpy as the sheep were about the loss of their sweet sugar treat, they didn't deserve what the Princess' threatening look promised. He started to quickly climb down the ladder to better explain the situation, but quickly climbed back up when several of the flock started to growl at him.

Safe once more on the top of the barn (but for how long, the farmer didn't know – several of the flock were off to one side, drawing up designs on how to build a sheep-friendly ladder), Farmer McSkooble quickly explained the sheep weren't an enemy in need of smiting, but were instead more like a group of naughty children in need of a good scolding.

"Ah," said the Princess, climbing back into the saddle. She sounded disappointed. "Well ... I'm afraid that's not my job. I am the Hero, you see, and not a sheep baby-sitter. I must admit I am a bit confused, for when you first spied me approaching, you announced you were glad to see me. Why else would you be glad to see the Hero of Mariskatania if there weren't some evil foe in need of smiting? I cannot spare a single, wasted moment, for there is a wretchedly, evil whale roaming the land, causing no end of mayhem and mischief and I must find it as soon as possible."

"A whale? I saw a whale come walking through here not long ago!"

"Ah!" cried the Princess, the deadly glint coming back into her eyes. "Oh, wait. I wonder if it is indeed the same walking whale I am following. I would hate to waste time tracking down the wrong whale."

Tupolev rolled his eyes. Whatever was going on

between Sir Nathan and the Princess, this sort of behavior was certainly very familiar to the horse. For all the courage and bravery the Hero usually possessed, sometimes the simplest of tasks were the most difficult. There was the one time Sir Nathan had made Tupolev ride all over Mariskatania, looking for the thief that took the Hero's Exploding Death Plumb Pie he had been saving for desert. Their search only ended after Sir Nathan finally remembered he had already eaten the pie.

"Your high- uh, I mean, Your Hero-ness," stuttered Tupolev, "I propose we proceed with the assumption that the farmer's whale is also the same whale we seek. After all, even if they're not the same whale, they probably know each other and we can ask the one where the other might be found."

"Capital idea, my fine steed! You have indeed proven yourself worthy of being the mount of the Hero of Mariskatania on this day!"

Tupolev kept his sarcastic reply to himself.

"Good farmer!" called the Princess up to Farmer McSkooble, who was nervously watching the sheep-ladder go from the planning stage to the construction stage. "Tell me more of this whale-spotting of yours and all that transpired!"

"Well, it wasn't much. He came ambling down that roadway there," he said, pointing at where the road would have been had it not been completely submerged, "mumbling to himself about floods and garbage and some sort of empire. He then threw me a friendly sort of wave and then kept on with his mumbling. After that, he dug two of them there crates out of his belongings. He tossed that one directly below me there and darned if it didn't just start pumping out water like it is now. I don't think it's ever going to stop."

Pointing at the other crate, the farmer continued, "Then he carefully set that second box over yonder. Unfortunately, he carefully set it down right on top of my sugar storage shed. That's why I'm up here, for you see —"

"Yes, yes, fascinating!" interrupted the Princess. "Now, I must not be disturbed, for I have some serious Hero work to do!"

A second later, she could be heard telling a smaller sheep that had approached her, "What's that? No, I'm sorry, I don't happen to have any water-proof ladder glue on me. So sorry."

With Sir Nathan whimpering the whole way, the Princess rode Tupolev over by the second crate. It sat perched atop the splintered wreckage of the sugar storage shed. She hopped lightly off the horse's back, landing with a splash in the rising water. With the hem of her dress swirling around her knees, she waded over to the crate.

"Curious," she muttered, walking slowly around the metallic box. "Why is this one still closed while all the others have opened up and are spewing water all over the place?"

The Princess thought they were maybe the exact same type of device, though it was tough to tell. With the walls and lid still shut, there was no telling what was inside. More gears and cogs and strange water-spitting pipes? Or something else?

"This is a perfect opportunity!" exclaimed Abbey after a long moment, straightening up from examining the crate. "Clearly this crate has failed to function. We can dismantle it and learn the secret of the whale-villain's mechanical abilities! We can then use this knowledge to stop the creature once and for all! Stand back, my faithful steed!"

Motioning Tupolev away, Princess Abbey lifted the Sword of Power high overhead. With a ferocious yell, she brought the sword swinging down, slamming it into the side of the crate. The magically sharpened weapon hewed into one edge of the box, cutting deeper than any normal blade could with a deafening clang. However, the mysterious crate was built well and the sword didn't penetrate more than a few inches.

Princess Abbey's assault on the box must have triggered some waiting thing, for at that very moment, a loud noise of grinding gears could be heard from deep inside. Just like the Cataclysm Crate in the Big Comfy Chair Room, the lid of the box flew off, cartwheeling away through the air. The wave of water thrown up by the falling cover drenched several of the sheep, making them grumpier than they already were.

However, instead of falling open, the sides of the crate remained where they were. Instead of a jumble of gears and pipes and pulleys, the interior of the crate was dark and hollow. Wrenching the Sword of Power from where it was embedded in the crate's wall, Princess Abbey stepped forward to peer inside.

With reflexes that only a true Hero possessed (even one who was normally in her *Advanced Mathematics in the Field of Princessing Class* this time of day), the Princess dodged away from the crate. She lifted the sword up and around in a flashing arc to bat away something that shot up out of the crate's interior, aimed directly for her face and riding on a jet of water. It was a thick, metal claw, like that of a lobster. The pinching edges were razor sharp and the whole thing looked solid enough to punch a whole week full of dizzy into a dragon.

The claw bounced off the hastily raised sword and fell with a splash into the water next to the crate. The Princess nodded, deeply satisfied with how she had defended herself. No knight could have done better nor reacted faster. Clearly, some foul creature was lurking inside the crate, armed with an equally foul claw-shooting weapon. Now that it's attack had failed, she wondered what other surprises her unseen foe had in store and looked forward to the challenge.

Too late, she noticed the fine chain attached to the back of the pincher. Before she could react, the slack snapped tight, pulling the claw up out of the water and back into the dark interior of the crate.

"Oh, ho!" quipped the Princess gladly. "Rearming ourselves, are we? It seems we have an enemy worthy of my attention! Good! I always hate it when the smiting is finished so quickly."

Banging the side of the crate with the flat of her sword, the Princess yelled in her best heroic voice, "Come forth and meet your doom, oh wretched villain! You should know that I, the Hero of Mariskatania, am here to put a stop to you and all your foul ways! You and your foul master, the whale known as Kale, shall not succeed! Good will *always* win out over evil and badness!"

From where he stood, Tupolev had to admire the way Abbey was handling the situation. She was certainly acting like the Hero would have in the same circumstances. The Princess rapped the side of the crate a few more times for good measure, causing the metallic box to ring like a bell.

From out of the depths of the crate's dark interior, something crawled.

It was foul.

It was terrible.

It was ... kind of goofy looking.

A metallic claw, possibly the same one that had flown straight at the Princess' face, reached out of the crate and clamped on to the box's rim. The grip was so strong, the thick, metal wall crumpled like a sheet of paper. A second claw rose up and grabbed another edge of the crate. The claws were attached to metallic limbs, much like the legs on the whale's walking contraption. Instead of bones, there were thick metal bars. Instead of tendons and muscle, the limbs had springs and chains and pulleys. Instead of skin, they had absolutely nothing, because the idea of fake skin had scared Kale the Whale too much and seemed really creepy and gross.

A monstrous, metal creature climbed quickly out of the crate's interior and jumped into the water, drenching the Princess with the large wave it threw up. With mud running unnoticed down her face and dripping off her chin, Princess Abbey stared at the odd foe before her.

For a moment, the Princess thought she faced a human foe wearing a peculiar set of armor. The enemy before her stood on a set of eight thin legs. Its body was long and rounded, with two massive arms ending in the dangerous-looking claws. Sets of gears and cogs covered the outer shell and a small, brass pipe stuck out its back like a chimney, spitting puffs of steam. An odd metal barrel was clamped to one arm, filled with what looked like long, slender pipes. Printed across its chest in crude lettering were the words *ThingamaBot 01*.

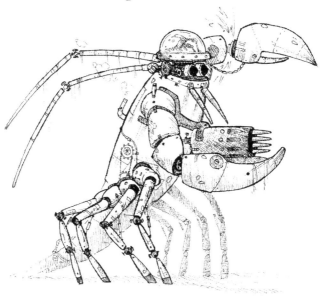

In the end, what passed for the contraption's head told her all she needed to know about the sort of enemy the Princess faced. Though she didn't entirely understand what she was seeing and couldn't understand how it worked, she realized she was facing one of Kale the Whale's minions.

Where a normal suit of armor would have a

helmet, the metal monstrosity standing before her had a clear, glass ball, bigger than a Wobble Melon. It was hollow and filled with water that sloshed around as the lumbering device slowly took one step towards her, then another. Inside the glass ball she spied a lobster, fat and red. It was pushing and pulling on a tiny set of levers.

The Princess quickly realized the lobster was controlling the evil gizmo and all she had to do was take care of the foul, little beast and the contraption would no longer be a threat.

"Easiest battle ever!" she declared, pleased with herself for finding the device's weak spot, but still disappointed the fight wasn't going to be that epic after all. "Lobster soup, coming up!"

Faster than anyone who knew the Princess would have thought possible, she whirled the Sword of Power around in an arc that sliced easily through the glass bowl, spilling the water to the ground and flinging the lobster through the air. It landed on the back of a nearby Licorice Sheep.

Or, at least that's what would have happened had the lobster not just as quickly pulled hard on one of the levers inside the glass bowl and raised one of the contraption's arms to block the blow. Her hands stung from the impact and the Princess was very surprised her attack had been stopped. There was no way way the metal arm should have been able to avoid getting sliced in half by her magically sharpened blade, but the sword did little more than gouge a small nick out of it.

As she stood there, her mouth slightly open in surprise, the lobster flipped a tiny switch and one of the claws shot out, striking the Princess in the forehead and knocking her backwards ten feet. The waves thrown up as she fell into the water hadn't even calmed before the lobster flipped another switch and the claw was drawn zipping back onto its arm by the chain connected to it.

Pushing and pulling on several levers, the lobster steered the contraption next to the Princess. The Thingamabot lifted a mechanical foot high out of the water and smashed it down on top of her. She was crushed and trapped beneath the waves, sure to drown! Or, she would have been had she been anyone other than the Hero, or at least someone who *thought* they were the Hero! As the lobster pressed its face up against the wall of the glass tank to watch the Princess drown, it failed to notice her silently rise out of the water behind it. With rivulets of muddy water streaming down her face, she raised the Sword of Power high and was about to bring it smashing down onto the glass bowl housing the lobster.

Before she could swing the weapon, it froze in her hands, immovable. No matter how she tugged and pulled, she couldn't budge the blade. It was as if its tip were encased in a block of solid stone. Turning, she saw the reason why. Unnoticed, a second contraption, identical to the first, had climbed out of the Critter Crate's interior. *ThingamaBot 02* was sloppily painted across its chest. While the Princess had been sneaking up behind the first lobster, a second had snuck up behind her. When she had raised her weapon, it reached out with a gigantic claw and clamped down hard on the blade. With a strength no regular lobster would have, the crustacean held onto the sword with an almost unbreakable grasp. The springs, gears, and chains in its arm gave it power, speed, and toughness beyond that of most humans.

However, the Hero of Mariskatania was *not* most humans, even if there was some temporary confusion about just who he (or she) really was.

With a dangerous look in her eyes, the Princess stared straight into the beady gaze of the lobster in the water-filled tank of *ThingamaBot 02*. The lobster was no expert on humans and their facial expression. If it had been, it would have realized the look on Princess Abbey's face meant it should seriously be rethinking its decision to ever crawl out of the Critter Crate in the first place.

Spreading her stance, ever so slightly, the Princess strengthened her leverage. Twisting her grip on the sword's pommel, she squeezed out a trickle of water that threatened to make her hands slip. Giving her head a subtle flick, she tossed a strand of hair up and off her forehead that was close to blocking her vision.

"You should have stayed in the box," the Princess said menacingly, almost too quietly for the lobster to hear. She pivoted on her left foot, ripping the Sword of Power out of the contraption's steely grip. The metal pincher dropped into the water, severed into several pieces. Pivoting back on her right foot, the Princess brought the Sword stabbing straight at the contraption's armored chest. As easily as Sir Nathan used the sword to chop through Princess Abbey's Smooshelberry bushes to get to the really juicy berries hidden in the thick foliage, the sword sliced through the metal and punctured the mechanical works deep inside. An ear-piercing shriek of ruined metal gears still trying to turn came from device's torn chest, along with a puff of black smoke.

As the second lobster frantically tried to operate its tiny controls and back away from the Princess, the first came stomping up behind her. There were one, two, three loud popping sounds! Puffs of steam shot out of the barrel-shaped contraption strapped to its arm. At first, the Princess didn't understand what the lobster was trying to accomplish, but then she heard a whizzing sound as something flew past her cheek, leaving a long scratch in her fair skin.

The long, slender pipes inside the barrel were a type of dart, riding on a geyser of steam and pressurized water. They flew through the air faster than an arrow, emitting a horrible shrieking sound as they streaked towards her.

"Get down!" yelled Tupolev from off to her right as the lobster aimed at her again.

*Pop! Pop! Pop! Pop!*

More puffs of steams and more whizzing sounds! The horse, covering the distance between himself and the Princess in one mighty leap, jumped to her side and knocked her out of the way as the darts shot through the space where she had been standing just moments before.

Three of the projectiles whizzed harmlessly past, but the fourth came close to piercing Tupolev's white flanks. Fortunately for him, Sir Nathan was still tied to his back and, fortunately for Sir Nathan, the knight was still wearing his plate mail armor. With a heavy thunk, the flying weapon bounced off the Hero's back, leaving a nasty dent. Sir Nathan screamed in terror.

While a normal Princess Abbey would haven been outraged at having the beautiful, clear skin on her beautiful, perfect head harmed by an attacking lobster, this Abbey only chuckled softly. It was an unnerving chuckle, a laugh the likes of which you'd only hear from the playground bully right before she beats you up and stuffs you in a garbage can for not sharing your Smooshelberry Desert with her.

Where the second lobster was completely ignorant about humans and their facial expressions, the first knew all too well what the dangerous smirk on the Princess' face meant. The crustacean had spent many years as the pet of a young girl who loved spending the day sewing silly, little costumes for it to wear. She would then force the lobster, whom she had named Pinchy, to act out complex and detailed scenes from all of the girl's favorite stories. The look on Princess Abbey's face was exactly the same as the one the little girl would get after reading a new fairy tale filled with all sorts of humiliating scenes for Pinchy to act out.

"Uh oh," said the lobster, a tiny trail of bubbles rising up from its mouth.

Kicking up a wave of water as she ran, the Princess charged straight at the metal contraption. She held the Sword of Power overhead in a firm, two-handed grip. The lobster pulled hard on his controls and frantically turned his armored machine, trying to put as much distance between himself and the angry look on Abbey's face as he could.

Princess Abbey leaped into the air with a bound, flying above the water's surface as easily as a Flip Flop Flamingo out for a leisurely flight. Feet first, she came down hard on the running contraption's back, the heels of her shoes actually puncturing the thick metal. *Blam! Pow! Smite!* The Sword of Power hammered down on the glass tank, time and again. Though no ordinary glass, because the ThingamaBot was built by no ordinary whale, the bowl couldn't withstand the repeated attacks. Long cracks spread across its surface, sounding like thick, winter ice breaking apart during a spring thaw. The pressurized water within squirted out through the fissures, soaking Princess Abbey even more than she already was.

The lobster within the cracked tank frantically tried to work the emergency escape hatch controls, but they were jammed by the force of Abbey's ferocious attack. With a wicked gleam in her eye, she raised the sword one more time and yelled, "For goodness and honor! Feel my smiting, oh wretched creature!"

She started to bring the sword down, the force of the swing sure to slice cleanly through the weakened tank (and possibly cleanly through anything inside), when suddenly the Princess was just ... gone.

One moment she was there, standing over the fallen ThingamaBot, the next she had simply disappeared. Looking out through the spiderweb of cracks in the glass, the lobster saw where she had disappeared to and smiled an evil, little lobster smile.

Tupolev had been watching Princess Abbey through the whole fight, amazed and shocked at the way she handled herself. Ever since they had left the Royal Palace, she had certainly been talking like the Hero. And a look at Sir Nathan confirmed the Hero was still acting like a frightened child. And now, with the Sword of Power in hand, the Princess was even *fighting* like the Hero. Her smiting was amazing to watch!

Tupolev had watched in awe as the Princess raised the weapon and started to bring it smashing down on the crippled ThingamaBot's tank. And then, as quickly as it to took to say, "Oops," she simply vanished from where she had been crouched on top of the fallen device.

The horse frantically looked all around, wondering where she could have gone. Had some sort of foul, whale-built magic whisked her away? Had she been rendered invisible by some sort of spell?

"Oh ... drat," said the steed in an embarrassed voice.

While he had been watching and wondering about the Princess and her newfound fighting skills, he had completely failed to notice a third ThingamaBot crawl up out of the crate. Where the first two were about the same size as Abbey herself, the third was twice again as tall and much more massive. At its very top, a bigger tank of water was perched, large enough to hold a pair of lobsters who were feverishly working side by side to control the contraption. Each crustacean wore a tiny shirt with the words *ThingamaBot 03* printed on the front.

With a gleeful lobster-giggle, they had pointed one of the massive, metal pinchers at the Princess. The claw shot off of the arm, riding on a jet of scalding-hot water and expanding steam. Just like on the other ThingamaBots, it trailed a thick chain behind it. With a clang and a grunt from the Princess, the claw had clamped around her waist just as she had brought the Sword of Power chopping down towards the first ThingamaBot. One of the lobsters quickly pressed a red button and the chain retracted back into the arm, jerking the Princess off the fallen lobster machine and pulling her skipping across the water like a thrown, flat rock.

"My bad!" called Tupolev in an ashamed voice. "I should have warned you about that one!"

As the Princess fought to free herself, Tupolev debated whether or not to run to her aid. On the one hand, she was doing a pretty darned good job of taking over for the Hero. On the other hand, the larger metal crab contraption she was fighting had now picked her up by the head and was spinning her around in dizzying circles.

Tupolev realized he was really going to have to figure out just what was causing Sir Nathan and the princess to behave so strangely as soon as he had a free moment.

He was about to charge into the fight, when he

realized having Sir Nathan tied to his back was going to be a big hindrance. The horse turned to quickly undo the knots holding the knight in place with his teeth, when he realized that once freed, Sir Nathan would most likely tumble pitifully into the water, making no effort in his misery to keep from drowning. In the past, the knight had spent considerably long moments under water without suffering any noticeable damage, but that was back when he had been acting more heroic than he was at the moment. The way he was behaving now, Tupolev was pretty sure Sir Nathan would just topple into the water and pitifully drown, held beneath the surface by his heavy plate mail and his depression.

The horse found the exact thing he needed nearby. Apologizing to the Licorice Sheep, he dumped Sir Nathan onto the work table they were using to assemble their sheep-friendly ladder. The knight fell in a clatter of armor and sobs and lay unmoving on the table. The flock eyed him with distrust.

Free of the cumbersome load, Tupolev turned and charged into the action. His hooves kicking up spray, he ran full-speed at the third Thingamabot just as it threw Princess Abbey flying through the air. She passed over Tupolev's head like a bird in flight, yelling something about how honor and goodness will win out over gravity.

His teeth clenched, a growl boiling up from deep back in his throat, the steed launched himself at the device. He came flying in, hooves first. Other enemies had learned the hard way how painful it was to be kicked in the head by Tupolev, especially when the horse was particularly upset.

All one-thousand pounds of Tupolev (though the horse would only ever admit to weighing no more than nine-hundred or so) crashed into the ThingamaBot. The impact between his hooves and the contraption's metal armor made a hollow sound as loud as the massive bells in the Palace Tower. Unfortunately, the monstrous gizmo was barely affected and, other than getting shaken around in their watery tank, the lobsters controlling it were unharmed. The thing was simply too strong and too heavy for the steed to knock over.

Impressively nimble for a horse, Tupolev flipped in mid-air as he bounced off the ThingamaBot and landed on his hooves, ready for another charge. Off in the distance, Princess Abbey was also back on her feet and ready for more.

By now, the second lobster had fixed some of the important gears and pulleys in his device and was once again advancing on the Princess. The first lobster had thrown some hasty patches on the cracked glass of his water tank and was moving in on her from the other side. Their sharp, metal claws snapped at the air as they advanced. She was surrounded and unable to help Tupolev as the third, larger mechanism lurched forward on its springy legs, ready to attack.

In a flash, the tide of the battle had turned. Tupolev was hastily backing away while Princess Abbey did her best to fight off the smaller ThingamaBots. Despite the ferocity of her attacks, the heavy armor and sturdy construction of the whale's metallic monsters was enough to stop most of her blows from causing any serious damage. It was clear Kale the Whale was a brilliant inventor. After all, who else could build a crate that produced a seemingly endless gush of water? If he hadn't been so determined to flood the world, he would have been welcomed as a genius inventor and could have made a fortune from his work.

With a vicious swing, Abbey managed to hack apart one of the dart-shooting devices threatening her. But still, she was forced to retreat from the ferocious lobster assault. Zinging darts from the other ThingamaBot and flying claws kept her off balance, driving her back, further and further from Tupolev. The horse was being pushed the other way, past the flock of Licorice Sheep as they contemplated what to do with the weeping form of Sir Nathan who was taking up all the space on their work table. Tupolev contemplated asking them for help, even though they had shown no signs of interest in the fight one way or the other. However, the sour look on their faces told him they still hadn't gotten over him dumping a weeping knight in their way.

Tupolev tried to dash right, then left, around the advancing ThingamaBot, but despite its hefty bulk and massive size, it could still move quickly. The pair of lobsters controlling it were experts at what they were doing and worked as a perfectly synchronized team. The horse was driven back.

Just as he was contemplating turning and making a break for it, hoping he could easily outrun the heavy contraption and somehow circle back around to help the Princess, there came the sound of rapid splashes and an angry yell that went something like, "For happiness and honor! Good will never fall to the dirty tricks of evilness, not when I'm around!"

The voice sounded similar to that of the Princess, but Tupolev knew better. It belonged to one of the newest knights in the service of Mariskatania, a young woman as determined as she was fierce. She was as dedicated to protecting Mariskatania from evil as Sir Nathan was.

She also went into combat swinging a soup ladle.

It was Amazing Grace, coming to their aid, and just in time!

Riding her chestnut-brown mare, Flopsy, through the water as quickly as if it weren't there, Grace blew past Tupolev like a Pigwiggle chasing the strong scent of frustration. The pair of lobsters operating the ThingamaBot didn't even have time to blink (nor did they have the eyelids for it) before a soup-ladle-sized hole suddenly appeared in their water tank. The water gushed out through the hole, carrying the lobsters with it. *Plop! Plop!* They dropped into the flood waters below and quickly swam off to avoid getting crushed by their deactivated contraption as it toppled over. The wave it created as it fell was so large, Tupolev was momentarily swept away.

Princess Abbey, cheered by the appearance of Amazing Grace, renewed her attacks on the other two ThingamaBots.

"For goodness! For victory! For honor! For

getting me wet!" she yelled with each mighty swing of her sword. "Amazing Grace, it is good to see you! Your arrival is at a time when it is most helpful! Come! Help me to dispatch these two villainous foes, in the name of Queen Gobbledeegook!"

Upon seeing the Princess wielding the Sword of Power masterfully and hacking chunks of metal from her fearsome enemies, Grace and Flopsy skidded to a halt and simply stood there, both their mouths hanging open in stunned surprise. Seeing Sir Nathan lying in a heap and sobbing uncontrollably didn't help to clear up the confusion.

Why wasn't he participating in the fight?

Amazing Grace had seen some curious things in her short career as a knight. She had met and befriended a dragon. She had seen an upside-down lake. She had seen Sir Nathan eat an entire bushel of Smooshelberries without even the slightest hint of a belly-ache. But nothing prepared her for what the Princess and Sir Nathan were doing now.

Eventually, the fact that there was still smiting to be done overcame her surprise and she spurred Flopsy into action. She rode up behind the two ThingamaBots, now in full retreat from the Princess' wrath, and threw herself out of the saddle. Her ladle flashed in the sunlight in an especially bright way since the sun loved nothing more than illuminating a good fight. Flipping in the air and then once more, she landed on one of the metal contraptions. Wrapping her legs tight around its chest, she pounded away with her ladle. Each hit sounded like a blacksmith hammering away at his anvil and the air was filled with the sound. *Ding! Ding! Ding! Ding! Ding!*

Faced with only one attacker, the Princess decided to use a trick from the Basic Knight Training Manual. This book was used in the training of the knights of Mariskatania and all thirty-two chapters had been written by the Princess as an extra-credit project for school. Chapter Twelve of the manual was called *Dirty Tricks Are Okay To Use Against Bad Guys Since They're Bad Guys And It's Okay To Trick Them* and described one of the most clever ways ever to defeat your enemy.

"Hey!" shouted the Princess, pointing behind the ThingamaBot. "Look over there!"

Turning around in his control tank, the lobster turned to see what she was pointing at, because surely no one would point at something if there wasn't anything to point to. At the same moment, driven by all the might and valor inside her, the Princess swung the Sword of Power in a gleaming arc and sliced cleanly through the chest of the ThingamaBot, cleaving through every bit of metal armor, steel gears, iron pulleys, and copper chains it was built of. The very top of the contraption, including the glass tank, popped up into the air and landed with a splash at Abbey's feet. The rest of the device crumpled into the waters, black smoke pouring out of its ruined innards.

The Princess turned to face the second ThingamaBot, but saw it was also sinking beneath the flood waters, dented beyond recognition by Grace's frenzied attacks. In one hand, she held a desperately wriggling lobster, struggling to get free.

"Well done, my faithful knight companion!" shouted Princess Abbey, saluting Grace smartly with her sword. "I always said that Mariskatania would benefit greatly from having you as a knight! Is that not so, Tupolev?"

The horse had walked up beside the two young women, grateful he had survived another hectic day of adventure. "Uh ... yes?" he answered slowly.

Looking back and forth between the Princess, Tupolev, and the sobbing Sir Nathan, Grace was extremely puzzled. "Though I am glad to be of assistance in dispatching these foul creatures, I don't understand a single thing I'm seeing."

"Whatever do you mean?" asked the Princess, smashing open the control tank on the ThingamaBot she had destroyed and pulling out the lobster from inside. It screamed angrily at her in a tiny, high-pitched voice.

"I mean ... *this*!" spat Grace, gesturing at basically everything all around her. "Why are the sheep over there scowling at Sir Nathan? Why is the Hero crying instead of smiting everything around him? Why are you able to hold the Sword of Power and fight as if you were the Hero himself? And, though not as important, why is that man up on top of a barn that appears to have been built with a giant crab shell for a roof?"

Farmer McSkooble tipped his hat at her in greeting. "Ma'am."

"Why, whatever do you mean, *as if I were the Hero myself*? I *am* the Hero! Do you not recognize me? Ho, ho, silly Grace! You have such a sense of humor and always tell the funniest jokes! Now, enough of your silliness. Tell me ... how did you happen to come upon us when our need was greatest?"

"Uh ... well, I had just returned to the Royal Palace from my special assignment. I was trying to get a straight answer out of a Junior Butler about why all of Mariskatania seemed to be slowly sinking when I received a confusing note from Queen Gobbledeegook. It said something about a whale and a lot of water and Sir Nathan wearing the wrong helmet and how you had all ridden off and that I was to track you down at once. I followed as quickly as I could, thanks to the amazing efforts of my fine horse."

"No problem," said Flopsy from where she stood.

From atop his barn, Farmer McSkooble had an excellent view of the entire battle. It had been quite dramatic, what with all the metallic lobster machines and the splashing of the water and the shooting of the darts. Fortunately, other than his smashed sugar-storage shed, the rest of his farm had remained undamaged, which is more than he could say for the last time Sir Nathan and Amazing Grace had been there.

It seemed to him as if something had changed since the last time he had seen the knights, which was right after their battle with the giant Grab Crab on whose shell he was currently sitting. Back then, Sir Nathan was walking around in nothing more than his underwear and the girl knight had looked as if her clothes had been both chewed on by a dragon.

Now, the Hero was appropriately dressed, but

was a lot quieter than usual. And rather than the homemade armor Grace had been wearing the last time Farmer McSkooble saw her, she was now dressed in some of the finest armor he had ever seen. It was a rich copper color that matched her flowing hair and had decorative patterns embossed into it. The breast plate was covered in a hammered design showing a spoon, a fork, and a butter knife held in an outstretched squid tentacle.

Her piercing, blue eyes glared out through the visor on her helm, which was curiously bucket-shaped.

Most curious of all was the weapon she carried. Instead of a sword, like most soldiers Farmer McSkooble had seen, she carried a soup-ladle made from the same gleaming metal as her armor. It positively glowed in the sunshine and, sword or not, Farmer McSkooble could only imagine what sort of bruise the weapon must cause.

"Your Highness, I really must —" Amazing Grace started to say, but she was cut off by the Princess.

"Hush now! We must question the prisoners so that we may discover the whereabouts of the foul whale and finish him once and for all!"

Grace gave Tupolev a "Is she kidding?" sort of look. He could only shrug in reply, which was pretty impressive for a horse if you stopped and thought about it.

Princess Abbey held the lobster in her left hand and pointed the massive Sword of Power at its tiny, black eyes with her right. The creature thrashed in her grip, but even the hardest pinches from its claws on Abbey's fingers got it no closer to freedom.

"Listen here, scum of villainy," said Princess Abbey in a menacing tone. "You'd better tell us what we want to know, or else it will go poorly for you. The Basic Knight Training Manual specifically says you can't torture prisoners, but I'm pretty sure it doesn't say anything about boiling them in a pot of water and serving them covered in melted butter."

The crustacean quit its wiggling and stared unflinchingly back at her. When it spoke, its voice was squeaky and hard to understand. "All hail Kale the Whale, he who is the master! All must serve the master!"

"Oh, I'll serve the master, all right ... I'll serve him up on a plate with a slice of pie right after a lobster-soup appetizer!"

However, the Princess' threats seemed to have no affect, even with the entire Sword of Power poised to skewer the lobster from head to tail. No matter what she demanded of it, no matter how she threatened it, the creature would only ever reply with the words, "All must serve the master!"

"That's it, I've had enough of this!" snarled the Princess. "Tupolev, go fetch me a big pot and some fire wood!"

Tupolev nodded and started off, but then stopped himself. The horse, a knight himself, knew it wasn't proper to boil prisoners, no matter how much they deserved it. Secondly, with the rapidly rising flood waters, there wasn't a dry piece of firewood for miles around, though he did know a great recipe for lobster and licorice stew.

"Wait a second," said Grace. While Abbey had been threatening the first lobster, Grace had been carefully studying the second. She was amazed at the way the creatures had been able to control the ThingamaBots. That certainly wasn't normal behavior for such an animal. Usually, all the lobsters Grace had ever met had just tried to convince her to loan them her favorite, big pot and all of her butter which they would take and never give back, for reasons she couldn't figure out.

"Yes, Amazing Grace? Have you thought of a better way to convince this villainous, hard-shelled, finger-pincher to tell us the location of Kale the Whale? Perhaps tickling it until it can't breathe? Or, better yet, lets make a sandwich out of it!"

"No, no, nothing like that." Grace pointed at the lobster's face, casually swatting away one of its claws as it tried to pinch her. "I see something weird attached to its shell, above the eyes. Does that lobster you're holding have the same thing?"

The Princess peered closely at the dark red crustacean in her hand. At first she didn't seen anything out of the ordinary. Its entire body, spindly legs and all, was covered in a mottled shell of blackish-red. Each claw was almost as big as the rest of its body. A pair of black, glossy eyes, like tiny glass marbles, stared back at her, beneath which were a twitching pair of antenna.

The lobster stuck its tongue out at her.

Then she saw what Grace was talking about. It was a small, dark object that easily blended in with the pattern on the lobster's shell, but it was unmistakably more of Kale the Whale's handiwork.

Atop the lobster's head, right above the eyes, was what was possibly the world's tiniest helmet. However, this was no metal headgear built to protect the wearer from tiny bonks to the noggin. Held in place with a tiny chin strap, this was a device made of tiny little gears driving tiny little chains, with tiny little puffs of steam coming out of tiny little brass pipes.

"All must serve the master!" the lobster was still screaming in its minuscule voice. "Serve the master! Serve the master!"

"Hush yourself!" snapped the Princess. Moving quicker than the eye could follow, she poked the point of the Sword of Power at the lobster. Grace cried out, figuring the Princess had finally decided to skewer the critter once and for all. Instead, wielding the sword as precisely as Sir Nathan ever had, Abbey merely sliced through the chin strap holding the bizarre contraption onto the creature's skull.

Its gears and cogs still whirring, the helmet slid off and plopped into the water below.

"Serve the master! Serve the master! Serve the ... uh ... what was I saying?" The lobster's tiny eyes looked around in confusion. "Say, where am I? And who are you? And why are you pointing that sword at me?"

"Ah, now I see the truth behind the evil actions of these creatures!" declared the Princess. "They were not acting like themselves, but were instead forced to act in an evil way by that horrid device perched atop their brains."

Grace tried to make sense of what the Princess

was telling her. Her mind was still whirling in a muddied confusion of its own, overwhelmed by the flooding land and the sobbing Hero and Princess Abbey acting almost entirely not like herself. She let out a sudden scream as the Sword of Power came swinging just inches past her face, humming as it cut through the air. Oh, no! Clearly whatever was affecting the Princess' brain had caused her to snap and she was attacking Grace!

But instead of a blood-thirsty, sneaky assault, the sword passed harmlessly by, neatly severing the strap on the second lobster's brain-control device. Seconds later, it was also free of the whale's control and asking numerous questions about what was going on, where it was, and what had happened to the stinky, dead fish it had been eating until a whale had swum up and stuck something on its head.

"Do you see, my brave friend?" the Princess asked Grace. "Yet another of the whale's inventions, designed to control these innocent, little creatures and force them to do his dirty work! Good has once again overcome the forces of evil! It is a time for celebration."

They released the lobsters into the water, with promises to explain everything to the confused creatures. Shaking their tiny heads, the lobsters swam over to where the sheep were working on a machine designed to dump the wailing Sir Nathan off their work bench so they could get back to building their ladder.

"Yes, it *is* a time for celebration," said Grace slowly, just to agree. She found herself as confused as the lobsters about everything that was going on.

Despite the Princess' impressive actions during the battle, Grace had grave concerns about Abbey's behavior and felt she needed to get her back to the Royal Palace for her own safety. "Tell you what ... we'll celebrate all you want and you can tell me everything that's going on and get me up to speed and then we'll *both* set out in pursuit of this whale you keep talking about. Okay? I truly don't understand what's going on here, but why don't you let me take and hold that sword for you, Your Highness, before you cut yourself."

"What?! Why, there is no need!" exclaimed the Princess. "A hero's arm is strong and powerful and never tires! Besides, no one is better at wielding the Sword of Power than me. What chance is there of accidentally cutting myself? Oh, you silly knight, you worry too much!"

As if to demonstrate, the Princess swung the weapon around in an intricate flourish of swings, thrusts, stabs, and parries, the sword moving so quickly as to be a blur.

Grace shook her head, puzzled. Whatever was going on, it did truly seem the Princess was somehow able to handle the weapon in a way she shouldn't have been able to. Perhaps there was no need to relieve her of the sword after all, especially so long as Abbey was able to take Sir Nathan's place while the knight was incapable of performing his duties.

"However," continued Abbey, "I have had a doozy of a time with my armor. It just doesn't seem to fit properly today." With her free hand, she tugged and pulled at her sopping-wet gown. "If you could be so kind as to hold the Sword of Power while I get myself adjusted, it would be most appreciated."

"Uh ... sure. Go ahead and adjust your ... uh ... armor." Grace wondered if the Princess actually thought her soaked dress was Sir Nathan's full suit of plate mail.

Trying to figure out just how she was going to get the pair of them acting more like themselves, Grace reached out and took the sword from the Princess. As the blade's pommel fit into her hand, there was a sharp flash of light, accompanied by a crackling buzz! Just like had happened with Princess Abbey in the Big Comfy Chair Room, the air filled with the sharp smell of a passing storm.

Grace froze in place. Her eyes grew wide as if whatever was happening was too much for her brain to understand. For a long, long moment, she didn't move. Next to her, Princess Abbey looked much the same.

Then, with a sudden intense look in her eyes, Grace thrust the Sword of Power high, pointing it at the heavens. "My work here is done!" she yelled. "We must continue forward on our mission to hunt down and defeat the evil Kale the Whale! Nothing bad can happen as long as I, the Hero of Mariskatania, am here to protect you all! Be safe, my good citizens!"

She saluted the flock of Licorice Sheep with the sword. They stared back, completely convinced all humans were crazy.

"Come, my fine steed, we must ride at once!" Grace called in a booming voice. Staring at her in confusion, Flopsy trotted slowly over to her side. "Oh, not you, you silly thing. You are not the mount of the Hero of Mariskatania. I need Tupolev, my faithful steed. Here, boy! Let us ride off and fight evil, wherever it may rear its ugly head!"

Tupolev had been over by the sheep, watching in fascination as their hastily assembled contraption lifted Sir Nathan off their work table and onto his back. The lobsters, though still baffled by what had happened to them, were happily pitching in and helped to tie the crying knight back into place.

Tupolev looked from Grace, her arm still holding the Sword of Power high in the air, to Abbey. The Princess now looked as confused as everyone else. He was about to open his mouth and start asking some serious questions to get to the bottom of things, when he was interrupted by Grace.

"The time grows short, my faithful steed! Now is not the time for delay! We must ride forth ... now!"

With a heart-weary sigh, he trotted through the deepening water to Grace's side. She vaulted into his saddle lightly, as if her armor weighed nothing. With an apologetic look back at Flopsy, Tupolev galloped off to the south, with Grace swinging the sword overhead and whooping about goodness and honor.

Back by the barn, the Princess was standing in the thigh-deep water. Her gown's skirt floated around her legs in a soggy tangle and her hair was plastered to her head in an unruly, damp mess.

She looked slowly around, as if surrounded by a

strange, bizarre land. She stared at the Licorice Sheep and their half-complete ladder. She gawked at the barn with its crab-shell roof and the farmer sitting calmly on top. She goggled around at the endless stretch of water covering the land.

Finally, she looked down at herself. Her gown was torn and tattered from her adventures. Her shoes were splitting open, the material coming unglued, the original color hidden under a thick layer of mud. Her hair was gritty and smelled like a murky bog.

The scream that tore from her throat was the fourth-loudest scream Mariskatania had ever heard. Interestingly enough, the top three loudest screams all belonged to Sir Nathan, all happening on days when he had put on his armor without first checking to see if the Royal Twins had filled it with stinging scorpions first.

"Where am I?!" Princess Abbey yelled. The sheep just stared at her. "What am I doing here? What happened to my clothes? Why is Sir Nathan tied to the back of Tupolev, crying? And why in the world did Grace just ride off like that without me?!"

Trotting up beside the Princess, Flopsy simply said, "Yeah, I'd like an answer to that last one myself. Come on ... I'll give you a ride home."

From atop the barn, Farmer McSkooble watched Abbey and the mare ride away, disappearing over a hill to the North East. Grace, Sir Nathan, and Tupolev had long since disappeared to the south. Below him, the sheep were putting the finishing touches on their ladder, sped along by some helpful advice from the pair of lobsters. The sun had decided it had been a full day and was starting to sink into a spectacular sunset in what was almost, but not quite, the exact wrong direction to set.

The farmer pulled his hat from his head and wiped the sweat from his brow with a checkered handkerchief. Looking around sadly and seeing his newly repaired farm getting destroyed once again, this time by a bizarre flood, and at the angry sheep down below, he said, "Perhaps it's time to get out of the farming business and go into something less stressful ... like dragon-taming."

\* \* \* \* \*

# PART III

The morning sun rose over a quiet, serene landscape, its orange light reflecting off the still waters of an inland sea that had unexpectedly appeared over the past day or two. The morning dew dripped off a small cluster of Huckle Nut Trees, practically drowning them in clinging droplets of water. Normally the morning dew was content to coat the grasses and flowers and bushes that dotted the landscape, but since all the grasses and flowers and bushes were currently deep underwater, the dew had nowhere else to go.

An entire family of Hobnobber Squirrels sat perched in one tree, all ninety-seven of them, each of them sad none of the branches were growing any Huckle Nuts. They were also depressed by the recent death of one of the family's great uncles, who had learned the hard way that Hobnobber Squirrels can't swim when he had set out to explore the other Huckle Nut Trees.

Things hadn't been made any easier by the pair of FlibbertyJibbits that were rough housing in the waters at the base of the tree. The fuzzy, white critters were making matters much worse for for the squirrels for two reasons. The first was that they had done nothing to assist the elderly Hobnobber Squirrel great uncle as he had been swept away by the floodwaters. The second was that they happened to be randomly saying the most insensitive things as they chased each other around the trunk of the tree.

"It's a shame the way that blue rodent didn't stand a chance of surviving," one would say, completely randomly and without any understanding whatsoever of the words coming out of its mouth.

"Truly a terrible shame that the squirrel should perish, especially since we are such fantastic swimmers and could have easily saved him with just the tiniest of efforts," the other would answer, no better at understanding what it was saying than a Hobnobber Squirrel understood how to swim.

"Did you ever notice how all the biggest cheeses in Mariskatania belong to the tallest blacksmiths?" the first would respond, while really its tiny brain was only wondering where it might find a nice bit of fish for lunch.

Suddenly, the FlibbertyJibbits stopped their play. The ripples from their antics faded across the water's surface. They clung to the tree trunk with only their white heads exposed and peered intently to the North. Listening with their ridiculously cute ears and scanning the shore for danger with their preposterously adorable eyes, they searched for the source of the sound they had just heard.

"I think it's best if we were going," said one of the otters randomly.

"Sometimes the juice of the Wobble Melon can

be used to fuel a magical craft capable of traveling to the moon and back," the other replied.

In a flash, they both disappeared under the water and swam off to safety. Up above, the squirrel family just watched, incapable of doing much more than keeping an eye out for the sudden appearance of a Huckle Nut.

"Onward, my faithful steed!" came the shout of a loud, bold voice from out of the morning mists that hovered over the water's surface like a lost cloud. "Onward! Ride like the wind so we may strike forth and smite our enemies! Ride!"

If the squirrels were expecting some fantastically muscled horse to come bursting out of the mist, galloping in a spray of water and carrying a bold knight on its back as they rode off to battle, they were disappointed. All that they saw was a fantastically muscled horse slowly plodding along, looking like the last thing he wanted in the world was to be anywhere near a battle. The knight mounted in his saddle looked exactly the opposite.

The knight's armor was a deep copper color that matched her long, glossy hair. A design of a squid holding several eating utensils was shaped into the breast plate. She kicked repeatedly at the horse's flanks with her heels, urging the steed to ride, ride, ride! The horse wore a look on his face clearly showing how incredibly tired he was of getting kicked all the time.

Behind the overly excited knight was a second. Where the first sat high and proud in the saddle, the second was tied to the horse's back in a thick tangle of rope. Where the first shouted constantly about honor and smiting, the second just sobbed and moaned pitifully.

As the horse and his riders passed under the Huckle Nut Tree full of squirrels, with all ninety-seven blue faces staring down through the branches at them, Tupolev took the opportunity to repeat what he had been saying for most of the past day. "You know, I could really concentrate more on getting us to where we're going if you'd stop kicking me, Amazing Grace."

"Onwards, my gallant mount! Onwards! On – what's that? Stop kicking you? But ... how else will you know that I, the Hero of *all* Mariskatania, am ready to ride forth and smite evil? The time is short, evil is afoot, and we must smite it down wherever it is to be found! So, onwards, my strong steed, and – hey, why do you call me *Amazing Grace*? Has some evil spell been cast upon you, forcing you to forget who I am? Do you not recognize me?"

It was clear to Tupolev that Amazing Grace had started to act bonkers right where Princess Abbey had left off. Though on a normal day she was easily as bold and courageous as Sir Nathan and just as likely to run around shouting about smiting, now she was acting just as incredibly bizarre as the Princess had been. Sadly, the horse was unable to figure out just what was causing them to behave so strangely.

"Perhaps there is an evil imp, living in your brain!" declared Grace boldly. "Fear not, my trusty steed! I shall smite the imp right out of your skull and have you back to your old self in no time at all!"

She raised the Sword of Power high, its sharp edges gleaming in the sunlight. The blade was capable of cleaving through solid metal and stone as easily as a spoon digging into a dish of Gumbleberrry pudding. Tupolev had no doubt what would happen if that sword came crashing down on his head.

"No! No, not necessary! Stop right there ... uh ... *Hero* of Mariskatania, I have recovered my wits and am under no evil spell!"

Grace lowered the Sword of Power. She glared at the horse suspiciously, always on the lookout for any of the dirty tricks evil was always trying to get away with. Patting Tupolev on the neck, she said, "It is good to see you are better, my fine steed. That awful imp must have realized it was no match for the likes of me and fled your brain straightaway."

"Uh ... yeah ... I'm *sure* that was what happened," agreed Tupolev. It was clear to him the same odd curse that had affected Princess Abbey was now affecting Amazing Grace. But what was it? What could cause them both to think they were the Hero of Mariskatania, while causing the Hero himself to act like a bawling child at the same time? Odder yet was the way Grace had picked up right where Abbey's odd behavior had left off, as if the mysterious affliction had jumped instantly from one to the other.

The horse felt bad about leaving the Princess behind once she had started to act like herself, but he was comforted by the fact that Flopsy would take good care of her and get her back to the palace.

If anyone was suffering from the trickery of an

evil brain-imp, it was clearly Grace and the Princess, though Tupolev wisely kept that thought to himself. The last thing he needed to be explaining to Queen Gobbledeegook was why Amazing Grace had tried to slice her own head open in a confused effort to rid it of tiny demons.

The horse pushed on through the deepening waters, his mind a jumbled mess of thoughts as he tried to understand all the goofy people around him. He found it difficult to figure things out, especially with Sir Nathan's constant moaning interrupting his thoughts.

Swiveling in the saddle, Grace turned and looked back at the Hero who was tied to the horse like a sack of mail.

"I say, you there," she called out to Sir Nathan. He merely moaned in answer. "I say, you appear to be a knight-like fellow, what with that suit of armor you wear. I do not see a weapon, but perhaps it has been lost in all this water. However, if you're indeed a brave, bold, warrior-knight, why do you carry on so? Why do you add the moisture of your tears to my steed's already-damp backside?"

His eyes bloodshot from crying, his nose red and running, Sir Nathan peered back at Grace through a puffy face. "Bold? Why ... *sniff* ... why would you think I'm bold?"

"Well, surely *any* knight would have to be filled with bravery and courage. That's what separates us from the ordinary citizens! Though, I am reminded of one rather ferocious young lady who lives in the Royal Palace. I would not wish to give her a reason to be angry with me."

"She lives in the Royal Palace?" asked Sir Nathan with a sob and a sniffle. "Sounds like you're describing ... *sniff* ... the Princess. Oh, she terrifies me!" He broke into another long fit of moans, each louder than the last.

"Ah, but she needn't do so! With boldness and honor, we knights can stand up to *any* enemy, be they a foul monster or merely a foul-tempered princess."

Sir Nathan's crying tapered off to quieter whimpering as he thought about what Grace was telling him. "But ... but ... what if she were to yell at me? I couldn't stand up to that. My heart would leap into my throat and my legs would turn to wobbly jelly and I'm sure I'd just collapse ... *sniff* ... collapse into a puddle of terrified goo."

"Nonsense!" cried Grace. "A knight doesn't know the meaning of the word *terror*. Nor does a knight know the meaning of the words *fear*, *horror*, *despair* nor *sphygmomanometer*! We laugh in the face of *fear*! We ignore the clutches of *horror*! We smite feelings of *despair*! We grab a dictionary when trying to spell *sphygmomanometer*! Nothing can hinder us!"

Sir Nathan looked at her doubtfully.

Grace reached out to Sir Nathan, having forgotten for the moment that his hands were tied (along with the rest of his body). She said, "Rise up! Take my hand and join me! Come and be bold and honorable at my side and together we shall rid the world of this foul whale and save the land we love!"

For a moment, it looked as if Grace had gotten through Sir Nathan's misery. He sniffed back a few tears and actually raised his head off Tupolev's back to take a look around. But then the site of the endless flood waters caused his own endless flood of tears to start once more. He shut his eyes tightly, shaking his head violently from side to side.

"No!" he cried. "No, it's too much! The world is too scary and I would surely only perish!"

Grace sighed heavily, disappointed. Whoever this strange man was they were carrying around with them (for reasons she didn't quite understand), he seemed forever lost in his feelings of doom. She turned and looked over Tupolev's head, gesturing with the Sword of Power at all the water in front of them.

"Somewhere, out there, is the villain, Kale the Whale," she said quietly to the horse. "He's out there and it's up to us and us alone to stop him. Our sad friend is beyond help and seems forever doomed, never to recover from whatever has frightened him so. Why, if I weren't so honorable and knightly, I'd be tempted to untie this chap, whoever he is, and leave him up in that tree with all those Hobnobber Squirrels."

When they heard this, the squirrels all chattered to each other excitedly. Though his understanding of the Hobnobber language was poor, despite having once been turned into a squirrel himself, Tupolev could tell the animals were all very interested to find out if Sir Nathan had any Huckle Nuts hidden somewhere inside his armor.

With the chattering of the Hobnobber Squirrels fading into the distance, Tupolev started forward once more, wading through the rising floodwaters.

Meanwhile, Grace continued to swing the Sword of Power around and shout vague threats to anything evil that might be listening. Sir Nathan only contributed more shameless crying.

With the lowest bits of the land around them buried under water, it was getting more and more difficult to tell exactly where they were. As usual, the sun wasn't being any help. On a *normal* planet with a *normal* sun, you could use its position in the sky to tell which direction you were facing. In Mariskatania, the only normal thing about the sun was that it was big, it was round, and it was hot. Everything after that was just kooky nonsense. Even so, Tupolev somehow knew they were riding South. Soon they should be passing out of the green lands in which Farmer McSKooble's farm was built and into what was normally the dry, hot plains of the Dangerous Desert of Disasters.

Tupolev's last adventure into the desert had been an exciting adventure, starting with the scorching, unforgiving heat and ending with an exciting battle against the savage members of the Eager Angry Ogre Tribe. There had been plenty of wonderful smiting. Now, he wondered what state the desert might be in. Would it still be a hot, dry, sandy place if it was sunk beneath the cool, refreshing waves of a flood?

Several hours later, he had his answer.

As they crossed the desert's border, the occasional grassy hills and tall trees poking up out of the water became occasional dunes of white, gritty sand. And, try as it might, the sun was really having a difficult time heating the desert up to its normal, scorching temperatures. With the entire region covered in a flood, there wasn't much that could be done to make it a dry, hot, miserable place.

Frustrated and pouting, the sun left in a hurry. It set hastily in the North, and the land was plunged into the darkness of night.

Still, Tupolev moved on. He found traveling through a flooded desert to be a bit easier than traveling through a flooded forest. The submerged sand compacted nicely beneath his hooves instead of turning into a thick, sticky mud and the flood waters ran much more clearly without leaves and grass and dirt to foul them.

Besides the fact that the whole world was slowly flooding, they were constantly reminded of the reason for their quest by the occasional Cataclysm Crate they passed. Every single metal box was producing a constant deluge of water, adding to the rising flood and driving them on in their effort to put a stop to Kale the Whale's horrible plan.

After a long while, weary from the difficult work of pushing his way through the water, Tupolev signaled that he needed to stop for the night. By his best calculations, he figured it was darned close to his regular bedtime anyway. When Grace protested, shouting angrily that she was ready to stay up the whole night if need be, Tupolev reminded her that he was the one doing all the work, while carrying not just one, but two riders.

Grace gave up, but not without a heavy sigh of disgust and a pouting look or two. Using his teeth to untie the knots holding Sir Nathan to his back, the horse dropped the knight on to the sands of a dry dune that poked up out of the flood waters. Sir Nathan instantly curled into a ball and cried himself to sleep. Grace looked at the knight without bothering to disguise the disgust on her face.

While Tupolev flopped to the ground and quickly nodded off, Grace paced around the borders of what was basically a small island. Sword of Power in hand, she vowed to patrol all night long to keep them safe, just in case they were attacked by sharks, or alligators, or sharks riding on the backs of alligators. A lone PigWiggle circled her head, feeding off her frustration and grunting contentedly.

"Once again, it is up to me, the Hero of Mariskatania, to protect the weak and the *tired*," she muttered. She spat the word *tired* like a curse. "Apparently, some people think there's plenty of time for a nap, despite the fact that the whole world is going to drown! Well, let me tell you ... when there's evil loose in the world and every single person is in danger, you would never catch *me* sleeping!"

\* \* \* \* \*

The Gasplort Vine wrapped its thorny tendrils around Grace's legs, catching her easily while she slept.

Gasplort Fruit hadn't been seen growing in the Dangerous Desert of Disasters for at least a thousand years. Back then, the whole area had been a lush, green place, filled with streams running with clear waters, endless grasslands, and thick forests that grew some of the tallest Jubb Jubb Trees the world had ever seen.

But then the Demon Herd of Kudzooey had come through, the hundred-foot-tall evil cows eating everything in their path, leaving the land a desolate, sandy wasteland. At the time, the Hero of Mariskatania had been a calm warrior by the name of Dame Maria the Infinitely Patient. She had calmly waited until the Demon Herd had fallen asleep after eating so much and then slaughtered every evil cow. She used their massive hides to make leather coats for every single citizen of the land, along with matching belts and fancy boots.

What most people didn't know was the plants that used to grow so abundantly in the region had left behind their seeds, buried and long forgotten beneath the shifting sands. When the flood came rushing through, the tiny seeds finally found themselves nurtured with the water they needed to germinate.

Impatient at having waited around for so long, the seeds burst open explosively and started to grow at astonishing speeds. While Tupolev and Sir Nathan (and yes, even Amazing Grace) slept, hundreds of plants wriggled their way out of the sands like countless, irritated snakes whose tails were anchored in the ground.

Even the normally calm plants, like Smooshelberries and Sodapopcorn, grew quickly and angrily. They thrashed around with their stalks, leaves, and flowers, angry at having been forgotten and looking for someone to take it out on.

In just a short while, the entire sandy island on

which the party slept was covered in a deep thicket of greenery. Fortunately, Sir Nathan's loud sobbing woke the others before things had really gotten out of hand when he cried out because the prickly leaves of a Wobble Melon vine were stuffing themselves up his nose in an effort to stop his terrible snoring. Having been kept awake by Sir Nathan's snoring on many a night, Tupolev had often dreamed of doing the exact same thing. It was hard work carrying the Hero all day, dressed in his heavy suit of plate mail, and it didn't help the horse any to suffer a terrible night's sleep because the knight's snarling, snorting snoring kept him awake.

"Leave me alone!" sobbed Sir Nathan as he feebly tried to push away the wriggling vines of the Wobble Melon. In just a matter of minutes, the plant had grown two large, black-and-white checkered fruits and was using them to bonk the knight on the head.

The commotion woke the others just in time. Grace's entire lower half was wrapped tightly in the clutches of the Gasplort vine and Tupolev was actually being passed, leaf to leaf, down the slopes of the dune toward the water's edge. Apparently, the plants were convinced the horse would surely gobble them all up for breakfast and so they had quickly hatched a plan to strike first and chuck him into the floodwaters.

"What sort of treachery is this?!" cried Amazing Grace as she woke and saw the wriggling vine coiling its way up her body. She reached out and grabbed the Sword of Power from where a nearby Smooshelberry bush had been trying to bury it in the sand. With a deft swing, she severed through the vine encircling her legs. The thick, green stalk fell to the sand, severed in half and writhing on the ground.

Tupolev woke much more slowly and was groggily trying to understand what was happening to him. Unfortunately, he didn't get the chance before he was tossed into the chilly waters. The shock cleared the last of the cobwebs from his mind and he violently kicked and splashed his way back to shore, choking on the water he had swallowed.

Grace hopped to her feet and strode over to where Sir Nathan was feebly pushing against the grasping stems of the Wobble Melon vine. Two quick swings chopped the melons in half and the fruit screamed in agony. Wobble Melons were one of those odd fruits that would yell and scream and make a fuss when they were first cut into and no one knew why. Someone cutting into a Wobble Melon for the first time, eager for a delicious snack, would most likely be quite surprised by a fruit that groaned in pain. But then the melon would yell "Just kidding!" and fall quiet.

It was very odd.

"On your feet, soldier!" yelled Grace, grabbing Sir Nathan by the arm and jerking him upright. He simply stood there, sobbing and trying to wipe the Wobble Melon juice from his face.

With a sticky-headed Sir Nathan on one side and a soaking wet Tupolev on the other, Grace loudly proclaimed, "You two should be ashamed of yourself! You fell asleep while on guard duty! We might have been killed! It's a good thing I was here to save the day!"

"But —" started Tupolev, but she cut him off with a sharp gesture.

"No time to argue about it, my fine steed! I forgive you. Now we must mount up and ride!"

"Yeah, but —"

"I said we must mount up and ride! Now!"

With a weary sigh, Tupolev helped Grace push Sir Nathan back into place and tie him down, muttering the whole time about how it seemed that acting like a hero always seemed to involve a lot of bossiness.

* * * * *

Globpimple the ogre was not having a very good day.

In fact, for as long as she could remember, she had never ever had a good day in her entire life. However, some days were worse than others and this day was one of them.

She figured her life was miserable mostly due to the fact that she was a member of the Eager Angry Ogre Tribe, or at least what was left of it. The tribe had once been proud, fierce, and strong, with many members. Now it contained less ogres than all of Globpimple's fingers and toes added up, which turned out to be exactly twenty.

Oddly enough, the total number of all her toes and fingers just two weeks ago was much higher than twenty, but then there had been an embarrassing accident involving a FlibbertyJibbit and a sack of day-old doughnuts. Now, other than a couple of missing toes and fingers, Globpimple was pretty normal looking for an ogre, which meant she had rough skin like the bark of a tree, a pair of tusks sprouting from her lower jaw and a spiky tail.

In the old days, the Eager Angry Ogre Tribe had gone where it wanted and took what it needed and there were plenty of chicken heads for everyone at meal time. Their three bold ogre chiefs had led them on many exciting adventures and things were generally pretty good. As one of the youngest members of the tribe, Globpimple usually had been assigned all of the cruddiest of the tasks, such as throwing away what was left of the chickens after their heads had been removed and convincing those chickens not yet turned into meals that everything was fine and they really shouldn't worry too much about why they hadn't heard from certain members of the flock lately.

And then the tribe had made the mistake of messing with a pair of humans from the North, all dressed in shiny armor and wielding powerful weapons. The ogres had been beaten and scattered. The few of them that ran away early in the battle and hid in the endless desert sands had found each other in the days that followed and formed a new, smaller tribe. The nastiest, bossiest ogre in the bunch took charge of the rest, now that their chiefs were gone, and she took great delight at yelling at all of her followers.

Especially Globpimple.

More than once, the young ogre had dreamed of running away. She had heard rumors that several members of the tribe had moved to the West after the battle and settled down peacefully, with a whole lot less shouting than there used to be. However, the one time Globpimple had tried to sneak away at night to try to join them, her new chief had caught her and punished her severely.

"Quits yer lollygagging, you lazy sack of lazinesses!" shouted Chief Glee, whipping a Hucklenut at Globpimple's head and interrupting her slow ogre thoughts. The chief had an amazing knack of always having a supply of nuts on hand, even out in the wasteland of the desert, and was capable of throwing them at blistering speeds, hitting her target every time.

Her target, more often than not, was Globpimple's head.

"Yes, of course, rights away, Chief Glee!" shouted the young ogre, taking up the slack on the thick, coarse rope in her hands and pulling with all her might.

The chief's full name was actually GleefulJoyPunchPunch, but everyone just called her Chief Glee.

"Listens to me!" shouted the chief to her tribe. They stopped and stared at her, drenched in sweat. Sand stuck to every exposed inch of their hides. "Alls of you, listens to me! You gots to work more harder! If we wants to survive, then you gots to pull them ropes with all your strengths! Now, get to work!"

"We *was* working – *Ow!* – until you stopped us to – *Ow!* – yell at us," muttered Globpimple under her breath, interrupted by the occasional thrown Hucklenut. She and two other ogres pulled hard on their rope, making slow progress through the Dangerous Desert of Disasters.

The land around them had changed in the last few days and the chief had ordered them to abandon the only home any of them had ever known in order to find a safe place to live. At first, the water that had come trickling through the dry sands had seemed like a miracle. Though rough and tough in nature, and able to withstand the heat of the desert and the scarcity of food, even ogres enjoy a refreshing drink every now and then.

But then the water had risen, faster and faster. Pretty soon what had been a small, trickling stream had become several streams, who then joined together into wider, more violent rivers. And even then the water hadn't stopped. Pretty soon the calm, dusty desert was nothing but a stretch of sandy island dunes, separated by an endless sea.

Desperate to save her tribe (because what good was an ogre chief without someone to shout orders to) Chief Glee had screamed at her followers, whipping them into action. In an amazing feat, the small tribe had built a fleet of gorgeous boats. After hammering a last nail into the bright orange and blue sailboat she had been building, Globpimple stood back and wiped the sweat out of her eyes and paused for a moment to wonder just where they had found all the wood and rope and canvas and nails and tools and paint and other things usually necessary to not only build a boat, but to build twelve of them, each more than twenty feet long with graceful curves and thick, strong masts. But a hurled Hucklenut had driven the wondering thought out of her head and Globpimple got back to work.

The tribe had loaded all of their belongings onto the boats and set forth to find a nice, dry, safe place to live. Unfortunately, they weren't making very good time.

"Uh ... Chief Glee, your most terrible ogre-ness?" called Globpimple as she tugged on her rope.

The chief was riding in the prow of the lead boat, her hands shielding her eyes from the sun as she searched the horizon. She turned and look down at the young ogre.

"What is it, you weak wretch of a thing!" shouted the chief, fingering a particularly large Hucklenut.

"I apologizes, oh mighty Chief Ogre, but I just can't help but thinks there might be a better way for us to be doing this."

"Listen, lowest of the low," screamed the chief, her over-sized face turning blotchy and red in anger. "Your jobs is nots to be thinking! Your jobs is to be pulling on that rope! I is the chief of the tribe and I is the one that tells you whats we oughts to be doing!"

"Okay, if you says so," said Globpimple agreeably. "It just seems like there's something we're missing."

With a massive grunt, the coarse rope burning her hands, Globpimple and the other ogres continued to pull with all their might. They finally managed to drag their boat up and over the crest of one of the dunes. The sharp, V-shaped hull left a

gouge through the soft sands behind them. Even now that it was pointed downhill, it still took quite a bit of effort to drag the boat along.

Globpimple looked at the rising flood, just a few feet away. "Say ... I wonder if the sands would be a lots more slippery if we were to coats it with water."

However, rather than risk getting another nut to the head, she just kept quiet, wondering what they were going to do if the higher, dry land they were traveling across ever ran out and they were forced to pull the boats through the water.

"As difficults as it is to drags these boats along," Globpimple muttered to herself, "it must be a whole lots more harder to drags them through that stuff."

* * * * *

*Boom!*

*Boom, boom, boom!*

*Boom, boom, boom, boom, boom, boom, splash!*

The sounds had slowly been growing steadily louder in Globpimple's ears. She sat up and took a long look around in the harsh, afternoon sunlight. The few members of the Eager Angry Ogre Tribe were taking a short break from the difficult chore of hauling their boats across the sand, not so much because their Chief was a wise and considerate ogre, but more because their Chief had tripped over her own, over-large feet and somersaulted head-over-backside down a particularly steep sand dune.

Her mouth full of half-swallowed sand, Chief

Glee had tumbled right off the edge of the island and fell with a loud splash into the rising flood waters. Dizzy and choking, she sank quickly below the surface.

The other ogres could only stare in confusion as their chief sank like some sort of craft designed to float on water that had gotten a hole in it and filled with water, whatever such a thing would be called. Without someone shouting orders at them and throwing nuts at their heads, they really didn't know what they should do in such a situation.

What if the chief *wanted* to trip and roll down the hill and sink underwater? If they were to go charging in, thinking they were being helpful and rescuing her, but were in fact only interrupting her careful plans, they'd surely be in a heap of trouble.

Besides, if someone so important as Chief Glee could sink so easily beneath the flowing waters, what chance did simple ogres like themselves have? Clearly there was more to swimming than any of them understood. If the chief couldn't handle it, her stupid followers (for that's what she was always calling them) were surely doomed if they so much as stuck a single toe in the water.

They decided it was probably better to just sit back and wait for Chief Glee to clearly tell them exactly what it was she wanted.

They plopped down in the shade of their boats for a rest.

After what had seemed like an awfully long wait, with Chief Glee giving them absolutely no orders on what they should do next, Globpimple noticed the faint booming and splashing sounds. In order to be able to see better, she clambered over the sides of one of the boats and climbed up its tall, wooden mast. Thirty feet above the ground, all she could see in any direction was the flooded desert surrounding them.

It was an unchanging scene of sandy dunes, rising up out of the water one after the other, a sea of desolate islands. Globpimple caught sight of an odd creature that appeared to be marching directly for them. It was a humongous beast, long and grey, riding on some sort of odd wood and metal contraption with more legs than she could count. That number wasn't very high, but Globpimple had never gotten past her *Counting To Three Class* back in Ogre Elementary School due to an argument she had with her teacher about whether or not the number *two* should be renamed something easier to remember.

The many-legged creature stomped down the side of the dune and, without pause, strode right into the waters, throwing up a terrific wave.

*Boom, boom, boom!*

*Splash, splash, splash!*

The massive beast was muttering to itself in a voice filled with anger. As it walked up out of the water and onto the island on which the ogres sat, Globpimple could hear it saying, "Have any of *them* flooded the world? No! Have any of *them* cursed the land's bravest knight? No! Have any of *them* invented a left-handed pencil? No! I'm the smartest one out of all of them, but do they give me any respect?! No! When I get back, I'll – oh, hello!"

The tone of the creature's voice changed

instantly as it saw Globpimple staring at it.

"I'm so sorry, I didn't see you there," he said politely. "My name is Kale the Whale and I'm pleased to meet you! I'd love to stop and chat, however I've got to finish destroying the world, so if you'll pardon me, I'd best get to it!"

With a cheerful little wave of a huge, metal hand that stuck out of its walking contraption, the creature stomped right on by, churning heavily through the soft sand.

As it approached the water's edge once more, it stopped, peering down into the depths of the flood. "Say, there!" it called back over what passed for a shoulder on a whale. "Did you know one of your kind is down here, under the water, looking like she's pretty darned close to drowning?"

With dozens of little gears and cogs on the walking contraption spinning and whirring, Kale reached down and plucked Chief Glee out of the water and deposited her gently back on shore. She collapsed to her knees and frantically sucked in great lungfuls of air. The whale patted her gently on the back with a mechanical hand bigger than she was until she was able to catch her breath.

Then, as quickly as if someone had flipped a switch controlling the whale's mood, he quickly resumed his angry grumblings. Globpimple heard him saying dark, dangerous things that scared her more than Chief Glee's anger ever had.

Using the same hand he had comforted the rescued ogre chief with, the whale reached back and lifted several metal crates off the frame of his walking device from where they had been suspended in special racks and nets hanging there.

Carelessly, he tossed two of the crates to the side. One of them flew through the air and smashed into the tall mast on which Globpimple had climbed. The thick wood splintered, snapping in half, but not before the force of the collision had fully tipped the sailboat onto its side. The ogre flew off her perch and hit the sand rolling. The second crate flew over the crest of the dune, landing out of sight on the other side.

However, the whale handled the third crate carefully. On its side an odd symbol was painted, perhaps meant to be a spider with wriggly legs or possibly a head with wild hair growing out of it. The crate was covered with a coat of algae and a rough blanket of barnacles. The whale gently placed it on the sand as carefully as if it were a newborn kitten and gave it a gentle, loving caress with one massive metal hand.

His voice was deep and rough, sounding exactly like Chief Glee's loud, rough, wet cough whenever she came down with a case of Ogre Pox (which was often). With a malicious-sounding chuckle, he said, "I'll just leave this here for anyone thinking to follow me. We'll just see how this ... *grabs* them!"

Chuckling loudly, he strode off into the waters and out of sight.

Chief Glee flopped over onto her back, spitting out wet sand and sucking in rasping breaths. "Why ... why ..., " she panted, struggling to control her breathing, "... why ... didn't you pathetic slobs come in and save me?"

Globpimple walked over and squatted down

next to her leader. "Well, it was kind of likes this. We was about to pulls you out of the waters, but we weren't sure if we should. Gluck over there yelled at you, askings whether or not you wanted us to grabs you, but you did nots answer him."

Finally catching her breath, Chief Glee growled at the members of her tribe. "If you simpletons thought I was hard on you before, you ain't seen nothing yet! There's going to be so many Hucklenuts whipped at your empty heads, you'll wish this entire desert would flood and wash us all away!"

In answer, Globpimple simply tapped her on the shoulder and pointed over at the rapidly unfolding Catclysm Crate, already starting to spew out a torrent of water.

"Too late," she said, as the gushing water washed down the side of the dune in a turbulent flow and swept the Chief back out into the rising sea.

\* \* \* \* \*

Tupolev was quickly growing tired of an entirely flooded Mariskatania, both physically and mentally.

Usually, the first half of any quest with Sir Nathan was nothing more than running around in circles long enough for the Hero to get tired of shouting about the sneakiness of evil. Tupolev knew they weren't going to get anything done until the knight had gotten some shouting and sword-waving out of his system. This wasn't much of a problem because the steed was in as fine a shape as any horse on the planet and loved the feel of the wind in his mane and the dirt under his hooves as he galloped from point to point, tirelessly.

Now, he found he wasn't pleased at all. This quest involved way more swimming than the horse was used to and he wasn't getting to gallop, trot, nor even canter. It was very frustrating.

On top of that, he was tired of being wet all the time. He was tired of the way Grace simply sat on his back singing heroic battle songs while he did all the work. He was tired of the unending stream of tears, drool, and possibly even snot pouring out of Sir Nathan and onto his hindquarters. He was quite convinced he'd have a permanent stain on his hide after all was said and done.

He was simply tired, inside and out.

It was clear the Dangerous Desert of Disasters was no longer fit to hold the name and at best could be called the Damp Desert of Disappointment.

More and more hilly dunes were sinking beneath the waves and those that remained were overrun with a frantically growing jungle of plants that flourished in the nourishing rays of the sun.

As they traveled on, Tupolev was left with few choices about which path to take, none of them good. He could either continue to wind his way around the dune islands, pushing his way through the deepening water and swimming in the spots where it grew too deep. Or, he could climb up onto dry land, only to be attacked by the thrashing plants that had sprung to life. Even with Grace wielding the Sword of Power and hacking a path, the trail before him was still a difficult one.

Though the sun was far from setting for the day (if indeed it was going to set at all – citizens of Mariskatania had learned long ago that the sun sometimes liked to stay up in the sky for hundreds of hours at a time just to see who it could fool into staying awake for that long) Tupolev was getting close to asking Grace if they could stop for the day. He climbed up the hill of a dune island that was relatively free of plants, despite a Cataclysm Crate just a few yards offshore, pumping out water. It looked like a great place to take a rest.

As he plodded through the deep, soft sand, they came upon a curious sight on the other side.

A second Cataclysm Crate was hard at work, adding its torrent to the flood and doing its best to drown a small, struggling group of ogres. Half of them were getting knocked off their feet over and over again by the crate's rushing torrent. The other half were busy trying to control a small fleet of beautiful sailboats that were trying to float away in the chaos. Surprisingly, the ogre method of regaining control of the boats appeared to be to chop ragged holes in the hulls with their axes, flooding and sinking the craft.

To add to the chaos and confusion, a jumbled mess of plants were writhing up out of the ground and they didn't look like they were in a good mood. One ogre (a pitiful thing with one giant eye in the middle of its face) was fighting off a Punkolantern vine that had grabbed hold of his axe. The sleek, red-hulled boat the ogre had been trying to sink floated away on the current.

"Here now, what's the meaning of this!" cried Grace.

"Oh, hello theres," said Globpimple, the nearest of the ogres. She was holding back an aggressive bush with one hand while holding onto a thick rope tied to a purple boat with the other. The floodwaters were rapidly rising up her legs. "Well, the meanings of this is that we is finding that these here awful waters is trying to steal our boats that we worked hard to build so we could push them across the desert so we could escape all this yucky water that is, as I believe I already mentioned, trying to steals our boats."

Tupolev shook his head sadly. He had dealt with ogres before and knew they weren't really cut out for thinking. Actually, they weren't cut out for much of anything at all except struggling to survive. Ogres had a *great* skill for making simple things, like living through the day without accidentally chopping off an important body part, extremely difficult.

"So, what you're trying to tell me," said Grace in a puzzled voice, "is that in order to be safe from the rising floodwaters, you built boats?"

"Yes, that is corrects. Hey, stops that!" She struggled with the bush as it tried to wrap itself around her throat.

"And, now that the boats are floating in the water, you're ... uh ... what is it exactly you're doing?"

"Well, since the ... *oof!* Knock it off, bush! Since we was just trying to get to a safe place. We builded these boats in order to keeps all our stuff in them and to make it easier to carry and then we was pushing these boats across the sands of the desert to avoid the mean waters. Since the mean waters is trying to steal our boats, we're chopping holes in them so they don't floats and that way the mean waters can't steal them. It's really a pretty good idea. I thoughts it up meself."

Grace frowned. "It never occurred to you that floating on water is what boats are *meant* to do? Why in the name of all that is good and honorable would you build boats and then chop holes in them to stop them from doing what they are supposed to do?"

Globpimple wrinkled her brow in concentration, taking a long, long minute to think about Grace's puzzling question. She looked at the rope in her hand and the boat it was tied to. She looked at the bush in her other hand. It looked back at her and shrugged, as confused about the whole situation as she was.

After a long while, she finally said, "Yeah, buts the mean water was stealing our boats. Why is that so hard for you to understands?"

Grace waved away her question. "Never mind, never mind. So, instead of building boats and then floating them in water to escape the flood, you were pushing them across the sand. Fine. Where were you trying to get to?"

"I tolds you already! Sheesh, you don't listen very much. Perhaps you needs some bigger ears, like an ogre. We was trying to gets to a safe place where the water wouldn't get us. We was living on the tall, tall mountain in the middle of the desert, but knew we couldn't stay there."

Grace scrubbed at her face with a hand, trying to wipe away the frustration. "I know I'm going to regret asking this, but why would you leave a tall mountain to get away from flood waters?"

Tupolev looked on eagerly, happily awaiting what was sure to be a very silly, entertaining answer. The horse had an ogre friend that worked back at the Royal Palace by the name of Garbuggle, who gave the same kind of answers all the time. The horse could never understand the time the ogre had accidentally set a pair of socks on fire as he was washing them. He had taken the time to pull them onto his feet before running out of the palace to find a stream or pond in which he could extinguish the flames. When asked why, Garbuggle had simply replied as if the answer should have been obvious, "Well, if I had *not* put the socks on my feets, then they would have been lefts behind when I ran outs of the palace looking for water."

Globpimple sighed, as equally frustrated with the human's complex questions as Grace was with her answers. "I should thinks it is obvious! The waters is rising, right? Well, us ogres is smart enough to know that rising means *up* and since the top of the mountain is also *up*, we is smarts enough to go *down*. Maybe we can find a nice cave or hole in the grounds where we can hide from all this mean water. Then we would be safe."

Globpimple paused for a moment to kick away a Wobble Melon vine that had crept close and was making a grab at her feet. "Now, you silly human ... *oof!* ... if you are done with your silly questions ...

*oof!* ... me and other ogre tribal peoples have gots to be getting on with the stuffs that we was doing!"

With a shout of rage and frustration, she ripped the attacking bush out of the ground and threw it as far as she could. Still holding onto the drifting boat with her other hand, she stomped on the Wobble Melon vine with all her might, causing the plant to yelp in pain. It slithered off like a snake, looking for an easier target.

"Tupolev, despite the rudeness of that spunky ogre, I believe she and her companions have need of the courageous services of the Hero of Mariskatania," said Grace, swinging down from the horse's back.

"Yeah, too bad he's too busy being a terrified wimp right now," muttered Tupolev, still very confused by everything that was happening around him.

"I'm sorry, my fine steed, I did not hear what you were saying!" cried Grace, giving the Sword of Power a few practice swings. "While I'm sure you were giving me a fine compliment about how brave I am, I have no time to listen to you tell me just how fabulous you think I am. Those evil plants are attacking and can not be tolerated! Goodness will always overcome evil, whether in the form of a giant or a crab or a whale or a plant! Stand back, faithful horse, and watch the Hero of Mariskatania in action!"

With a ferocious yell, Grace charged into the mayhem of attacking plants, gushing water, and confused ogres, swinging the sword wildly. Tupolev was positive she was going to get confused in all the

chaos and slice a few ogres in half while protecting the plants, but each and every swing was as precise as any Sir Nathan had ever landed. Bits of bush, vine, and flower flew into the air, neatly severed by Grace's attacks. In her wake, she left behind a trail of puzzled ogres and destroyed foliage.

Finding themselves free of the marauding bushes and vines, the Eager Angry Ogre Tribe started to get organized. They hauled their fellow members out of the water and regained control of their tiny fleet. Chief Glee was hauled up out from underwater for the sixth time, sputtering and coughing, and gently placed to recover in one of the boats.

Without their chief to scream orders at them, the tribe was actually getting things accomplished for a change. Globpimple waded through the water, giving firm commands here and there, while Grace patrolled around the group, fighting off any plants that came too close.

"Okay, you ogre peoples!" yelled Globpimple, climbing onto one of the boats. With one hand on a rope dangling from the mast, she pointed out at the endless sea filling the desert. "You see all that waters that is outs there? That waters is our enemy! Sadlly, all those green plants that is growing here is also our enemy, and so we can not stay here on this here land. Chief Glee bravely led us from the danger of the very, very high mountain top which was way, way, way, way up in the sky and enormously much taller than this here sand dune. Since all of this dangerous waters is going up, too, we would have surely been sunk had we stayed there, though ... now that I think about it ... it looks like it would have taken about seven years for the water to gets that high. Hmmmm."

She paused, clearly having second thoughts about their whole adventure. As an ogre that rarely had *first* thoughts, this was more than her simple brain could handle.

The normal thought process for most ogres was something like:

*One. I is hungry.*

*Two. Oh, look! A chicken head! (or cup of worms, toenail trimmings, Chief Glee's right hand, etc.)*

*Three. Eat chicken head (or worms, trimmings, hand, etc.)*

*Four. I is not hungry no more.*

But now, Globpimple's simple brain was having to deal with complicated thoughts like:

*One. Why did we ever leaves such a high mountain top where it seems like it was never, ever, ever, going to ever get flooded by all this waters because it is so high and the water is not so high and oh my gosh all this thinking is really making the insides of my head hurt and speaking of heads I wonder if there are any chicken heads left over from lunch because I is hungry.*

It was almost more than she could handle. But ogres were nothing if not tough, inside and out, so Globpimple just brushed away the nagging doubts she was having and did what ogres did best, which was to blindly go forward with whatever plan they were currently following, even if it meant their certain doom.

"So, listens to me! So that we don't die, we must gets busy!" yelled Globpimple.

"Yes!" shouted Grace in full agreement, swiping away a thorny tree.

"We must gets organized!"

"Right you are!" hollered Grace, stabbing her sword through a Wobble Melon, which tried to scream in pain, but couldn't keep from giggling.

"We must hurry up and chops holes in all these boats!"

"You better believe – wait, what?!" cried Grace, fending off the rather aggressive attacks of an Exploding Death Plumb plant.

Grace yelled at the ogres, ordering them to stop destroying their only means of rescue, but once they had a clear goal in mind, nothing was going to keep the tribe from plunging ahead, *especially* if it meant their certain doom. Ogres were nothing if not easily convinced to march right off a cliff, or into the jaws of a monster, or anything else easily resulting in their doom.

In the end, Grace found the only way she could stop the ogres from destroying their small fleet was to step back and let the hastily growing plants recapture them. Unhindered, the plants flowed quickly over the sides of the boats, trapping the tribe members hand and foot in tightly clinging vines and branches.

Once they were ensnared and she had their full attention, Grace quickly laid out a complex plan for how the entire ogre tribe could use the boats to sail away to safety. Seeing the blank, confused stares on each of the ogre's faces, she then quickly laid out a *very simple* plan for how the entire ogre tribe could use the boats to sail away to safety. Certain important facts about how to actually sail a boat were left out of this new plan, but Grace realized she only had about ten words or so before their simple brains overloaded with information and just started to think about a nice snack of chicken heads. As she carefully cut the ogres free from the attacking foliage once more, one ogre had already gotten confused about the difference between water and air and was hastily trying to throw himself overboard.

A simple, precise punch right behind the ogre's right ear rendered him unconscious, leaving the other ogres to organize their remaining boats. Soon, they were sailing away in a more or less steady fashion and Grace knew they would be safe long enough for her to finish tracking down and smiting the villainous Kale the Whale.

She was about to turn back and remount Tupolev when she saw that somehow, someway, with nothing but the clothes on their backs, a small sack of chicken heads and a few poor-quality weapons, the ogres had quickly managed to set half of their boats on fire.

As ogres jumped from the burning boats and were pulled from the water by the other tribe members, Grace carefully turned her back on the whole scene and pretended not to notice a thing.

She, her horse, and Sir Nathan were alone on the sandy island. The dune was steadily growing smaller as the floodwaters rose and would soon be completely submerged. Afraid of Grace and the

170

magically sharp Sword of Power, the remaining plants were hurrying to get elsewhere. They bunched themselves together into a ragged clump and swam away like a giant, green FlibbertyJibbit.

"Our work here is done!" exclaimed Grace, making to get back into the saddle on Tupolev's back. The horse stopped her with a look.

"I'm not so sure," he said. "What about that?"

He gestured with his head towards the odd crate that remained closed.

Grace turned and gave the crate a thoughtful look. Tupolev studied her carefully as she studied the crate carefully. It was amazing how there seemed to be absolutely no difference how Sir Nathan usually behaved and the way first Abbey, then Grace, was carrying on. It was as if the Hero's brain had been plucked from his head and sewn into their skulls. The horse was beginning to suspect that some strange magic was causing all the goofy behavior. By the way Grace was acting, Tupolev could tell Abbey's memories of opening the Critter Crate at the farm had been passed into Grace's head somehow, along with the belief she was the hero.

With a firm grip on her sword, Grace cautiously approached the metal box. Like all the others, it was covered in clinging sea grasses, barnacles, and clams, and dripping a slime of algae and seawater. The only thing that seemed different was the crude icon painted on the side.

Before Tupolev could even ask Grace what she thought the symbol was supposed to be, she raised the Sword of Power overhead and brought it slashing down at the lid of the crate. However, before the blade could even get close, several things happened, so fast Tupolev had difficulties understanding what he saw.

As the blade's magically honed edge streaked towards the crate, the lid blew up and off the crate just as quickly. The two met, midair, and the blade passed easily through the metal cover. As the two halves of the lid went whirling harmlessly off into the floodwaters, something shot up out of the crate and grabbed hold of the descending blade with an iron grip.

Grace grunted at the shock of the blade stopping so suddenly. Tupolev cried out a warning, thinking there were more ThingamaBots lurking in the crate. He was sure it was one of their metal claws that had grabbed the Sword of Power. Then he got a better look and saw it was no metal pincher wrapped around the weapon.

It was a thick, rubbery tentacle, as big around as a stout tree branch. The top of the tentacle was wet with slime and covered in a mottled green and brown pattern. The underside was coated in countless suction cups, each as big around as a Happyfest Hullabaloo Summer Fair souvenir plate (or, as Tupolev would put it, "Big enough to suck your face off!").

As Grace retightened her grip on the Sword of Power, tugging and twisting the blade as hard as she could in an effort to free it, another tentacle flopped out of the crate's interior like a writhing snake, then another. Soon, it seemed as if a whole forest of massive tentacles were growing from the dark innards of the metal box. They uncoiled and spread out, groping blindly in the sand. Tupolev was forced to take several steps back as a pair of them came dangerously close to grabbing ahold of his legs.

In the middle of the thrashing nest of tentacles, Grace stood fast, refusing to abandon the Sword of Power. Bracing her legs wide, she gave one final, pushing twist of the blade. With a sickening, wet sound, the blade sheered through the rubbery tentacle holding it. Grace fell back, brandishing the sword and fending off several attempts to grab her.

The severed tentacle fell to the sand, writhing and thrashing in apparent pain. Suddenly, it coiled itself and raised its tip just like a Battle Snake readying to strike. Tupolev was more afraid of snakes and snake-like things than he was of just about anything else and would have sworn that the tentacle's suction cups looked just like eyes, staring at him with a vicious hunger. He felt his legs go weak and his stomach rumbled nervously. He would have run away if his terror-stricken brain had remembered how.

Faster than the eye could see, the tentacle uncoiled like a bolt of lightning, striking for the horse's face. The suction cups made little, wet kissing sounds as they reached for Tupolev's skin. Just as quick, Grace was there between the steed and the tentacle, brandishing the Sword of Power. She pushed Tupolev out of the way with one hand while swinging the blade wildly with the other. In less than a second, the whole attack was over and the tentacle lay on the wet sand in dozens of quivering pieces.

As mighty as her courage and honor made her,

Grace was still amazed at how easily she had flung Tupolev out of harm's way. Talking horse or no, he still weighed considerably more than she did (especially with all the Huckle Nut cupcakes he had been eating lately). But then she realized she hadn't so much pushed the horse to safety as he had happened to faint in fear and fall to the ground at the exact same time.

Humming a small tune of satisfaction to herself, Grace nodded. Results were what counted in Hero-work, no matter if from bravery or from horses with a silly case of snake-o-phobia.

Sir Nathan, on the other hand, wasn't so happy. He was already stricken helpless with fear and it didn't help matters any being strapped to a horse and jostled painfully about as they travelled all over the land. When Tupolev had fainted, Sir Nathan had fallen off the horse's back to land with a painful thud on the wet sand, still trussed tightly in the ropes. He moaned mournfully from the jolt, then again as he realized he had fallen incredibly close to the water's edge. Since the flood was rising faster than ever as the whale travelled the land, sprinkling it with countless Cataclysm Crates, it wouldn't take long before the waters rose up and covered the knight, head to toe.

"Come, now!" Grace shouted to Sir Nathan in a voice thick with disapproval. "It's bad enough that my faithful steed has fainted dead away! We can't have you crying over a little thing like water! What kind of knight does a thing like that?"

However, just as she was about to pull Sir Nathan away from the water's edge, a dark, looming shape behind her caught her eye. She turned back towards the crate and noticed, not too happily, that the owner of the severed tentacle was standing there and looking very displeased about having one of its limbs painfully removed.

It was easily the biggest octopus Grace had ever seen. But then again, the only other octopus she had encountered was the pet Huggo kept in his small shack behind the Royal Palace. Come to think of it, in addition to being considerably smaller, Huggo's octopus only had four tentacles. And, as Grace stared at the massive, slimy enemy before her, she remembered that his pet octopus didn't so much have tentacles as it had legs. And instead of being slimy, it was actually kind of furry and didn't live in water at all but lived in a nice dog house Huggo had built it, which really was kind of an odd thing to build for an octopus.

Either way, Huggo's pet was considerably smaller than the one threatening her now.

It stood ten feet tall or more. Its bulbous body was bigger around than the biggest Hootentoot Tree, with seven and a half tentacles protruding from underneath. It wore an enormous helmet, shiny and silver, topped with a sharp spike. Its enormous eyes were big and round, like dinner plates, and covered with goggles filled with what Grace assumed was sea water.

With bits and pieces of armor strapped here and there, the octopus glared at her. It was an unnerving look that surely would have terrified anyone not filled with bravery and courage. Grace, on the other hand, merely looked at the octopus' severed tentacle and said, "Looks like this winter you're only going to need seven mittens instead of eight."

The hateful glare in the creature's eyes grew darker and more sinister. The beast was clearly enraged. A gurgling sound emanated from somewhere amidst all the tentacles, but Grace couldn't tell if it was meant to be a threatening growl or just the regular workings of whatever contraption was letting it breath out of water.

Its tentacles writhing, it reached into wherever an octopus keeps its belongings and pulled out a thick, wooden club.

Grace glared at the octopus.

The octopus glared right back, another wet burble coming from deep inside somewhere.

"Same to you, mister!" shouted Grace, assuming the evil creature had just called her a naughty word. "I will not let you roam across this land that I love, hurtling wet insults at the good people of Mariskatania! Goodness and courage and a sharp sword will *always* beat evil, sneaky, treacherous beasties like yourself! Prepare to suffer my smiting!"

With sword held high, she raced at the octopus. Its seven and a half tentacles whirling in a frenzy, the octopus flew towards Grace. They collided in a frenzied assault of twirling steel and pounding wood, with a few thousand clutching suckers thrown in.

On the sand, Tupolev started to recover from his fainting spell.

"Snakes," he muttered dizzily. "Anything but snakes."

His head still spinning, he struggled to a sitting position. That was when he noticed the whirling combat going on just a few feet away. To the horse's mind, it looked exactly like Grace was in the middle of a twisting, constricting nest of thick, slimy serpents, all trying their best to suck her face off."

"Here we go again," was all he said as he fainted once more.

There was a series of heavy clunks, like an axe striking a tree, accompanied by a triumphant shout from Grace. She hopped away from the octopus, the Sword of Power held protectively in front of her.

In one tentacle, the villain was holding the stump of his weapon. The rest of it lay in several neatly sliced chunks on the sand.

"Victory is mine!" shouted Grace, thrusting her blade into the air. "You cannot stand against the might of the Hero of Mariskatania! Now that I have disarmed you, you'd best just surrender!"

The octopus just stared at her, the weird gurgling sound it made going on and on. Was it laughing? For a long while, it simply stared at Grace. The anger and hatred in the look was clear.

Grace sighed, wondering why the bad guys never chose to surrender. Couldn't they tell how poorly things were going to go for them when they ran up against a true Hero? The beast was clearly defeated. She had lopped off one tentacle. She had diced apart its weapon. What chance did it have?

But if it was so beaten, why was the octopus suddenly smiling at her with a wicked grin? And, maybe more importantly, how was it smiling at her all? Grace didn't know much about octopus body parts (other than what she knew about the one Huggo kept as a pet), but she was pretty sure that a foul beast with nothing more than a hooked beak for a mouth, buried deep beneath its blobby flesh, shouldn't be able to smirk at her in that unsettling way.

Grace took a moment to peak over at Sir Nathan. The pitiful knight was doing nothing to squirm away from the rising floodwaters, but merely lay there sobbing as the the first waves started to wash up against his head. She considered making a quick dash to drag him up to dryer ground, but was sure the octopus would take that moment to strike.

Its tentacles twisted and squirmed, making sickening squishy sounds as they slimily rubbed against each other. And, quick as that, Grace knew why the creature was smiling (but just not how).

"Oh, dear," said Grace as the octopus lifted all seven and a half tentacles into the air. Each was now holding a different, dangerous weapon. Tiny throwing knives, wickedly curved swords, a trident, and a variety of spiky maces – the creature had them all and more. It was even using its severed tentacle to hold a heavy chain which it was strong enough to use as a whip.

"Fear not, my brave steed!" she called over her shoulder. Unconscious, the only thing Tupolev had to fear was sand fleas crawling up his nose. "The battle is just beginning, but in the end, honor and goodness will be victorious!"

Once again she raised her weapon and rushed at the octopus. As the Sword of Power came hammering down, the octopus swung just about every weapon it was holding right back at her. They came together in a deafening crash, sparks flying as metal ground against metal. According to the Royal Register of Everything, a fight like this had never taken place in the entire history of Mariskatania, unless you count that one time things had gotten out of hand at Professor Xoot's retirement party. Professor Xoot had been in charge of the Department of the Study of Rough-housing at the Royal Institute of Hocus Pocus and, 109 years old or not, he really knew how to throw an exciting party.

It had taken three weeks just to get the demons that normally haunted the Institute's basement to quit hiding in the broom cupboard.

The battle between Grace and the octopus was so ferocious, it raised a cloud of sandy dust around them thicker than any sandstorm. They splashed back and forth along the shore line, kicking up so much water that a damp, grey cloud formed in the air over their heads. The sparks thrown off by their clashing weapons charged the air with static electricity and soon the cloud was spitting out tiny bolts of lightning in all directions.

The booms of thunder shook Tupolev awake from his fainting spell. The horse rolled to his feet, his head still dizzy and spinning. It didn't help his confusion any having the lightning-filled sand storm raging not more than twenty feet in front of him. He could feel the hairs of his mane and tail standing on end from the highly charged air.

A tremendous crack of lightning split through

the cloud of sand and fog, brighter than the sun (which decided to go off and pout about the whole thing behind some clouds) and dazzled Tupolev's eyes. It was accompanied by a deafening blast of thunder that shook the ground and rippled the water's surface.

A curved sword, shattered into pieces, came flying out of the cloud to land on the sand at the horse's feet.

Another crash of lightning, another blast of thunder, and a broken trident followed after.

Up and down the beach the battle raged, Grace and her enemy obscured deep inside the flying sand. The floodwaters continued to rise, turning the once fair-sized dune island into a small bump of sand no more than twenty feet across and a few feet high. The raging battle forced Tupolev off the sand and into the rising sea.

Sir Nathan, consumed by whatever fears and terrors were haunting his mind, didn't even make the slightest effort to keep his head above the water and Tupolev had to trot over and lift him up by getting a good mouthful of his hair. If this caused Sir Nathan any pain, he didn't show it by crying any louder or moaning any more often.

"Yuck!" spat Tupolev around a mouthful of the knight's tresses. "When ish the lasht time he washed hish hair?"

Bits and pieces of shattered weapons continued to fly out of the cloud, the waters rose, and soon the combatants had only the very tip of the submerged sand dune to stand upon. Tupolev stood in knee-deep water, watching from a safe distance while holding Sir Nathan.

Slowly, the whirling maelstrom of combat slowed. The dark cloud faded away and the dusty air drifted back down into the water. Grace and the octopus were left facing each other, just a few feet apart. Both were breathing heavily, the octopus gurgling loudly through his breathing contraption.

Every single one of the evil cephalopod's weapons were destroyed. Even the long chain it had carried in its half tentacle had been sliced into dozens of tiny bits of metal. The creature's shiny helmet was dented and scarred, the long point on the top bent over at an awkward angle.

Soaked in sweat from the exertion of the battle, Grace pulled off her helmet and shook out her hair. Pointing at the octopus with her sword, she shouted, "Victory is mine! One again, we see how goodness and honor and courage and a whole bunch of other stuff has defeated the yuckiness of evil! You must surrender, because *all* of your weapons are destroyed!"

The octopus made no move to surrender, but just stood there silently glaring at Grace.

"I said, *all* of your *weapons* are destroyed! You positively, absolutely *must* surrender!" Grace was starting to sound a little less sure of herself.

Still, the octopus made no move.

"Hey!" cried Grace, lowering her sword and pointing an accusing finger at the creature. "Why aren't you surrendering?! All of your weapons are broken ... aren't they?"

The octopus flashed her that unsettling, impossible grin once more. After it pulled out just one more weapon, the rest of Grace's confidence disappeared like a child running off to avoid a long list of weekend-chores.

From a hiding place Grace was pretty sure she didn't want to know about, the cephalopod had pulled forth a weapon that surely had to be the workings of the evil Kale the Whale. But if it was a weapon, how did it work? It was big, big enough that it took several tentacles just to hold. Grace certainly wouldn't have wanted to get bonked over the head with the thing.

However, the new weapon didn't look like the sort of thing used to clobber someone over the head. It was mostly a set of pipes, maybe six or seven total, all clustered together in a bunch. Each one was a few inches across and several feet long. The

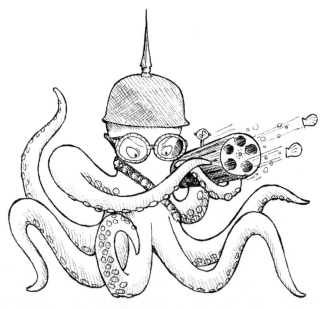

pipes were held together in a frame of metal and wood and covered with gears, chains, pulleys, and all the other bits and pieces involved in any of the whale's contraptions.

She wondered how it worked.

With a wet, gurgling chuckle, the octopus showed her *exactly* how it worked.

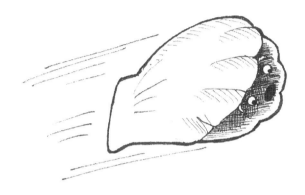

Within the frame, the cluster of pipes began to spin and make loud popping sounds. Something was shooting out of them, like a cork out of a bottle of Smooshelberry soda! Grace heard something go whizzing by her ear, and then another and another!

As the pipes spun in a blur, flashes of steam were popping out of their open ends, shooting clams and mussels and scallops as fast as an arrow fired from a bow! The shellfish zinged through the air, screaming in terror as they went. Most of them missed Grace and skipped across the water behind her. But the octopus finally got control of the wildly bucking device and his aim improved. A terrified clam smashed into Grace's hand, knocking her grip on the Sword of Power loose. The blade dropped into the water at her feet. Before she could bend over and retrieve it, an oyster came whizzing through the air, barely missing her head. It clamped onto her long, coppery hair with its shell as it flew past, jerking her head back as surely as if she had been punched. Another hit and another, each projectile pinching her with its shell as it clamped onto her skin, clothes, and armor. The force of each strike knocked her back.

*Pop! Pop! Pop! Pop!*

The contraption in the octopus' arms seemed capable of firing forever! No matter how Grace ducked and ran, her enemy kept firing at her, pinning her down in a hail of shellfish.

There was nothing for Grace to hide behind and no place for her to run to. The rising flood made it difficult for her to move and the relentless attack drove her back into deeper waters. Tupolev knew something had to be done.

With a jerk of his head, he flung Sir Nathan around by his hair and tossed the knight onto the his back. The Hero howled in pain and flopped like a rag doll when he landed. Tupolev had a lot of experience holding Sir Nathan in place while he ran, since the Hero was usually too busy shouting about smiting to hold on properly. The horse dashed through the water, kicking up a wall of spray as he ran to where Grace had dropped the Sword of Power. He hoped that if he could get the weapon to her, she'd be able to defend herself and put a stop to this annoying seven-and-a-half-tentacled creature once and for all.

He plunged his head into the cold water, bubbles streaming from his nose, and searched desperately for the fallen blade. Where was it? Wasn't it right where the horse was standing?! Or was it further to the left?! Maybe to the right!

Suddenly, he felt the weapon with a hoof. He raised his head from the water and sucked in a deep breath. A quick glance showed him Grace was in bad trouble. She had been knocked off her feet and was lying in the water with just her head and one arm above the surface. Clams, mussels, and scallops covered her, pinching her painfully. It would only take a few more hits from the octopus' powerful weapon to finish her off.

If the enemy had been watching Tupolev, he would have seen the horse plunge his head beneath the waves as a stream of bubbles gurgled to the surface from the steed's nose. The rubbery creature would have been able to see the horse suddenly freeze as the water around his head flashed white as if a bolt of lightning had erupted from underneath. The octopus would probably have wondered what was causing the water around the horse's submerged head to suddenly erupt into a frenzied boil, just like in Huggo's biggest soup-cooking pot as it hung over a raging fire.

However, the octopus wasn't watching. It was glaring at Grace with a sinister look in its eyes. It giggled in its watery voice. The beast carefully lined up its clam cannon, ready to deliver the final blow that would destroy Grace once and for all.

Grace gasped for breath, barely able to hold her head out of the water. There were at least twenty different shell-fish clinging to her head, ears, and hair. Their hammering blows as they had slammed into her had driven her to the brink of exhaustion and knocked her almost completely senseless. One eye was completely swollen shut. It didn't help matters any that a tiny crayfish was clinging to her eyelashes on that side.

Too late, she remembered the soup-ladle hanging from her belt, though she couldn't exactly remember why it was there. The Hero of Mariskatania only ever used the fabled Sword of Power, right? Why would she have any other weapon? She couldn't think clearly through the pain.

Pushing her head up out of the water with one hand, she fumbled at her belt with the other. Trembling fingers pulled the ladle from its loop and raised it weakly.

*Pop!* The octopus fired off another shell. A clam flew through the air, smashing into the ladle with a loud clang and knocked it out of Grace's weak grip as easily as if she were no stronger than a Hobnobber Squirrel. It flew through the air and landed with a splash dozens of feet behind her, lost.

A pair of FlibbertyJibbits swam by, floating on their backs with their pink bellies sticking out of the water.

"Oh, my, that poor girl is in terrible danger," said the first.

"My stars, you're right," said the second. "Sometimes wearing a diaper on your head *does* make cooking easier."

Through the fog of her battered mind, Grace

wondered just how she, the Hero of Mariskatania, had come to be in this position. How had she been defeated? How was it even possible? Off to her right, her faithful steed was so concerned, he appeared to be hiding his head underwater, unable to watch.

What a wonderful friend he had been, so loyal and trustworthy. Grace thought back to all the time they had spent together. The Hero and Sir Tupolev had been through many wonderful adventures and she knew that ... she knew that ... what was it exactly she knew? Her brain seemed to be having trouble remembering any of the adventures they had ever been on. Why was that?

It was if she couldn't recall anything they had ever done together. Grace assumed this was just because of how badly beaten up she was.

Suddenly, there was a bit of a commotion off to the side and a flash of bright light. Grace's head spun dizzily and she suddenly felt like she had been ripped out of her own body and then slammed back in. Where was she? Why did she feel so terrible? What was this crayfish doing clinging to her eyelashes? She was hopelessly confused.

Worse yet, why was there a ferocious-looking octopus staring at her? Why was it holding such a sinister-looking weapon? Why was it leering at her with an eery smile? How was it managing to smile in the first place?

She couldn't quite remember how she had come to be in such a horrible state, but by the look of things, she was doomed. With a glint of evil in its eyes, the octopus raised the bizarre weapon and pointed it straight at her head.

Grace closed her eyes, unable to look.

Nothing happened.

A few moments later, she peeked cautiously out of her good eye. "Am I dead?" she whispered.

There was a sudden terrible racket, a noise Grace was positive had to come from the cephalopod's weapon. It was accompanied by a terrific splash. Waves rocked over and around her, threatening to sweep her away. She felt too exhausted to fight them and started to slip beneath the water.

Then someone was there, supporting her and lifting her to her feet.

It was Tupolev! The horse had never looked more beautiful, more dashing, or more gallant than he did at that moment. The steed held himself proudly, water dripping from his coat. It was the sort of image the Royal Portrait Painter was always trying to capture, but since she was terrified of anything more deadly than an angry kitten, she was never around to witness such majestic sights. As a result, her paintings of Tupolev, while all quite beautiful, usually depicted the horse doing nothing more dramatic than buttering his toast at breakfast.

For reasons Grace was having a difficult time understanding, Sir Nathan was lying on the horse's back and crying loudly. Maybe that was why the horse was holding the Hero's sword in his teeth.

"Jushtish hash won the day!" the horse proclaimed as best he could with the massive weapon in his mouth. "That evil octopush was

shoundly defeated and goodnesh and honor again proved to be unshtopable!"

Nearby, the octopus floundered in the water. Its shiny helmet floated nearby. Grace could see the creature's shell-fish-shooting weapon, hacked into dozens of pieces and slowly sinking under the waves. The beast looked as confused as she felt. A dim memory wanted to make her think they had been battling just moments before, but Grace couldn't remember for sure.

Rubbing its blubbery head with a tentacle, the creature looked around as if it couldn't remember where it was either. "Excuse me," it said, "I was wondering if you could possibly tell me what happened to my shop?"

"Your ... your shop?" asked Grace weakly.

"Yes. My shop. I run a shell-cleaning and fin-straightening shop. Perhaps you're a customer?" Seeing that neither Grace nor Tupolev had shells nor fins, the octopus shook his head. "No, perhaps not. Either way, the last thing I remember was working on a rush-order for one of my regular customers – a snail who was late for his own wedding, believe it or not. He was in need of a complete shell cleaning and polish. I was just finishing the initial scrub down and was getting to work on his undercarriage when another customer came in."

The creature got a far away look in its eyes as it struggled to remember.

"The new customer, he was big. I remember that. Huge, even. Couldn't even fit through my doorway, but just stood outside in the alleyway, talking to me ... something about needing me for something important. I ... I remember wanting to tell him no, that I was busy, but ... but suddenly I couldn't. I knew I needed to finish my customer's shell-cleaning, but something was holding me back. I don't remember anything after that."

The octopus looked around, seeing nothing but the last of the rapidly sinking tops of the dunes of the Dangerous Desert of Disasters.

"Uh ... where are we, anyway?" it asked.

"Here ish where evil hash been shtomped out and goodnesh and honor have again shaved the day!" cried Tupolev, the Sword of Power still clutched in his teeth. "Be not shcared! I, the Hero of Marishkatania, will shave you from any dangersh!"

Tupolev spun in a complete circle, carefully checking the flooded land around them for signs of trouble. Grace could barely stand. She was exhausted and confused and couldn't figure out why a bunch of shellfish were clamped onto her. The clams, oysters, and scallops made little squealing sounds as she tugged them free and dropped them into the water.

Where was she? What had happened? Why was the land all under water?

The flood! The memories of Kale the Whale and his devious contraptions rushed back into her head so quickly it hurt! She remembered chasing down Princess Abbey and finding her at Farmer McSkooble's farm. She had arrived just in time to help with some fantastic smiting against some of the whale's henchmen. After the battle was over, they had discovered the lobsters they had been fighting had only committed their evil acts due to tiny mind-controlling helmets they were wearing.

She and the Princess had freed the lobsters from the whale's control and set them on their way. But then what? She could not recall.

Now she was somehow in what appeared to be the Dangerous Desert of Disasters, or whatever was left of it. It was clear the villain's Cataclysm Crates were still hard at work, spilling their unending stream of water across the land. With most of Mariskatania under water, how would they ever track the whale in order to find him and put a stop to his shenanigans?

"Thish way!" proclaimed Tupolev confidently, pointing with the Sword of Power towards the South. Grace looked in the direction he pointed, but saw nothing to indicate that way was better than any other. However, Tupolev was one of the best trackers in the land ... perhaps there was something the horse could see that she could not.

Sir Nathan merely lay on the horse's back, whimpering. He clearly wasn't going to be any help.

Without even looking to see if Grace was following, Tupolev plunged off into the water. With barely an effort, he steadied Sir Nathan on his back, preventing the armor-clad knight from sliding off and sinking beneath the waves.

As the octopus slowly swam away in search of his shop, Grace stood and watched Tupolev moving in the opposite direction. She knew she needed to go along to help, but felt so confused and so beat up she could barely move.

As if it was the boost she was looking for, her

soup ladle floated by, riding on the back of a sea turtle out for a casual swim. She plucked the weapon off its shell and enjoyed the familiar feel of the grip in her hand.

Sliding the ladle into the loop on her belt, she nodded once to herself. She knew she had to follow Tupolev. She knew she had help him track down the evil villain and save Mariskatania. She knew she had to figure out what odd curse was affecting Sir Nathan and find a way to restore his courage and bravery.

She also knew she better get a move on if she didn't want to get lost. Horse or not, even carrying Sir Nathan, Tupolev was swimming along as fast as any FlibbertyJibbit. In a few moments, he'd be out of her sight.

"Hey, wait up!" cried Grace, plunging into the deep water and half swimming, half wading after him. "Wait and let me catch up!"

Without slowing in the slightest, Tupolev looked back over his shoulder. "Evil will not shlow down and wait, Amazing Grashe! We musht move quickly, with honor and goodnesh, and shwim forward to victory! I, the Hero of Marishkatania, shay thish ish sho!"

Turning to face forward once more, Tupolev spied the octopus' helmet as it bobbed along, floating away from the scene of the battle on a strong current.

"Ooh!" he proclaimed happily. "Sho shiney!"

\* \* \* \* \*

## PART IV

In Mariskatania, far to the South of the Royal Palace, there was a beach.

It was a quiet, peaceful place, made of long, rolling dunes built from white sand like fine sugar. The beach hugged the shores at the edge of a bright blue sea. Day after calm day, the beach was an isolated and restful place, the only sound the rustle of the waves breaking upon the sand.

After what was about to happen, the beach was going to wonder what it had ever done to get treated so poorly.

It started with a sound. Faint at first, the sound grew and grew in volume. It was like a trickle of water pouring from a fountain, but on a much bigger scale. Coming from somewhere far inland, a rivulet of water wound its way through the sugary dunes and ran down the beach into the sea. It was as if someone hundreds of miles away had left their bathtub faucet on and the overflow had spilled out the window, across their lawn and down the street, eventually finding its way to the beach.

Shortly after, another trickle of water came flowing through the dunes, much like the first. Then another, then another.

Soon the beach was awash in steadily flowing channels of water, rushing heavily from the land and pouring into the sea. Eventually the growing streams started to drag bits of floating debris along with them. As the running water carved deep channels into the sand, these bits and pieces were dumped onto the wide beach or carried away into the choppy waves of the sea.

Most of the debris was clumps of grass, piles of leaves, and bushes and trees ripped right out of the ground. However, more than one surprised farm animal found itself rudely dumped onto the sand, along with whole sets of furniture, entire wagons full of water-logged goods, and complete families of confused FlibbertyJibbits.

Over the roar of the rushing streams, another sound could be heard. It was much more mechanical in nature, sounding like massive blocks of wood and metal grinding together along with a rhythmic booming. Soon, the source of the sound came walking over a distant dune, following one of the heavier streams as it flowed out from the flooded lands to the North.

It was Kale the Whale, stomping along on his complex walking contraption. The heavy, metal feet left deep prints in the sand and his tail wiggled excitedly, like a puppy excited about a new bone. It was pretty clear the evil villain was eager to return to his beloved sea, where he could be free to swim and frolic in the waves. Plus, there was a spot where his walking contraption was chafing him, right beneath his left pectoral fin and even a generous application of dragon spit hadn't soothed the raw and tender skin.

Kale stomped down to the beach, stopping momentarily to look around. A huge smile was plastered on his wide face and another of his thick, menacing chuckles erupted from far back in his throat.

Picking up a washed-away Cuddle Cow in one of his mechanical hands, Kale the Whale said, "The lands of the humans will soon be totally under water! They will pay for the way they have treated the wilderness! Once the Cataclysm Crates have done their thing, the whole world will be mine and belong to the Empire of the Waters! Now ... to my super secret fortress!"

He carefully set the cow back down on the ground, giving it a gentle pat on the head. The Cuddle Cow was as confused by this as it had been by anything that had happened to it that day and just wandered off to be by itself for a while and think things over. Perhaps it would quit being a farm animal and go back to school like his mom wanted.

Without hesitation, Kale the Whale strode purposefully into the crash of the surf until the waves swallowed him up and he was gone from sight.

\* \* \* \* \*

"Slow down!" yelled Grace. It was the seventh time she had screamed for Tupolev to wait in just the past hour. "I can't keep up with you! Slow down!"

The horse swam tirelessly on, not slowing in the slightest. In addition to carrying the Sword of Power in his teeth, he was also now wearing the shiny helmet the octopus had dropped in the Dangerous Desert of Disasters. The weapon in his mouth made him look like he was sucking on an odd-shaped lollipop. Sir Nathan moaned and sobbed in his usual place on the horse's back.

"There ish no time to shlow down, Amazing Grashe!" Tupolev called back over his shoulder. "Evil waitsh for no one! Goodnesh and honor musht hurry and catsh up and then we shall shmite that treacheroush whale into the middle of next Tueshday!"

He cleared his throat and tried to say the word more clearly. "Tueshday! Ahem ... *tuesh*day! Uh ... I guessh shmiting him into the middle of next Monday would be okay, too."

"Yes, yes, I want to shmite ... uh, I mean *smite* ... the whale, too! It's just that I'm exhausted and can't go on without a rest. Tupolev?! Are you listening to me?!"

"Tupolev?" called the horse in a confused tone. "Who ish Tupolev? You keep shaying that name. I am not he, though he shounds like a fine fellow. Nay, indeed I am the Hero of Marishkatania, you shilly pershon! Now, come along! There ish shmiting to shee to."

They had been traveling South for countless hours, following some trail that only the horse seemed able to sense. Grace was about as good a tracker as there was, but there was no way she could find any trail of the evil whale, as huge as he was, in a world that was nothing but water.

Lately, she had noticed the flood waters had been forming currents, which had been steadily growing in strength. They all flowed to the South. There had also been a growing amount of debris floating in the waters around them, which made being in the water that much more dangerous. Swimming more often than walking was hard enough. It didn't help matters any to get stuck in the backside with the horns of a Gobble Goat as it washed past.

However, farm animals were the least of their concerns. Grace was still amazed they had managed to avoid injury when they had looked behind them to see an entire kite-maker's shop ripped free from its foundations and washing along on the current. The building had nearly run them both over and only a last-minute dodge by Tupolev had pulled them all out of harm's way.

As the two-story shop had floated past, the kite-maker had stuck his head out of an upper story window. The look on his face was one of confusion. "That's odd," he could be heard saying as he floated out of sight, "I don't remember anything in today's schedule about getting washed away in a flood." He looked about for a moment more, then shrugged and went back to work.

Exhausted and covered with reddish welts all over her body for reasons she couldn't quite remember, Grace finally managed to catch hold of Tupolev's tail. She held on tight and the horse pulled her along as he moved effortlessly through the ever-deepening flood waters. The current around them grew more and more wild, the water frequently churning and spinning in the growing rapids.

In between coughing out mouthfuls of splashing water, Grace said, "You know, making our way through all this could be so much easier! If only I had three Punkolanterns, twenty-seven pieces of red wire exactly ten inches in length, half a barn door and a purple umbrella!"

They were nearing the Southern borders of the Dangerous Desert of Disasters, a region of Mariskatania made up of knobby hills of barren rock. The floodwaters piled up against these hills, like a river being held back by a dam. The flood crashed against the rocks, crashing through the narrow channels between the hills in a raging torrent. Without hesitation, Tupolev plunged into one such channel and they were swept along in the angry flow along with the rest of the debris.

Grace screamed in horror, sure she was going to lose her grip on Tupolev's tail and be forever swept away to a watery grave. The horse just kept his head held high, the Sword of Power clenched in his teeth, humming a song about Huckle Nuts.

A few brave PigWiggles flew near, but decided the flavor of Grace's terrified worrying was a little too bitter for their tastes and they buzzed away, their tiny tails whirling in a blur.

After what seemed an endless time in the chilly waters, getting banged off submerged rocks and floating garbage, they squirted out of the south side of the hills. The water fell onto a broad, quiet beach. With room to spread out, the flow calmed and slowed, falling into deep channels carved into the sand.

Grace, Sir Nathan, and Tupolev were roughly dumped onto the seashore. Pushed by the force of the raging torrent, Grace rolled over and over across the flat beach, finally banging to a stop. Her clothes were drenched, her armor leaked water at all the joints, and her coppery hair was plastered across her face like a damp beard. Sir Nathan tumbled to a stop beside her, head first, digging a furrow across the beach with his face. A lesser man would have found this very uncomfortable, but the knight was made of stronger stuff, even with his courage missing. He merely lay where he had fallen, having plowed up a two-foot high wall of dirt with his head. His pitiful crying was muffled by the sand covering his face and by the crashing of the waves.

Unruffled, Tupolev bounded to his feet. He took off galloping down the beach as fast as he could, streams of water flying from his soaked mane. Small bursts of sand exploded from beneath his hooves. He disappeared into the greyish-white haze of mist coming off the sea, his hoof beats fading away to silence. Just as quickly, he reappeared, galloping hard in the opposite direction. He went barreling past Grace just as she rose unsteadily to her feet. In just a few seconds, he had disappeared into the haze again.

Not really knowing what the horse was up to (and, as exhausted as she was, not really sure that she cared), Grace stumbled over to Sir Nathan and worked to pull the knight out of his sandy ditch. Soon he was laying on his back, his face plastered with clinging grit. Despite quite a bit of sand in his ear, up his nose, and stuck between his teeth, he merely lay there, sobbing.

The Hero's sadness made her uncomfortable. She had never seen him act in such a way. He was clearly the bravest person she had ever met and sometimes made her feel like a coward by the way he would charge into danger without a moment's hesitation. To see him just laying there, unmoving and nearly hysterical with tears, especially when Mariskatania was threatened, was almost more than she could take.

She was trying to convince Sir Nathan to sit up, without much success, when Tupolev came charging out of the mist. The horse skidded to a halt, showering them in a spray of wet sand.

"Come, Amazing Grashe!" he shouted, oblivious to the glare she was giving him as she shook the damp grit out of her hair. "And come, you, you knight pershon who ish jusht laying there, whatever your name ish! Danger lurksh near and the daylight ish fading and we musht be up and on our way!"

"Duh ... danger?" mumbled Sir Nathan. He looked cautiously around as if he thought the sand itself might suddenly rise up and attack.

"Danger, yesh, of courshe! We *love* danger! We laugh in the face of danger, ha-ha! We dance carefully planned little jigsh whose only purposhe ish to make danger angry at the way we're dancing and laughing at it! Come! Let ush arm ourselvesh and go off to battle and to victory!"

Sir Nathan sniffled loudly and wiped at his

running nose with a gauntlet-covered hand. He dabbed at his tear-soaked eyes with the other gauntlet-covered hand. Needless to say, his gauntlets were starting to corrode from all the facial fluids the knight kept wiping on them.

Grace was surprised to see Sir Nathan push himself to his feet. A bit of his old self could be seen in his face. His eyes took on a stern look, his mouth was set in a grim, tight line. Grace held her breath, eagerly hoping his odd behavior was finally coming to end.

He looked at the Sword of Power, clenched between Tupolev's teeth. He started to reach out for the weapon, but then changed his mind at the last second and just pet the horse's nose.

"What kind of foolishnesh ish thish?" asked the horse, but not in a rough tone. "You know, few people would get away with reshting their hand, eshpecially one ash filthy ash yoursh, on the noshe of the Hero of Marishkatania! I will let your shilly behavior go without punishment ... thish time."

Sir Nathan didn't seem to notice or understand what the horse was saying. Instead, a little bit of the lost look came back into his eyes as he studied the Sword of Power.

"I ... I remember ..." muttered the knight. "I remember something, but it's so hard to get a firm picture in my mind! There's an image ... this *all* reminds me of something, but I can't *see* it! It's like the memory is just a ghost, floating around in my brain and it keeps fading away through the walls of my skull. But ... but this all seems like there's something I should know, something I should be doing. What could it be?!"

With a cry of despair, Sir Nathan buried his head in his hands and sank back to the ground. He sat there, rocking back and forth and making a pitiful moaning sound.

Grace dropped down and tried to comfort him, but Sir Nathan acted as if he didn't even know she was there.

"It jusht ish not important! Leave him, for we don't have time for chickensh!" spat Tupolev. "There are lotsh of indications that treacheroush whale wash here! I have found his tracksh from hish walking contraption. He hash come from the land and returned to the watersh, out there!"

He gestured at the churning sea with his head.

Grace took a long moment to study her surroundings. The skies over the beach were overcast, a haze of white thrown up by the warm moisture of the sea stretching out before her. It was clear the raging torrents streaming out of the rocky hills were all the floodwaters draining out of the lands of Mariskatania. For as far as she could see, both up and down the beach, debris carried by the flood littered the sand. Broken bits of trees and bushes, boards and beams from shattered houses, furniture, children's toys, even a whole wagon or two littered the seashore.

Suddenly, Grace realized where they were. She had memorized the Basic Knight Training Manual from cover to cover and could repeat back to you any section you asked about. She could describe in detail any of the seventy-two color illustrations, including the full-color, fold-out map of

Mariskatania. But she had been having a difficult time figuring out exactly where they were since most of the landmarks were submerged underwater. It had all started to look pretty much the same.

"What does Farmer McSkooble's farm look like?" one might ask.

"Like an endless lake," would be the answer.

"What about the Dangerous Desert of Disasters?"

"Yep, another endless lake."

"What about the Downside-Up Lake of Most-Terrible Screams?"

"An endless lake with an upside-down one floating over it."

However, the puzzle pieces finally fit together in Grace's mind and she realized exactly where they were. The endless stretch of water at the beach's edge was not just more flooded land – it was the Sea of Silliness. She instantly told Tupolev what she had discovered.

"Ekshullent!" cried the horse. "Fantashtic work, my young friend! We have travelled through the Dangeroush Deshert of Dishashters and emerged here on thish beach, which ish called ... which ish called ... shay, what ish thish beach called, anyway?"

"It's not called anything," answered Grace.

"What?! Why, it musht have a name! Every place in the land hash a name! There ish the Shea of Shillinesh, the Valley of Cupcakesh, the Flying Hillsh of Blort ... why, there's even a name for that dead tree near the Royal Palace."

"You mean the Dead Tree of Wammerling? Or,

are you talking about the Lifeless Tree Of HrunkerDoo?

"No, the other one – the Ugly Tree Of Barren Branchesh And Despair ... you know, right next to the Shidewalk Of A Million Footstepsh. Sho you shee, *everything* hash a name."

"Well, not this beach, apparently."

Tupolev stared hard at Grace as if blaming her for the fact no one had ever thought to label the sugary stretch of sand. She shifted uncomfortably, squirming under his accusing glare. Hero or not, the horse was really good at giving her the same harsh look Sir Nathan always did when he thought she was keeping him from some nice, cheerful smiting. If the horse had stared at her any longer, Grace would have broken down right then and there and confessed about the piece of gum she had stolen from her best friend, back in second grade.

Finally, he looked away, focusing his gaze out at the Sea of Silliness. Why it had that name, Grace didn't know. It certainly didn't seem very silly at the moment. Its water was a dark gray in color, like dirty socks. Through the haze, she could make out a solitary, gloomy cloud hovering far out on the horizon. Was it a storm? She couldn't quite tell, but there seemed to be a waterspout spinning out from the cloud's belly, reaching down to the waves below.

She wondered if the storm would blow their way and hamper their efforts to track the whale.

Tupolev's gaze was more keen than hers and he could clearly see that indeed there was a turbulent tornado of churning water that twisted out of the bottom of the cloud. It spun down to the sea's surface, whipping the water into a frenzy of mist and haze.

"Ash far ash I can shee," said the horse as he stared intently off into the distance, "the shtorm cloud ish unmoving. I don't think it will be any bother to ush."

Grace shivered, a chill of worry shaking her still-damp body. "But, what could cause such a storm? What kind of cloud just sits in one place? I don't like it, not one bit."

"Fear not!" cried Tupolev, his teeth clinking on the Sword of Power's pommel. "All we need ish bravery and courage! Evil and itsh shilly waysh shall shink into nothingnesh like a shtone shliding shlowly beneath the fathomlesh wavesh!"

"Huh?" Grace hadn't undershtood a shingle word the shteed had shaid.

"Nay, the shtorm concernsh me not," said Tupolev, a menacing gleam in his eye. "But that dishturbance there, in the water. What ish that? Besht we be on our guard, lesht there be danger."

Even though he was disgusted with Sir Nathan's pitiful behavior, Tupolev trotted over to stand next to the knight where he lay crying on the beach. The horse stood guard over him, all the while intently watching a line rippling through the waves not too far off shore.

Slowly yet steadily, something was moving under the water, heading directly for them. Despite the turbulence of the churning sea, something was headed towards the beach, unmoved by the push and pull of the current.

Grace moved to stand on the other side of Sir

Nathan, drawing her ladle from the loop on her belt. Though she was tired, bruised, and soaking wet, she was still brave and courageous and would never falter in her protection of the land she loved. She only wished she had a better idea of what was going on with Sir Nathan and his horse. It frustrated her that she couldn't find the time to puzzle through the mystery of their odd behavior.

The disturbance in the crashing foam, caused by something swimming steadily just below the surface, moved closer and closer to the beach. As it neared the shore, they could see a small object, now visible amidst the churning of the waves. It was small, yet clearly had the strength to swim without getting swept away by the crash of the surf. Grace wondered what it could possibly be, sure it had to be yet another of Kale the Whale's contraptions.

Was it a mechanical shark that could shoot razor-sharp teeth at them? Was it a Nipper Fish on springs so it could bounce across the ground and threaten them with its bite, a chomp known to be strong enough to tear through armor? Was it a Smelly Fish, which was a blob-like creature that floated in the water, stinking like a pile of dirty diapers rotting in the hot sun? People who accidentally touched a Smelly Fish got its stink on them so bad, they weren't allowed indoors anymore.

Nope, it wasn't any of those.

It was a Hobnobber Squirrel.

Its wet fur was plastered to its body, making it look more like something a dog had dug out of the

garbage instead of a cute, fuzzy rodent. It walked up out of the crashing waves and stopped on the hard packed sand, just staring at Tupolev and Grace.

Tupolev and Grace stared back.

It was immediately obvious this was no ordinary squirrel. Mainly this was because of the well known fact that Hobnobber Squirrels didn't swim. The other odd thing about the squirrel was the small helmet it wore on its head. It was rounded, much like a Huckle Nut itself, and held in place with a leather chin strap. A few tiny gears stuck out of its side and they turned in lazy circles. Puffs of steam occasionally popped out of a small vent on the top.

The squirrel just sat there, staring.

After a long, quiet moment, Grace said, "That has got to be the weirdest thing I have ever seen."

Tupolev nodded in agreement, the Sword of Power in his mouth bobbing up and down.

As they stared at the unmoving squirrel, they didn't notice that another had calmly crawled out of the surf. It moved a few feet onto the beach and stopped to stare, just like its cousin. It wore an identical helmet on its tiny, blue head.

Then another swam out of the waves, and another. Soon there were dozens of squirrels, all wearing helmets, all just standing on the hard-packed sand and staring at Grace and Tupolev.

"I don't know about you," said the horse carefully, "but thish whole shquirrel thing ish kind of freaking me out."

At that very moment, a tiny red light located on the front of every one of the helmets blinked on. It reflected out of the rodents' unblinking black eyes, giving them an evil look. In his many adventures with Sir Nathan, Tupolev had seen ferocious demons that looked more pleasant than the squirrels did at that moment. Why, one would only really know the Rabid Demon of Splotch was truly evil only if you spent the time getting to know it. On the inside, it was a churning mass of terror and fright. On the outside, it kind of looked like a cross between a kitten and a bunny and a duckling, though fuzzier and with three eyes.

Moving as one, the squirrels all raised their tiny paws from their sides. At first, Grace thought they might be pointing to something behind her. But then she quickly realized they were pointing directly at her and Tupolev, with tiny little squirrel weapons clutched in their paws.

Before she could utter a warning, the entire horde of squirrels attacked and a ferocious battle broke out on the sands of the shore of the Sea of Silliness. Afterwards, Tupolev kept repeating, "There wash a shavage battle on the shands of the shore of the Shea of Shillinesh," and giggling, over and over again, until Grace threatened to shave his mane off and use it to gag him.

Grace leaped to defend against the mob of squirrels attacking from the left. Tupolev jumped to defend against the mob of squirrels attacking from the right. Sir Nathan lay on the sand like a beached fish, crying. The tears were washing tiny trails down his sand-caked cheeks.

The first wave of squirrels charged in, wielding small pointy sticks. Grace recognized the sticks as coming from the wood of a Tangle Twig Tree. The wood of the trees was some of the hardest in the land and could be whittled into points as sharp as any dagger. With her ladle, she knocked aside the first few jabbing attacks as the squirrels tested her defenses, looking for a weakness.

They spread out, a handful of blue rodents each moving to her left and right, hoping to get past her longer reach and duck in close to attack. She knocked a few of the squirrels back with vicious swings of her weapon, but the others pressed in close, their pointy sticks held high.

Grace dropped back a few quick steps and, before the squirrels could react, ran forward and jumped over the whole group. Tucking her legs, she flipped a fast somersault in mid-air and landed stumbling on the far side. She was still very exhausted and fell to her knees in the damp sand. With a grunt, she struggled back to her feet and turned to face the squirrels.

"Ow!" she cried as something flew through the air in a blur, bonking her in the head. "Ow! Hey! Quit that!"

Off to the side, unnoticed in all the confusion, a trio of squirrels were operating a slingshot. Two of the rodents held the weapon while the third loaded another Huckle Nut into the elastic band and pulled it back. Communicating in a rapid, high-pitched chattering, they aligned themselves for another shot and let fly. The nut whizzed through the air and managed to hit her in an ear already tender and bruised from having an oyster clamped onto it earlier in the day.

Another slingshot crew setup behind her and started firing. Rocks, small shells, and anything else they could find on the beach came hurtling towards Grace. Some projectiles she could duck, others she could knock aside with her soup ladle, but a third of them were easily finding their target. Getting hit on the head with one Huckle Nut was annoying. Getting hit on the head with two or three was painful. Getting hit, over and over again in a relentless barrage was enough to take down even the strongest of warriors.

Squealing in pain, Grace was driven back by the continuous onslaught. Ducking to stay below the slingshot's projectiles, the stick-wielding squirrels ran forward, looking for a chance to slip past Grace's defenses and overwhelm her.

Hurled by a slingshot, a small shell flew through the air, much to the surprise of the crab that still lived inside it. When it hit Grace's face, the crab did what any crustacean would do in its situation – it lashed out and pinched whatever it could reach, which in this case turned out to be Grace's lip.

"Ouch!" cried Grace, her lip already swelling and puffing up. "That'sh not fair! You can't fling shellsh that have crabsh in them! Oh, no! Now my shpeech shounds jusht like Tupolevsh!"

A yell of anger and frustration erupted out of her throat, scaring the crab so much it let go of her lip and fell back to the sand. It hastily scurried into the protective waters of the sea and found a big rock to hide under. For years and years to come, it would tell its children, and then its grandchildren, about the day it had magically flown through the air and attacked the face of a red-headed giant.

None of them would believe him.

Striking aside a flying Huckle Nut, Grace ran forward and aimed a kick at one of the slingshot crews. The squirrels dove to the side as her boot came smashing down. The slingshot splintered into pieces and, for some strange reason, exploded and burst into flames.

Chattering angrily, the squirrels ran off in search of a different weapon. Grace turned her attention to the other slingshot, ignoring the poking jab of a stick-wielding squirrel that darted in to attack her calf. Seconds later, the other slingshot was broken apart, the shattered bits and pieces flying through the air to land in the crashing surf.

Soon the rest of the squirrels were in full retreat, running down the sand and screaming in fear in their high-pitched voices as Grace chased after them, ladle held high.

At the other end of the battle, Tupolev was caught up in a similar fight. Sword of Power held firmly in his teeth, he attacked and blocked and parried, the whole while shouting things like, "Victory ish mine! Shurrender, you shtupid rodentsh!" and "Shally shells shea-shells by the shea-shore!" just to see if he could.

Few other horses could have been so bold and ferocious in a battle in which they had to try to attack with a sword held in their teeth (especially while shouting tongue-twisters). But Tupolev was no ordinary horse and had learned many things while riding with Sir Nathan. On any day of the week, especially Tuesdays, he was quite impressive in the heat of battle. Now, with the courage of the Hero of Mariskatania flowing through him, he seemed unstoppable.

Those squirrels armed with nothing more than a stick, no matter how pointy, were no match for the horse's speed and power. He wielded the Sword of Power with precision, cleaving through their weapons easily without touching a single, blue hair on their bodies. Evil or not, no one wanted to see what a Hobnobber Squirrel looked like after it was peeled open with the Sword of Power.

The slingshot-wielding squirrels didn't do much better. More often than not, their projectiles merely bounced off the shiny helmet Tupolev wore. This only resulted in the horse getting a slight headache from the constant clanging sound the flung rocks, nuts, and shells made when they struck.

Quickly, Tupolev had the squirrels on the run. He chased them down the beach, yelling, "Honor alwaysh winsh! Marishkatania ish shaved! Ahem ... *shaved*. No, not shaved ... *shaved*. Oh, forget it! Marishkatania ish reshcued!"

Running the other way down the wet sand was another band of disarmed squirrels, retreating before Grace and the vicious, whooshing attacks of her ladle. The two groups of squirrels ran into one another, each knocking the others off their feet.

"A-ha!" cried Tupolev triumphantly. "Thish little battle ish at an end! Shurrender!"

Now, if someone had ever asked Tupolev if he had ever expected a fuzzy, blue critter to attack him, he would have answered, "No."

If someone had ever asked Tupolev if he had

ever expected an innocent-looking rodent to crawl out of the sea and attack him with pointed sticks and slingshots, he would have told that person they were crazy.

If someone had ever asked Tupolev if he had ever expected a Hobnobber Squirrel to look him calmly in the eye and throw a pinecone at him that would explode, sending the horse flying through the air, he would have asked, "Have you recently been struck on the head hard enough in such a way as to cause you to ask really ridiculous questions?"

These thoughts flitted through the horse's mind as he flew through the air on a blast of wet sand and pinecone bits. He couldn't quite figure it out. He had been just standing there, confident that victory was at hand when a squirrel had stood up, brushed itself off, and pulled out a small, harmless-looking pinecone. The next thing Tupolev knew, the critter had somehow lit the stem of the pinecone and chucked it at the horse's feet. Before he could comprehend what he was seeing, the pinecone detonated. The force of the blast threw the horse through the air as easily and as far as a Cuddle Cow could spit a Wobble Melon seed (which is pretty easy and pretty far).

He landed hard and merely lay there, stunned.

Grace was enraged at the sight of her dear friend being attacked! Pointy sticks were one thing, but trying to blow up her companion was quite another. She raised her ladle high and charged, determined to end the battle once and for all.

Exactly one explosion later, she found herself laying on the sand, not far from Tupolev, wondering how she had gotten there and why her ears wouldn't stop ringing. She rolled to her side and was surprised to see that the horse had managed to keep his grip on the Sword of Power, despite having been flung through the air and bounced hard off the wet sand. It reminded her of Sir Nathan in so many ways. The knight had proved just how tough he was, over and over again. A mere explosion would have done no more than keep him out of a fight for just a moment or two and soon he'd be charging back into the thick of things, shouting about courage and smiting and honor.

She was about to praise the horse for his bravery, when another sizzling pinecone landed between them. They both scrambled to their feet and ran in opposite directions. The pinecone exploded with a thunderous *BOOM!* and threw sand twenty feet into the air.

It seemed as if every one of the squirrels suddenly had an endless supply of exploding pinecones, which were surely yet another of Kale the Whale's clever creations. Grace and Tupolev were kept busy for several minutes, dashing this way and that to avoid one explosion after another. Soon the beach was covered in dozens of craters, each easily ten feet wide and several feet deep.

Another detonation sent Grace diving face first into one of the deeper craters for protection. Spitting sand, she peeked carefully over the rim just in time to see Tupolev go diving into another, a series of detonations trailing behind him.

She slid down to the bottom of the massive hole, trying to think of a plan. Though they were the best warriors in the land (other than Sir Nathan when he was feeling more like himself) there seemed to be nothing they could do to get anywhere near the squirrels as long as they had a supply of the pinecones. It looked like they would never run out! Grace remembered a day when she and Sir Nathan were fighting an entire nest of rabid Battle Snakes that had been easier than this. She and Tupolev were both exhausted and ready to collapse. If the squirrels kept chucking the exploding pinecones at them, it was inevitable they would meet their doom and wind up in tiny, gross pieces splattered all over the beach.

A trickle of sand down the slope of the crater caught Grace's eye. She looked up to see a squirrel standing at the rim. The gears on its tiny helmet spun rapidly like a windmill on a breezy day and the red light shone like a drop of wet blood. In one paw, it held another pinecone, the stem sizzling and sputtering with sparks. The squirrel just stared at her with unblinking eyes.

She was trapped! There was no way she could scramble out of the crater in time to avoid the explosion. Without a moment's hesitation, she cocked her arm and threw the soup ladle. It flew end over end, smacking into the squirrel's head with a hollow, metallic sound like a ringing dinner bell.

As the squirrel fell backwards, propelled by the blow, its helmet flew off its head and the smoking pinecone tumbled across the sand. Both of them fell into a nearby crater, where a massive detonation shattered the helmet and threw a plume of sand high into the air. Most of it landed on Grace, filling her already filthy hair with grit and running down her neck and inside her clothes and armor.

Shaking the sand out of her ears as best she could, she scrambled up to the lip of the crater. She dove over the rim, hit the sand in a somersault, snatched her ladle off the ground on the roll and jumped to her feet. The dazed squirrel lay where it had fallen, rubbing its furry head with a paw. Grace ran up to the creature, her weapon ready to strike. However, it made no move to attack. Instead, it sat up slowly and looked around in confusion.

After a long moment, it looked up at her and said something in the chattering language Hobnobber Squirrels use that was clearly a question.

Though Grace couldn't understand its words, she could clearly understand its confusion. "It's okay," she said. "You're on the shores of the Sea of Silliness and you were ... not yourself for a little bit. But, you'll be okay now."

The squirrel pointed behind Grace at where Tupolev was running away from a group of its kin, a trail of explosions in his wake.

"Oh, yeah. That. Well, they're only doing that because of those helmets they're wearing."

The rodent chattered another question, a worried sound to its voice.

"What's that? No, we won't make you fill in all those holes in the beach. That's the whale's fault, not yours." Seeing the squirrel was only growing more confused, she just held up a hand. "It's a long story."

She ran off after Tupolev, shouting at him to try to knock the helmets off of his attackers. Behind her, the Hobnobber Squirrel gently rubbed its bruised head. Looking around, it noticed all of the Huckle Nuts littering the beach, left over from the slingshot attacks. It squeaked with joy and started gathering all the nuts it could find.

With some way to finally stop the deadly pine cone attacks, Tupolev and Grace fought back. They knocked the mind-control helmets off the squirrels one by one and eventually the battle was over. The beach was filled with squirrels chattering to each other in confusion.

Grace leaned against Tupolev, tired to the bone. She was exhausted beyond belief and covered with wet sand from head to toe. The horse wasn't much better. They had managed to track Kale the Whale to the shores of the Sea of Silliness and beaten back his small army of squirrels. But their quest wasn't over. It was clear the whale had gone into the sea and they had to find some way to follow and stop him once and for all.

"I don't know about you," said Grace, dislodging a small sea shell that had gotten lodged up her nose in one of the last explosions, "but I don't think I've got the energy to swim out into those churning waves and find that evil villain without drowning in the process. Even if we had a boat, which we don't, the whale is probably deep under water. How are we going to find him? It would take a magical spell to help us hold our breath long enough to track him down and we don't have the time to go all the way back and find the Prestidigitator Porter or the Warlock Christofer. The whole land is almost flooded and we're running out of time!"

"Fear not, my trushted companion! It ish ash I alwaysh shay ... goodness and honor will alwaysh shtay shtrong and never shurrender to the shtinky enemiesh of evil! Beshides ... I don't think we're going to need a magic shpell. Look."

Grace turned to see the horse gesturing to the squirrels, who had quickly put off their confusion and were frantically searching the beach from end to end for Huckle Nuts. They carefully piled all the nuts they could find in one crater and were throwing everything else in another. The second crater was mostly filled with rocks and shells, but the pile was topped off with all the small helmets the squirrels had been wearing.

Other than a few of the mind-control devices that had been destroyed in the fight, the rest were intact. Their gears whirred and clicked, the lights on the front of each helmet now blinked on and off in blue.

"The shquirrels were able to shurvive beneath the wavesh, jusht fine," said Tupolev. "It had to be shomething in those helmetsh that helped them breathe underwater – just like thish helmet that I'm wearing helped the octopush breathe on land. I'll bet we can modify them to work for ush and then we can shwim down and put a shtop to that whale, for once and for all!"

"I think you're right!" cried Grace. She scooped one of the helmets off the pile and inspected it closely. There was no way she could get it to fit her, but since there were so many, she hoped there was some way to use them to get to the whale.

She quickly set to work. She pulled all the helmets out of the crater and lined them up on the sand, clearing a spot amongst some spilled Huckle Nuts the squirrels hadn't claimed yet. They chose one helm to take apart so they could figure out how they worked and, though they could never have built such a device themselves, they were pretty sure they could figure out which part of the contraption was involved in controlling the squirrel's minds and which part helped them breathe underwater.

Tupolev used the fine tip of the Sword of Power to dismantle all of the mind-control parts of the helmets. It was impressive just how accurately he could move the long weapon with his nimble lips, even when working on something as tiny as a squirrel helmet lying on the sand at his feet. With one part of the helmets disabled, they figured out how the rest of the contraption produced a steady flow of air that was then fed into a small tube. The tube was flexible enough that a squirrel would have been able to bend it to fit into its mouth. They found the same thing was true with the helmet the octopus wore, though it was designed to feed the creature a steady flow of water to breathe. Tupolev quickly figured out how to reverse its mechanism and the tube started blowing out a steady stream of cool air.

They rigged together the air-supply contraptions from several helmets into a single unit, all the tubes twisted together and emitting a continuous flow of air much in the same way the Cataclysm Crates produced a steady flow of water without any apparent source. Grace tore a strip of cloth from her pants and tied the device around her neck, shoving the ends of the combined tubes between her teeth.

She waded out into the crashing waves and disappeared beneath the water for several minutes. Just as Tupolev was about to go in looking for her, she rose up out of the surf with a big smile on her face.

"It works!" she cried. Tired though she was, she was excited they had found a way to use one of Kale the Whale's devices against him. She was also happy to have had the opportunity to wash some of the grit and grime out of her hair. If she was going to go into battle, she at least wanted to go in clean.

They fashioned another collection of helmets into a breathing-apparatus for Sir Nathan, tying it around his neck with only a tiny, moaning protest from the miserable knight. Grace thought that, if nothing else, having the breathing tube shoved in his mouth might just stop him from complaining all the time. With Tupolev's help, she shoved the limp knight back onto the horse's back and lashed him into place.

"Tupolev, we're going to have to tie your helmet on to your head," said Grace as they finished up adjusting the device. "Otherwise, it might fall off while we're underwater."

"Yesh, I agree," said Tupolev.

With yet another torn strip of fabric, Grace placed the helmet on his head and started to tie it into place. Pretty soon she had a tangled mess of knots and straps, none of which were doing any good.

"Here, let me hold *that* one," said Tupolev,

dropping the sword so he could hold the loose end of one of the straps in his teeth. "Then you take that other one and bring it underneath my chin."

The sword fell to the sand, the wonderfully sharp blade sinking halfway up its length into the beach, neatly slicing in half a Huckle Nut that it landed on.

Nearby, one of the Hobnobber Squirrels was standing back to admire the collected pile of nuts they had all gathered. It was looking forward to the feast they would all enjoy that night! Now, if only there were some way to start a fire on which to roast the nuts, with a little Smooshelberry butter, they would have themselves quite a treat!

When the squirrel saw the sword easily cleave the Huckle Nut in half, its heart skipped a beat. It was the most amazing thing it had ever seen! It just so happened one other reason more Hobnobber Squirrels hadn't died over the years from eating the poisonous nuts was due to the fact that they have one of the hardest shells found amongst all the nuts of the world. Their shell was thicker than that of the seeds of the Stone Skin Bush found in the tropical islands of the Malachite Archipelago. They were harder to shuck than the nuts that grew in thick clusters on the Hinder Binder Trees that grow on the high peaks of Mount Thunder. They were even tougher to open than the delicious, teeth-shattering Num Nuts grown only by rare-nut collectors and dentists.

Quite often, a Hobnobber Squirrel's teeth just weren't up to the task of chewing into a Huckle Nut and they often resorted to trying to bust them open by dropping rocks on them or leaving them in the road to get run over by passing elephants. Now, the squirrel had found just the tool they had been searching for! With that long, beautiful, shiny piece of sharp metal, the squirrels would be able to slice open *all* their nuts in no time at all and have a wondrous feast!

It rushed over to collect the freshly sliced halves of the nut, drooling a little bit in excitement. As the squirrel triumphantly held one half of the Huckle Nut over its head, its call to the other squirrels died in its throat when its bushy, blue tail brushed up against the Sword of Power.

There was a tiny, bright, little flash of light accompanied by the stink of burned fur.

A long, quiet moment of confusion passed.

Finally, the squirrel shook its head as if to clear away cobwebs of confusion. Tupolev did the same. They both looked around, wondering where they were and how they had got there.

"I don't feel so good," moaned Tupolev.

"Oh no, not again," moaned Grace.

"In the name of all that is honorable, goodness shall always overcome evil!" cried the squirrel in a high-pitched voice.

Like a streak of blue, fuzzy lightning, it climbed the immense Sword of Power faster than any Hobnobber Squirrel could climb a tree, standing on its pommel and holding one tiny paw over its heart.

"I, the Hero of Mariskatania, am the sworn protector of the land and I shall smite that evil whale so hard, he'll be wearing his tail for a mustache! To victory!"

Somehow, even while standing on the hilt of the sword itself, the squirrel reached down and lifted the blade out of where it was stuck into the sand. Even a normal sword would have been too big for any squirrel to carry around and the magical, mysterious Sword of Power was too heavy for even the strongest citizen of Mariskatania to lift unless their heart was heroic and pure.

However, the squirrel held the weapon aloft in one paw as if it were as light as a puff of smoke. It gestured wildly with the blade as it carried on and on about goodness and honor and a whole lot of smiting.

The other squirrels just stood and stared, wondering just what exactly their fellow rodent was doing and why he was no longer gathering Huckle Nuts.

"If he thinks he's getting out of helping us gather food, just because he's armed," said one squirrel to another in their squeaky language, "I'm going to shave his tail and paint him orange!"

"Come my trusted steed! Come, my brave companion!" the sword-wielding squirrel called to Tupolev and Grace. "Let us adventure onwards and put a stop to this menace once and for all!"

And, without another word, the squirrel plucked up one of the tiny, modified helmets, plopped it on his head and shoved the breathing tube into his mouth. Without a backwards glance, he marched stoically into the crashing surf and was soon out of sight beneath the waves.

Grace and Tupolev looked at each other, both their mouths hanging open in shock.

"Did I really just see what I thought I saw?" asked the horse.

"Yes, I'm afraid you did," answered Grace, frantically gathering up their supplies. "And I don't have time to explain everything right now. You're just going to have to trust me and follow that squirrel and I'll explain everything later." *That is, if I can explain it to myself first*, she thought to herself.

She finished lashing the horse's helmet into place, shoved the breathing tube in his mouth and pointed out to sea.

"Buh wha uh-bow awe buh —" Tupolev started to ask as best he could around the breathing tube, but Grace just shushed him with a harsh gesture and pointed once more at the water.

Shoving her own breathing tube into her mouth, she made sure her soup ladle was secure in her belt and waded out into the waves. Tupolev had no choice but to follow. The squirrels on the beach waved to him as he walked into the crashing surf of the Sea of Silliness.

As the water rose up over his legs, he wondered if it was too late to pretend he was coming down with a cold so he could go home and hide under his blankets.

\* \* \* \* \*

# PART V

Far, far from the shores of the Sea of Silliness, a solitary storm cloud hung suspended over the water. Dark and angry, the cloud hovered over the exact same spot on the sea's surface, despite the strong winds that whipped the water into an unbroken string of large waves. Lightning flickered through the depths of the cloud, illuminating its dark interior with a flash brighter than the sun (which the sun really didn't appreciate).

A twisting, violent waterspout hung from the bottom of the cloud, reaching all the way down to the water below. Spinning faster than the whirling tail of a PigWiggle, it sucked water from the sea and pulled it up into the belly of the dark cloud.

Where the tip of the waterspout touched the surface, the sea was twisted into a raging whirlpool, one hundred feet across. Any ship unfortunate enough to blunder into it would have no chance to escape. The ship and her crew would surely get pulled deeper and deeper into the whirlpool's twisting throat and sucked down to a watery grave.

A flock of Flip Flop Flamingos flying too close were struck by a flurry of lightning bolts that arced out from the cloud like jagged spears of burning light. Dazed and confused (and a little bit toasted) the birds dropped out of the sky and were caught by the water spout. Around and around they were flung, whipped through the sky like a rock tied to the end of a string and whirled around a child's head. Half the flock was sucked up into the belly of the cloud, never to be seen again (or at least not until later that afternoon) while the other half struggled out of the twisting winds only to fall from the sky and land clumsily in the middle of the raging vortex of the whirlpool. Down, down, down they spun, spinning faster and faster as they were pulled closer and closer to the whirlpool's center.

Just before they were sucked beneath the waves, doomed to spend all eternity as wandering ghosts beneath the water (or at least until later that afternoon), one Flip Flop Flamingo said to the others, "Farewell, my friends! Before I die, I just want you to know ..." It paused, to choke back a few sad tears. "I just want you to know ... that I blame Fred for all this nonsense! I *told* you we should have taken a right turn at the Valley of Cupcakes, but oh, no! You all said, *Listen to Fred, he's got a shortcut*. Well, we took Fred's shortcut and look at us now! We're going to die and it's all his fault!"

The Flip Flop Flamingo named Fred looked hurt and managed to blurt out, "Hey, it wasn't *my* idea to try out this new thing called *Migrating* that we've been hearing about!" before getting sucked forever into the dark and chilly depths (at least, until later that afternoon).

While the storm raged overhead, things were quiet down in the depths of the sea.

A few Nipper Fish swam silently along, keeping an eager eye out for any unsuspecting prey on which they could feast. They had noticed the waters of the sea had grown a bit cluttered in the past day or so. The oddest things could be seen drifting about, none of it normal underwater-type stuff. There were various bits of furniture, a large amount of confused trees and shrubs, farm tools, wagons, and even a few houses and other buildings which the sea creatures found very useful for busting up into firewood, until they sadly remembered how difficult it was to keep a fire burning under water.

The other peculiar thing the fish all noticed was the way the water seemed to be getting deeper and deeper. None of them could tell where all the new water was coming from and they didn't like it one bit.

Several ideas had been proposed (and rejected), such as digging holes in the floor of the sea in which to hide all the extra water or getting every fish to drink twice as much water as they normally did as a way to get things back to normal. The first idea was rejected because no one in the land of Mariskatania had ever invented the shovel and the second idea was tossed out just as quickly once it was realized the results would be a whole lot more fish pee and no wanted that.

The Nipper Fish swam along, their extremely sharp teeth gleaming white even in the dim light of the sea's depths (because they always brushed and flossed after meals). Suddenly, they scattered, darting for the protective depths as something dangerous came swimming along.

It was a Hobnobber Squirrel, it blue fur waving in the water's currents. It wore an odd helmet on its head, out of which ran a small tube, the other end of which it had stuck in its mouth. With no effort whatsoever, it carried a massive sword in one tiny paw. Big even for a human, the sword was huge for something so small as the squirrel. However, it held the weapon with no more difficulty than it would hold a Huckle Nut as it swam tirelessly along.

Struggling to keep up, Grace and Tupolev swam along behind the squirrel.

Grace had been through an awful lot in the past few days and despite her brave, heroic ways, even she couldn't go on forever without a rest. She was ready to collapse.

Tupolev swam beside her, his hooves kicking at the water. The horse was quite capable of running without a rest, from one end of Mariskatania to the other, however even he was having a difficult time keeping up with the squirrel. He wasn't really built for swimming and had also been through quite a bit recently, including getting nearly exploded into smallish bits back on the beach. It also didn't help having Sir Nathan tied to his back, wearing his heavy armor.

The horse's hooves were too small to be very effective at paddling through the water, but Tupolev found he could get a little boost in speed by twirling his tail in a clockwise spin.

The squirrel led them onwards and with each passing minute they swam further and further from the shore and deeper and deeper into the sea's depths. With gestures and a lot of odd faces, the squirrel had indicated to Grace and Tupolev that it wanted to investigate the area below where the dark storm cloud hovered. Grace had figured that was where they were headed and had her own suspicions about a cloud that never moved. Since they had followed the whale to this region, there had to be some connection between the Sea of Silliness and the villain's watery attack on Mariskatania.

Eventually, they reached the muddy sea floor. Very little light penetrated through the sea's murky water. As deep as they were, every rocky outcropping and cavern was cast into a dark gloom of shadow. For the most part, there was nothing to see. Mud and rock and more mud and rock, stretching on and on and on.

Half swimming, half walking along the muck-covered sea floor, Grace followed Tupolev and the Hobnobber Squirrel. The rodent was making it all look effortless as he kicked through the water, his tiny hind paws a flurry of motion. The whole time, he pointed the way with the Sword of Power though the large metal weapon had to weigh one-hundred times more than the squirrel did.

Instead of swimming, the horse simply walked behind the squirrel, his hooves stirring up thick clouds of mud from the sea floor.

Eventually they came to the top of a steep, underwater cliff where the sea floor sloped sharply downwards. The squirrel stopped and pointed with the Sword of Power, up towards the surface of the water and then slowly down to the floor of the crevasse before them.

Grace and Tupolev followed the squirrel's gesture and both almost gagged on a mouthful of seawater when they gasped in surprise. Above them, massive and dangerous-looking, was the swirling whirlpool. Seen from below, it looked like a giant, watery tornado, but much bigger than any storm they had ever seen. The sunlight shining down from above pierced the the violently churning surface of the vortex, causing weird bursts and flashes of light that pierced the darkness.

Down, down, down the vortex reached, narrowing as it twisted into the depths.

The squirrel motioned for them to follow, then swam confidently down into the darkness, following the steeply sloping crevasse below them. Grace and Tupolev exchanged a nervous look, then followed hesitantly after.

Grace found descending the steep slippery sides of the slope to be much easier than it had been to find her way across the flat bottom of the sea floor. It was almost *too* easy and soon she was sliding quickly down the slick mud, doing all she could to slow herself. Off to her right, Tupolev was doing much the same, digging in his hooves as they both slipped down into the darkness. An avalanche of mud and rock was dislodged by their feet and tumbled down the slope in front of them, while behind a cloud of disturbed muck filled the water, blotting out what little light was reaching them from the surface.

It grew very dark and very cold. The weight of all the water pressing down on them was like the crushing footstep of a giant.

As the last of the light faded into darkness, Grace realized she couldn't have stopped moving if she had wanted to (which she kind of did). The best she could was to keep herself from tumbling head over heels in what would have been the second longest series of somersaults ever recorded in Mariskatania.

The first longest series of somersaults ever recorded belonged to Sir Nathan and happened on the day he had just finished climbing to the top of Mount Thunder to return a pair of socks he had borrowed from his friend, the Warlock Christofer. The entire climb up the mountain, Tupolev had been nagging the Hero about his untied boot laces, but Sir Nathan hadn't been listening. Just as they were about to knock on the Warlock's door, the knight tripped over his own feet and fell back down the entire mountain, somersaulting the entire way. It took a little over thirty-seven minutes for him to reach the bottom and it was tough to say which was more dented from the long fall down the rocky slope – his armor or his head.

Long after they had been plunged into absolute darkness, the group reached the bottom of the steep slope. Grace stumbled as she tripped over a rock and gently tumbled to the sea floor. The muck beneath her hands was cold and slimy to the touch as she pushed herself back to her feet.

For a long moment, she just stood there, unsure of where she was or where her companions were. In the dark, she had no way of telling which way they might have gone and, with the breathing tube stuck in her mouth and a considerable amount of water surrounding her, no way to call out to them.

She jumped when Tupolev's nose nudged her arm, catching her completely by surprise. The horse, just as lost in the darkness as she was, had never moved from the bottom of the slope and had been standing next to her the whole time.

But where was the squirrel?

Overflowing with heroic bravery, he might have just swam away without them, ready to smite the whale all by himself. Grace wondered if she and Tupolev were stuck forever at the bottom of the Sea of Silliness, with no way to see where they were going! Their air could run out any second and they would be doomed!

Sucking hard on her breathing tube, Grace calmed herself. She realized these weren't very heroic thoughts and was glad that, in the darkness, no one could see the panic on her face.

"Fear not, my faithful companion," said the squeaky voice of the squirrel right in her ear and startling her so much she spit out her breathing tube. "I can tell by the look on your face that you have concerns, but you need not worry so long as the Hero of Mariskatania is here, at your side, ready to smite evil!"

Grace fumbled for the tube, but was unable to find it in the dark. How had the squirrel been able to see the terrified look on her face? And, weirder yet, how was he talking to her?

"Uh ... Grace?" came Tupolev's deep voice. It was calm and clear and didn't sound at all as if he were sucking on a thick metal pipe. "Why don't you try opening your eyes?"

Grace realized that, in her fear, she had closed her eyes tightly and been holding them that way to the point where her face muscles were starting to ache. Cautiously, she cracked one eye open, then the next, and was startled to find that she could see quite clearly after all.

A faint light filtered through the water. Though not as bright as sunlight, it was enough for her to see by.

Feeling foolish, Grace opened her eyes all the way. "Oh, sorry," she said, then instantly wondered how she had managed to speak. With her eyes open, she could see to find her breathing tube and was about to stick it back in her mouth when she realized she was no longer surrounded by water. Or, at least her head wasn't.

Though she was still standing on the sea-floor, her feet slowly sinking into the ooze and muck, her head was poked into a perfectly round bubble of air, maybe three feet across. Tupolev had his long nose shoved into the air bubble as well, up to his eyeballs. Through the shimmering wall of the bubble, Grace could see the squirrel swimming about, Sword of Power in hand.

"Pretty cool, right?" asked Tupolev, his voice filled with wonder as he looked around at the bubble surrounding their heads. "That squirrel did it somehow. While you were just standing there with your eyes shut, he pulled his breathing tube out of his mouth and let a long stream of bubbles gurgle out into the water. But, before they could all float away up to the surface, he swung that massive blade around and around in these fast, tight circles. It was amazing! He stirred the bubbles like Huggo stirring a batch of pancake batter and made this one, single, giant ball of air. He then pushed it over and stuck it onto our heads. Pretty cool, right? I mean ... do you think Sir Nathan could have ever done that?"

Grace peeked out through the transparent wall of the bubble at where the knight lay strapped to the horse's back, occasional moans bubbling up out of his nose. Despite his current miserable condition, Grace was confident that on a better day, Sir Nathan would have not only been able to force the bubbles into a single, large air-pocket with nothing more than a stern look, but could have also forced it to polish his shield and make him a sandwich.

Grace thought the similarities between Sir Nathan and whoever happened to be holding the Sword of Power couldn't just be a coincidence. Whether it was a princess, a horse, or a ridiculous blue squirrel, there was an over-powering presence in each of them as they ran around, shouting about smiting. It was as if the fury of a 10,000 pound dragon had been shoved into the flesh of a hundred pound body and all the extra power and ferocity was trying to force its way out.

She was starting to realize there was more to what was going on than just some people acting oddly.

The squirrel swam back over and wriggled his head through the wall of the bubble. At first, the thin skin of the air pocket stretched without breaking, like the wall of an inflated white balloon, but then it gave out with a tiny little pop and the rodent's face broke through.

"The coast is clear," he announced, sounding disappointed there was nothing around that needed a good smiting.

"So where do we go now?" asked Grace. "I see no sign of the whale and have to admit that I wouldn't have the first clue on how to track a creature as it swam through water."

"She's right," agreed Tupolev. "The only thing I see besides all this muck on the sea floor is that massive underwater mountain over there kind of shaped like a castle with the light glowing out of it and the whirlpool spinning up out of its top."

Grace looked where the horse was staring, noticing for the first time the mountain he was describing. How had she missed seeing it? It was still a good ways away from them, down yet another slope, but was clearly no normal pile of rock. It towered high above the flat sea floor, its rocky walls rising to a tall peak. The jagged mountain looked scary and unnatural and reminded Grace of Mount Thunder.

"At long last, I have found it!" cried the squirrel. "This is clearly the fortress of our enemy! We must move forward, right this instant, to put a stop to his madness!"

"Wait, wait!" cried Grace. "Just slow down for a second. What's the rush? Let's take a second to come up with a plan before we just go marching in the front door of the villain's lair. You know, the Hero was always doing that sort of thing and it got him in trouble more often than not."

"What do you mean, *the Hero was always*

*doing that sort of thing*? I *am* the Hero! And none shall stand before my might and honor! We can't sit around and talk! We must march *now*, before further evil can be done! Oh ... and this air bubble is about to collapse, in three ... two ... one ..."

Right on cue, the giant pocket of air popped and the cold water of the sea rushed in to fill its place as it disintegrated into a million tiny bubbles that floated quickly away. Grace had to scramble to get her breathing tube shoved back in her mouth and then rushed to help Tupolev with his.

The squirrel swam off towards the fortress, his fuzzy tail twirling in rapid circles. Grace and Tupolev shot each other a shared look of concern, then followed after as best they could.

As they moved closer to what was most likely the whale's mountainous hideout, they were amazed at the complexity and enormous size of the thing. Half carved from natural rock, half built from concrete and steel, the fortress was bigger even than twenty Royal Palaces. Thinking about it, Grace realized it would have to be big for a whale to live inside. However the massive structure wasn't just big enough for the whale to fit into – it was so large, it could easily have held dozens of whale-sized rooms and hallways and other whale-related structures. Grace wasn't quite sure what a whale's bathroom would look like (or how it would even work) but she was quite positive it would need to be huge.

The entire outer surface was haphazardly decorated with countless metal statues. Grace could see they were figures of mermaids, each holding a

spear or trident. No two were the same. Some were posed like they were swimming, others like they were at rest, while still others appeared in a wide variety of tasks.

There were countless statues and they all seemed randomly scattered across the surface of the fortress.

The squirrel lead them straight towards what was apparently the entrance to the whale's lair. It was a giant set of sliding doors, made of metal and built into one flat face of the rock. Grace tried to get the squirrel's attention in order to tell him to slow down and find a different, sneakier way in, but she realized there wasn't much of a choice. The sea floor all around the fortress was plain and bare, with nothing to hide their approach. Anyone keeping an eye out for an attacking force of squirrels, horses, and humans was going to see them coming from a mile away.

Soon they were standing at the foot of the massive door. It towered over them, as tall as the Palace Tower. A whole family of whales, stacked ten high, could have swam through the doorway without even having to scrunch together. At the moment, the massive doors were closed and, if there was a knob or a latch or even a simple button that could be used to open them, it was not sitting out in plain sight.

The squirrel hammered on the metal with the Sword of Power, the bang echoing loudly through the water. Grace could tell from the heavy, dull thud that the doors were thick and probably too strong to be cut open with the magic sword. That didn't stop the squirrel from trying. As he chipped away at the metal, hacking away tiny slivers that sunk to the sea floor, Grace turned to Tupolev to explain to him with gestures that she was going to try to swim up along the door frame and see if she could find a way in.

That was when she noticed the trident sticking out of the horse's helmet, like the stem sticking out of the top of a shiny, silver apple.

"What is that?" Grace tried to express to the horse, through wild, flailing gestures of her hands and odd, surprised looks of her face.

"Did you just call me fat?" Tupolev tried to express back. Not having hands, he had to do most of his gesturing with his eyes, lips, teeth and tongue. He wasn't very good at it.

"No, I don't think you look like a bat," Grace gestured back, frustrated at her inability to get her message across. "I was simply asking you about the trident on top of your head!"

"Why would you say *fly dent on mop of door bread*?! That's very rude! Also, I have no idea what it means."

They would have gone on like that for quite some time if, at that moment, another trident hadn't come swooshing down through the water. It stuck in the muddy sea floor, just a few inches from Grace's foot. She looked at the still quivering shaft, then glanced up just in time to see a spear come plummeting through the water, aimed straight at her head.

She backpedaled quickly, swimming away as fast as she could. Suddenly, it was raining spears, tridents, and more, and Grace darted this way and that to avoid the attack. Tupolev found himself doing much of the same. Unable to swim as nimbly as Grace, he couldn't change directions quickly enough and was forced to use his helmeted head as a shield to block some of the attacks. Tied to his back, Sir Nathan waved his hands frantically. He swatted away one spear that almost impaled the horse, but two more hit the knight in the chest and were deflected by his armor.

As she parried aside an odd-looking spear, Grace saw the attack was coming from the countless statues adorning the mountain. They were not mere decorations, but were instead more of the whale's fantastic inventions! She could see each of the figures was built of moveable pieces instead of a solid chunk of metal like she thought. Like living creatures, the statues followed Grace and the others with glowing eyes.

Instead of running away, the squirrel swam quickly up the face of the mountain, striking out at each statue he passed. Soon, Grace and Tupolev not only had to dodge the sharp projectiles raining down around them, but also the heavy chunks of hacked-apart statues that came plummeting down through the water. Grace knew a bonk on the head from one of the heavy pieces would be just as deadly as any sharp spear or trident.

She looked over at Tupolev and Sir Nathan and saw they were having a difficult time. Even after throwing its weapon, each statue was rearmed through a fancy system that fed a new trident or spear into its hand through a pipe jutting up out of its base. It was really quite an impressive defense, for the statues would never tire and could continue to fight on for so long as they were equipped with projectiles. The repeated attacks were taking their toll on the horse who just couldn't move through the water very easily. Unable to dart out of the way like he could on land, Tupolev had two more spears stuck in his helmet and another was lodged in Sir Nathan's breast plate.

Thinking of all the times the horse had helped her when she was too tired to go on, Grace swam quickly over to him, knocking aside a volley of tridents raining down. She made a mental note to apologize to the horse later for what she was about to do, then grabbed him firmly by the tail and started to swim upwards with all of her might. A normal person wouldn't have stood a chance at pulling this off, but then a normal person wouldn't be breathing air from a goofy squirrel helmet at the bottom of the Sea of Silliness while fighting mechanical statues.

Straining with the effort, she lifted the horse and Sir Nathan off the sea floor and swam up to where the squirrel was busy turning big statues into small chunks of metal. Grace knew they'd only be safe from such an attack by working together.

Dangling beneath her, Tupolev was helpless. He couldn't do much but just hang there and wait. Suddenly, he felt his helmet shift on his head. The added weight of the spears stuck into its thick metal were trying to tug it off his skull and hanging upside-down wasn't helping the matter either. Without it, he'd be exposed to getting holes punterured in his pretty hide from all the weapons flying at them. He wasn't terribly pleased with the idea. Worse yet, without his helmet, he'd have no way to breathe.

Underwater, he had no way to tell Grace he was in trouble and, being a horse, he had no hands to hold his helmet in place. Another trident bounced off the helm and Tuoplev knew it was over. The straps holding it in place snapped and the helmet started to slide off his head and towards the sea floor, far below.

Suddenly, the helmet was shoved firmly back onto his head. Hands quickly tied the straps with secure knots and then plucked away the heavy spears and tridents stuck into it. Craning his neck, Tupolev looked behind him to see just how Grace had managed to do all that *and* keep swimming. What he saw surprised him more than anything before in his life, including that time he had walked in on the Royal Twins as they were pulling one of their countless pranks on the Hero by shaving his head while he napped and gluing a FlibbertyJibbit to his scalp. It had taken Sir Nathan a week to figure out that his hair hadn't suddenly learned to talk and another for him to figure out how to get his helmet to fit while he waited for the glue to wear off.

It was the Hero! Free of the ropes that had held him in place, Sir Nathan was clinging to the horse's back by clamping his legs around the horse's chest. He gave Tupolev a weak smile and a small wave, then reached out to finish tying one last knot in the helmet's straps.

Seeing Sir Nathan up and moving about, after

so many days, brought more joy to Tupolev's heart than even the time the Queen had surprised him with a giant Huckle Nut cake, baked by Huggo and the size of a small shed, for his birthday.

"Oh, shucks," Huggo had said in an embarrassed way in reply to Tupolev's enthusiastic thank-yous. "It most certainly weren't nuthin'. I just had to stay awake ter bake it for twenty-three days in a row. I was gonna be up anyway, you know, because me Auntie Broadbottom is in town and you know how she likes to stay up late and talk."

Half swimming, half climbing up the craggy side of the rock and metal fortress, Grace finally pulled the horse up to where the squirrel was tirelessly smiting away. He had sliced through a trio of mermaid statues positioned on a flat, horizontal slab of rock and was intently studying something about the fortress itself. An overhang of stone kept them shielded from the attacks of the statues above and Tupolev was able to stand on his own on the flat stone.

Grace's eyes showed her surprise when she saw Sir Nathan, free of his ropes and sitting on the horse's back. She was so stunned, she didn't notice the massive shark swimming out of the darkness, her massive mouth filled with rows upon rows of teeth and ready to attack!

As the shark's shadow blotted out the light, Sir Nathan lunged off Tupolev's back. He landed on the shark's head and wrapped his legs around her as tightly. Using the only weapon he could find, he ripped the modified squirrel helmet from where it hung around his neck and started to bash the shark on top of the head with it.

It all happened so fast, Grace wasn't even sure what was going on until it was all over. The shark had twisted and rolled, trying to dislodge Sir Nathan from her back, but the knight never faltered for one second and continued hammering away.

Suddenly, it was over. Sir Nathan let go of the shark and the weight of his armor pulled him down through the water until he was standing next to Grace on the rocky shelf. The shark was floating just ten feet away, a confused look on her face. She slowly looked over at where Grace and Sir Nathan stood. Grace readied her soup ladle for an attack, but it never came.

Sir Nathan raised his hand and then Grace understood. In it he held the mind-control helmet the shark had been wearing, now smashed and broken beyond repair.

Flashing Sir Nathan and Grace the most dangerous smile either of them had ever seen (and that included the nightmarish grin of the Masticating Monster of Many Maniacal Smiles), the shark turned and swam off into the darkness, intent on getting back to her home in time for supper.

Grace could barely restrain her desire to rush to Sir Nathan and knock him over with a tight hug. Her tears of joy went unseen, blending in as they did with the surrounding sea water. She was so amazed to see him acting like his old, brave self again that if she didn't need the breathing tube stuck in her mouth, she would have shouted with joy.

When Sir Nathan started to frantically gesture to Grace, she couldn't understand what he was trying to say. Perhaps he was trying to apologize for not being his normal, heroic self lately. Or maybe he was trying to congratulate her for the fantastic job she had been doing. Or, more likely, he was trying to say things like, "Evil shall never win so long as goodness and honor was around!".

He kept pointing at his mouth, which Grace just assumed meant he was eager to shout something about smiting.

She kept nodding in agreement, until he held up his other hand and Grace saw the modified squirrel helmet that had been feeding him air. It was as smashed apart as the one that had been on the shark's head.

He couldn't breathe!

Grace tried to swim several directions at once. Part of her wanted to shoot to the surface, yanking Sir Nathan along to get him some air. Part of her wanted to swim to the beach and grab another one of the squirrel helmets for him to use. She ended up merely swimming in panicky circles.

Sir Nathan simply stood there. He looked over at the squirrel, who had been watching the whole thing with a calm look on his face.

"What is wrong with our companion?" the squirrel's expression seemed to be asking of Sir Nathan.

"She's been handling a lot of different things, ever since this whale showed up, and I think she's a bit worn out," Sir Nathan's look seemed to answer.

"She is indeed a brave and honorable companion," the squirrel indicated with a twitch of his lips.

"She is at that," replied Sir Nathan with a single, lifted eyebrow.

"I wonder what has in her such a tizzy," the squirrel's wiggling whiskers pondered.

"Oh, she's just glad to see me up and about," answered Sir Nathan's shrug. "That, and the fact that I don't have any air to breathe right now."

"Oh," the squirrel said simply with a blink.

Sir Nathan, the squirrel, and Tupolev watched Grace for a few moments more as she tried frantically to fix Sir Nathan's broken breathing device with nothing more than her soup ladle and a clam shell pried loose from the rocky walls of the fortress.

With a shake of his head, the squirrel simply turned to the wall behind him and used his tiny paws to rip open a steel panel he had found built into the rock. An explosion of air burst out of the opening, bubbling violently upwards. With barely an effort, the squirrel grabbed his companions by the hand (and hoof) and fought his way through the boiling stream of bubbles, pulling them through the open hatch.

They tumbled through the opening and fell onto a smooth, rock floor. The hundreds of gallons of water gushing through the opening washed them across the stone and down a long hallway. As she slid along like an upside-down turtle with a waxed shell shooting across an icy pond, Grace was surprised to find the interior of the fortress dry and not completely filled with water like she expected. However, the water pouring through the mangled hatch threatened to change all of that very quickly.

Grace struggled to get to her feet. Beside her, Sir Nathan was doing the same, coughing up mouthfuls of swallowed water.

The squirrel stood before the hatch, engulfed in the overwhelming jet of sea water pouring through the opening, as unmovable as one of Mitzy's very tasty, very *heavy* Smoosehlberry cakes. His rear claws dug into the stony floor and he held his ground easily, despite the powerful rush of water trying to wash him away. His head was completely submerged by the flow yet he still didn't budge. Though Grace could see no sign of the squirrel buried beneath the rushing torrent, she saw the Sword of Power rise up out of the water like a majestic mountain peak thrusting through the clouds.

The blade dipped, just once, as if to point at the hatchway and the water rushing through it. Instantly, the flow cut off as surely as if someone had somehow shut the mangled hatch cover. The water already inside the fortress drained away, gurgling and streaming down countless other side corridors and passageways. The squirrel stood before the hatch, his fur wet and plastered to his body, the sword held firmly in his tiny paw.

Grace slowly walked over and was amazed at what she saw. It appeared as if a piece of glass had been fitted over the opening. She could see out into the sea water that surrounded the fortress, but not a single drop trickled in through the hatch. Cautiously, she reached out with her hand. It was if she was reaching down into the surface of a still pond – her fingers easily passed through the opening and into the water outside.

She withdrew her hand and rubbed her wet fingers together to prove to herself she wasn't imagining things. Beside her, the squirrel was staring at the water with a meaningful glare on his face. Grace then realized why the water was no longer pouring through the still open hatch. There wasn't a single person in Mariskatania that would willingly mess with the smiting rage of the Hero, not even if it was currently stuck inside the blue head of a squirrel. The water of the surrounding sea was silly, but not stupid, and it suddenly remembered it had better things to do than flood some stupid whale fortress.

The squirrel gave a little satisfied nod and stomped off down the hallway, waving the Sword of Power over his head. "Come, brave companions! Goodness must rise up against evil! Our quest is far from over! We must ride forward and finish off this treacherous whale once and for all!"

As the squirrel disappeared down a side passage, Grace took a moment to look around. The hallway they were in was half metal, half stone and quite impressive considering it was built hundreds of feet under water. The passage was very wide and tall, as big as many of the rooms in the Royal Palace. It occurred to Grace that all the hallways would probably be big in order to allow the massive body of Kale the Whale to fit through them easily.

Wherever the passage walls, floor, or ceiling were made of stone, the rock was smooth and polished. Where they were metal, they were made of massive plates a dozen feet across and riveted together at the seams. Here and there, she could see sets of gears and pulleys, sprouting out of the walls and spinning for reasons she didn't understand. A constant sound of gurgling could be heard whispering from behind the thick panels, like the drain on the world's largest bathtub emptying the last of the bath water.

If the mechanical gears sticking out of the walls were part of some vast pumping system, built to keep the interior of the fortress dry, they weren't quite keeping up with the job. Here and there, trickles of water ran down the walls or dripped from the ceiling. Patches of slick algae covered parts of the floor and one rusted seam hosted a whole colony of giggling barnacles thriving in the damp conditions.

Grace walked over to where Sir Nathan was tenderly wiping sea water from Tupolev's damp mane. Normally, the knight would have been rushing down the hall, seeking action, but now he seemed almost bashful, as if he was just waiting to be told what to do.

"Are you okay?" Grace asked in a soft tone.

"I don't know," Sir Nathan answered after a hesitation. "It's as if I feel like I'm two people. There's the part of me that remembers being a bold knight, charging off to confront danger, but then there's a part of me that's terrified and can't believe I would ever have done anything more dangerous than going outside on a cold day without wearing mittens."

Grace could see the hurt confusion in Sir Nathan's eyes. All his life, he had charged recklessly into action, never once considering what the dangers might be. It had to be awful for him to feel so helpless.

She looked down the hallway in the direction the squirrel had disappeared, a wondering look on her face. All of the odd things she had seen ever since catching up with Princess Abbey at the McSkooble Farm were starting to make an odd sort of sense. First the Princess and her strange behavior, then a whole period Grace herself could barely remember, followed by Tupolev charging around like he was immortal. Now, a random Hobnobber Squirrel was carrying the Sword of Power as if it were nothing more than a toothpick.

Time and again, she had seen the whale accomplish amazing things using nothing more than wood and metal and his own smarts. Even the simplest of his inventions was far more complex than anything anyone else in the land of Mariskatania could create. There was the walking contraption, big enough to carry the whale around, yet nimble like a spider's legs. He had made helmets that controlled the wearer's brain, forcing them to do whatever the whale desired. And then this, a fortress deep beneath the waves, protected by mechanical statues.

The most impressive thing the whale had built was the series of Cataclysm Crates that were currently flooding the lands of the country she loved. Grace was pretty sure there was some connection between the violent whirlpool spinning down into the top of the fortress, and the water twister rising up out of the sea into the dark, dangerous-looking cloud up above. It seemed the walking, wicked whale had somehow found a way to siphon the water out of the Sea of Silliness and send it streaming out of all of the Cataclysm Crates. The sea was so big and so deep, all of Mariskatania would be twenty feet underwater before anyone noticed any of the sea's water was missing.

If the whale could do all those impressive things, then how difficult would it be for him to make one of his mind-control helmets in such a way as to suck all the bravery and courage right out of the Hero the way Tupolev could suck the juice out of a Wobble Melon with a straw? Grace didn't think it would be that tough.

Somehow, all of the wonderful things that made Sir Nathan the wonderful Hero that he was had gotten dumped into the Sword of Power in the process. Grace didn't know if that was the whale's plan, but if so, it was backfiring on him. Whoever happened to hold the magical blade seemed to be getting all of the knight's stolen bravery, turning them into the Hero, or at least someone who acted like him.

And maybe that would be enough to defeat the villain.

In one encounter after another, against all the mind-controlled minions the whale had sent against them, goodness had prevailed and evil had been defeated. The lobsters, the octopus, even the army of Hobnobber Squirrels on the beach – all of them had been stopped and freed from the clutches of the villain. And Sir Nathan hadn't done anything to help, other than keep Tupolev's back moistened with a steady flow of tears.

"If your bravery, borrowed temporarily and stuck into someone else, was enough to succeed in all of our battles so far," said Grace slowly, pointing to Sir Nathan as she finally figured out why he had been acting so pitifully, "then there's no way we can fail, now that you're back on your feet!"

Upon hearing this, Sir Nathan promptly got back *off* his feet by collapsing to the floor and curling into a ball.

"Oh, no," said Grace angrily, "we're not doing this whole sad-knight routine again. Get up."

"No," came Sir Nathan's muffled reply, his head buried in his hands.

"Get up!"

"No!"

"So help me, if you don't get up right this instant and march your butt down that hallway and help us defeat this evil whale, I am going to take this soup ladle and bonk you in the face until you cheer up!"

All the anger and frustration that had built up in Grace since the adventure to defeat the whale had started poured out of her in a gush. Her cheeks were flushed and red, her breath came in heaving gasps and the glare in her eyes could have been used to cut through steel. A few barnacles, clinging to the ceiling near a steady stream of leaking sea water, fainted and fell to the floor in a clatter.

Sir Nathan peeked through his fingers and looked up at Grace. The look on her face defied him to utter so much as one single, tiny sob.

With a deep sigh, he pushed himself back to his

feet. He looked at her with a weak smile on his face. "Sorry about that."

"Don't be sorry," snapped Grace. "Be angry. Be angry at that whale for tearing his way into the Royal Palace. Be angry that he threatened the Queen and put the Chief Butler in a grumpy mood that will take years to go away. Be angry that he wants to drown all of Mariskatania!"

She looked at him with a critical eye. "So ... are you angry?!"

"Uh ... yes?" His meek answer wasn't quite what Grace was hoping for, but for now, it would have to be enough.

"Good. Then lets go."

She turned sharply and headed down the hallway in the direction the squirrel had gone. Sir Nathan looked over at Tupolev and started to say something, but the horse interrupted. "Look, you can apologize by baking me a thousand Huckle Nut cupcakes later," the steed said with a grin. "Right now, we better get moving or you-know-who is going to wallop us in the face with her soup-ladle so hard, she'll knock our hair off. You're just an ugly human, so it wouldn't make much difference, but me ... I'm gorgeous and people expect me to look my best."

Sir Nathan managed a weak chuckle. Though he was no longer tied to the horse's back and filled with tears, he still had a long way to go before he was back to being his old self.

They walked down the hallway, side by side, and for a quiet moment both of their hearts flowed with the joy of their friendship.

Then Grace poked her head back around a corner and ruined everything.

"Alright you two, happy hug time is over!" she screamed back at them. "Move your tiny little legs and get down here before I feed you to the whale myself!"

They hurried to catch up, each avoiding Grace's angry glare as they scampered past her. To emphasize her mood, she bonked them both on the hindquarters with her ladle, firmly but gently.

The new passageway they turned into was much like the last. The parts of it that were chiseled out of the stone were smooth, the rest was massive plates of steel. Leaking water trickled out of loose rivets, imperfect joints in the steel, and cracks in the rock. Small patches of aquatic plant and animal life thrived in the moisture.

The passageways were dimly lit by ugly, toothy fish swimming in glass tanks sticking out from the walls. Each fish glowed with a dim light that shone out of the transparent walls of their bodies. They glared at the companions menacingly as the group walked by or bit ferociously at the glass of their tanks in an effort to chew their way free and attack. One crossed his eyes and stuck out his tongue at Tupolev, who returned the gesture and added a rude comment.

Besides the occasional gears and pulleys that decorated the hallways here and there, there was always some random assortment of glass and metal pipes arching up the walls and branching overhead through which water seemed to be constantly gurgling.

They moved through an endless collection of hallways, each looking identical to the last. Some contained broad sets of stairs, but the party didn't seem to be making any progress, whether they chose to go up or down.

The squirrel constantly scampered ahead of the group, checking at every corner and crossing hallway, keeping an eye open for signs of danger. Behind the squirrel, Grace and Tupolev quietly asked Sir Nathan questions about what had happened to him and why he had been acting so afraid. At first, Sir Nathan didn't say much. It seemed as if it was all he could do to keep himself walking deeper into the whale's lair, putting one foot in front of the other without breaking down into another fit of tears. After a bit of kind coaxing from his companions, the knight finally started to answer their questions.

"I don't remember much," he admitted in a quiet, sad voice. "I recall being awoken from a nap ... uh, I mean I was disturbed from some heroic training I was doing. The bells in the Palace Tower were ringing, summoning me. I ran to the Big Comfy Chair Room as fast I could. I remember being a little confused because my helmet fit a little differently, but I had no time to worry about that because the Queen needed me."

"Once I reached the Big Comfy Chair Room, I *immediately* confronted the evil villain I spotted there, threatening the Queen. A lesser man would have failed to notice him since he was in disguise, but to my trained eye I could immediately tell he was filled with treachery and nastiness. I launched what I'm sure was a fearsome, devastating attack on the villain, but ... but ... "

He walked in silence for a long moment. Grace noticed a lone tear sliding down his cheek.

"Yes?" she asked gently. "What happened then?"

A sob or two escaped from Sir Nathan's chest, which he quickly tried to disguise as nothing more than a cough. However, his face showed a memory of fear as he thought back to that day.

"I'm pretty sure ... yes, I'm pretty sure that my attack must have smote the enemy quite hard," Sir Nathan finally said. "However, after that, I don't remember much."

He stopped walking and leaned up against the wall, not caring for the trickle of sea water that flowed down the stone and soaked into the crevices of his armor. The knight covered his face with his hands. Grace and Tupolev could clearly hear his quiet, muffled crying. Grace patted him gently on the shoulder and Tupolev nuzzled his cheek.

"I just don't understand!" Sir Nathan said angrily after a bit. "All I can remember is terror and fear and sadness after that! How can that be possible?! I have never felt afraid before, never not once in my entire life! Not even that time I faced those Blorpian Pirate Raiders that were trying to steal the golden trophy given out on Higgledee Piggledee Eve for best pirate voice, and *everyone* knows that Blorpian Pirate Raiders are some of the scariest pirate raiders in the world due to the way they leap out at you and shout nasty insults when you're not expecting it."

Tupolev shivered at the memory of the Blorpians and the fight to retrieve the trophy. The enemy had jumped out at the horse no fewer than seven times during the fight, shouting "Boo!" and startling him terribly. He had had nightmares for a week and jumped every time anyone had said his name.

"There's no way any of this is possible," mumbled Sir Nathan, shaking his head in confusion. "There's just no way I should feel fear. There's no way I should feel sad and frightened. I've been battling all sorts of evil ever since I became a knight, but nothing in my experience has taught me how to fight being afraid. And I *can't* be afraid! I just can't! I'm the Hero of Mariskatania!"

"Whoa, hold up there a second!" came a bold voice. They all turned to see the squirrel standing nearby, the Sword of Power casually held in one tiny paw. "I'm glad to have you here helping out and all, but let's not forget who is who. Everyone knows that *I* am the Hero! I'm tall and brave in my shining armor and nothing can stop me!"

The squirrel pointed behind him, down the hallway he had been exploring. "Now that we have that straightened out, I have found what is sure to be the hiding place of the treacherous villain. Come, my fine companions! Let us ride forth and stomp out this evilness once and for all! Nothing can stop goodness and honor, especially when I, the Hero of the land, am here to save the day! Come!"

He turned and scampered down the hallway. Sir Nathan, Grace, and Tupolev looked at each other, then broke out into giggles.

"What an odd sort of character," the knight said in between chuckles.

"You're right about that," agreed Grace, taking Sir Nathan's arm and pulling him off the wall. "I think I've only ever met someone like him once before in my life."

"You have? Well, then I feel sorry for you, because the way that squirrel talks is ridiculous."

Grace and Tupolev shared a quick look, then broke into another uncontrollable fit of laughter. Sir Nathan didn't know what they were giggling about, but at least their happy mood brought a small smile to his face.

\* \* \* \* \*

Deep inside the mountain fortress of Kale the Whale, there was a room unlike any other.

First of all, it was big.

Huge.

Enormous.

To merely call it a room was like calling the Sea of Silliness a little puddle of water. Where the hallways in the fortress were clearly built to give the whale plenty of room to get around, the room was large enough that dozens of whales could have thrown a party inside and still had room for a herd of dancing elephants. Grace thought the sun and a full set of clouds would have fit inside without any problems.

Glass pipes ran alongside massive iron and copper tubing, covering most of each wall and quite a bit of the ceiling. Even the floor had patches of

thick pipes jutting out of it. Poking out from amongst the pipes were huge turning gears and cogs, several feet across. Their intermeshing teeth clacked together loudly, driven by some unseen power throbbing behind the thick walls.

Up in one corner of the ceiling there was a complex set of metal rails, like an upside-down railroad track. In Mariskatania, railroad tracks had been invented a long time ago and sets of gleaming rail criss-crossed the countryside. Unfortunately, no one had ever invented anything to ride *on* the tracks and so most people just used them for a nice place to have a picnic and fly a kite. Every three minutes and thirty-three seconds, an odd contraption would shoot out of a hatch in the wall, hanging upside-down from the rails on wheels made of oyster shells. It would zip out, flying through a set of zig-zagging turns while making a loud clattering sound. Once it reach the end of the tracks, a mechanical claw would reach out from the device and flip a giant switch labeled "Do Not Touch" in letters so big, the companions could read them easily in the gloomy light.

Having accomplished its bizarre purpose, the contraption would ride quickly back and disappear back into its hatch. Thirteen seconds later, a much smaller hatch right next to the switch would open and a tiny gear-driven mechanical turtle would pop out and flip the switch back using its mouth.

Sir Nathan and the others stood watching in silent confusion. On the fourth or fifth trip out of its metal hatch, the metal turtle noticed the group standing far below and threw them a small, friendly wave with one copper flipper before disappearing back into the wall.

Oddly enough, this was only the seventh weirdest mechanical device in the room.

The most peculiar, most confusing, most bizarre contraption sat in the very center of the floor. It was a massive device, as big as some of the large houses built near the Royal Palace. Other than its size, it looked a little similar to the Cataclysm Crates scattered across the land, currently pumping out an endless supply of water to flood Mariskatania. Gears as tall as Tupolev meshed together, spinning pulleys and cogs and metal bits of all sorts. The noise was incredible. The entire device was built over an open section of floor, a hatch one hundred feet across that was open to the sea. Rapidly spinning metal shafts, as thick as a tree trunk, plunged down into the water from the bottom of the beastly device. Unseen paddles at the bottom of the shafts mixed the sea water violently, stirring it into a churning froth. Had Huggo seen the device, he would have used it to mix up gigantic batches of cake batter. The Royal Baker and Cake-Maker thought, and rightly so, that cakes were only their most delicious when they were as big as a barn.

Thick glass pipes, several feet across, gurgled with greenish sea water as they rose up out of the open hatch and fed into the base of the device. One of those pipes alone could have drained a good sized pond in less than hour. All of them combined had to be sucking up so much water, only a body as big as the Sea of Silliness could keep up without going dry.

The inner workings of the device gathered the water together into a central holding tank as big as the Breaking Fast Room in the Royal Palace. From there it was pumped under high pressure out of a nozzle at the top, shooting towards the ceiling faster than Tupolev rushing to the Royal Kitchens for a fresh-baked batch of Huckle Nut muffins.

The horse, Grace, Sir Nathan, and the squirrel couldn't understand what they were seeing. The water jetting out of the top of the contraption hit a rapidly spinning corkscrew that twisted the water into a tight column and shot it up into the mouth of an inverted funnel that carried the water away in a series of waiting, dark tubes.

"I can't believe it," mumbled Tupolev, his eyes wide with shock.

"Look at all that water," said Grace in a voice filled with awe. "I can't believe the sea hasn't been completely drained. Where is it all going?"

"The evil beast has created a machine of great evil," said the squirrel. For the first time since handling the Sword of Power, the rodent's voice was barely a whisper instead of his usual boisterous tone. "Could it be ... is it possible ... is that machine ...?" His voice trailed off into silence.

Sir Nathan finished his thought. "Is that machine taking thousands and thousands of gallons of water a minute, spinning it into a whirling vortex and spitting that out of the top of the fortress, which forms a giant whirlpool that feeds a water spout up on the surface of the Sea of Silliness that lifts the water up and into that massive, dark, stationary storm cloud floating overhead, which somehow sends the water to gush out of the countless Cataclysm Crates currently flooding Mariskatania?"

Grace, Tupolev, and the squirrel turned to face the knight, more in shock at the words coming out of his mouth than at anything they had seen in the whale's fortress.

"Yes," Sir Nathan said in reply to his own question. "That's exactly what's happening."

"Uh ..." said the squirrel.

"But ..." said Tupolev.

"Oh-kay ..." said Grace.

"Yup, my thoughts exactly," finished Sir Nathan.

They all stood there, unmoving and silent, watching the mesmerizing process of the water getting sucked from the sea and sent on an impossible journey to flood the country they loved so dearly (except the squirrel, who didn't really care where he lived, so long as there were plenty of Huckle Nuts to find).

"Well then, we know what we have to do!" shouted the squirrel suddenly, startling them all. "We must disable this infernal contraption! We must shut it down, for once and for all, using all the goodness and honor we possess! I, the Hero of Mariskatania, armed with my fearful Sword of Power and protected by my gleaming suit of armor, assisted by my less capable companions, by which I mean you guys, shall smite that bizarre monstrosity until it can pump water no more easily than a pig can fly! Any questions?!"

"Yes. What about PigWiggles?" asked Tupolev, raising a hoof. "Do they count as flying pigs?"

"Quiet! None of your backtalk! Now, are there any *other* questions?! Any *serious* questions?!"

"Yes," said Grace quietly. "What does *infernal* mean?"

The squirrel just glared at her until she looked away. Grace made a mental note to just look the word up in the Royal Register of Everything when she got home.

Confident he wasn't going to get any more of what he considered "sass", the squirrel picked his way across the room, heading towards the giant water-pumping device. It wasn't an easy thing to do, considering all of the pipes and valves and turning gears that sprouted from the floor. Some of the obstacles the tiny squirrel could just squeeze under, but the rest were too big for him to climb over and he had to find a different way around.

Twice he had to remind himself not to get distracted by the mechanical turtle waving to him from the ceiling.

The others followed and soon they were scattered across the room, each trying to find their own way to the center.

At one point, Tupolev got his tail pinched in between two gears and yelped with the pain as a large clump of hair was pulled loose. Grace brushed up against a set of hot copper pipes and got a nasty burn on one leg. The squirrel tried to squeeze through a very narrow gap between the rough stone floor and a coarse steel plate and had a patch of blue fur scraped off his belly, leaving behind a raw, pink spot.

Never taking his eyes off the wondrous,

monstrous, massive contraption, Sir Nathan strode through the litter of obstacles as if they weren't there. His feet seemed to find the right places to step on their own, his legs hopped and twisted and slid at all the right times to avoid anything in his way. Like a person possessed, he practically floated through the room, unhindered.

Eventually they were all standing next to the device. Up close, it was much larger than it had seemed from the edge of the room. The glass pipes rose up out of the floor next to them like transparent trees whose sap flowed and bubbled with an angry gurgle.

Grace stared at all the pipes, gears, and pulleys. The contraption was so massive, so sturdy, so solidly built, it looked indestructible. "How are we ever going to destroy this thing?" she asked.

"You aren't!" came a deep voice from behind them.

They whirled around, surprised to see Kale the Whale had entered the room unnoticed. Grace and Tupolev had yet to meet the whale and, despite the fact that he was standing there before them, they had a difficult time believing what they were seeing. Just the size of the whale alone was frightening. Seeing the whale on a nasty looking walking contraption, most normal people would have run for their lives.

Unfortunately, there weren't any normal people to be found.

"There is nothing you can do to disable my wonderful Sea Slurping System!"

A small giggle escaped from Grace's lips as she

thought about what Tupolev would have called the contraption, back when he was running around with the Sword of Power clenched in his teeth.

"Surrender to me now, oh wretched whale, oh scum of evilness!" said a voice that any other time would have belonged to Sir Nathan. This time, however, it was the squirrel that spoke. He hopped up onto a section of heavy pipe. With one tiny paw he pointed at the whale, with the other, he held the Sword of Power lifted towards the heavens. It was quite a ridiculous sight. "We meet again and this time, I shall smite you so much, I'll knock your teeth down your throat so hard, they'll shoot out your tail!"

The naughty smile the whale wore faded and was replaced with a look of confusion as he stared at the small, blue, fuzzy rodent yelling at him. "Oh, hello there," Kale said in a friendly tone. "I don't believe we've met."

"Oh, we've met before!" shouted the squirrel. "Though I can understand why you would wish to forget me, since I'm so awesome! But make no mistake, it is I, the Hero of Mariskatania, here to stop your evil ways!"

The whale stared at the squirrel for a long moment, then looked up at Sir Nathan. Ignoring the rodent for the time being, he asked the real Hero, "How did you manage to escape from the control of one of my wonderful Head-Holding, Brain-Bending Helmets of Horror? I designed that one very carefully, especially for you. There should have been no way for you to get your courage back!"

It was then the whale noticed the look on Sir

Nathan's face. Normally, any villain that challenged the Hero saw only brave, raw, angry courage in the knight's eyes. But now the whale could plainly see Sir Nathan was uncertain and even afraid.

"Oh, ho!" chuckled the whale, his deep voice echoing in the large room. "I see that you *don't* have your courage back! This is *very* interesting, very interesting indeed. Here you are, the great and wonderful Sir Nathan, out to stop the most terrible enemy Mariskatania has ever seen, yet you are shivering in your armor with fear. How delightful! The Empire of the Waters will not be stopped, especially by a hero that's afraid of his own shadow!"

"Look at my face when you are speaking to me!" shouted the squirrel, his tiny voice almost lost among the noise of the huge Sea Slurping System. "I'm not sure what odd games you are playing, but I, the Hero of Mariskatania, stand before you! My courage is pure and right where it's always been and I am afraid of no silly fish!"

Kale the Whale looked back and forth, from the squirrel to Sir Nathan. Finally it all made sense. "Oh, ho! So that is what happened! Fascinating! Somehow, there's been a differential trans-disposition that ameliorated the courage-continuance. That is good to know. I shall adjust my Head-Holding, Brain-Bending Helmets of Horror in the future to make sure that doesn't happen again."

"Speak plainly, you foolish fish!" shouted the squirrel. "I am the Hero and I will tolerate no nonsense!"

"I'm not a fish, you simpleton! And you're not

the Hero! That cowardly fool standing behind you is! But, none of that matters! You can't stop me, especially here in my own fortress! And, as you can see, I'm wearing my super-fantastic Pummeling Paraphernalia of Perambulation. It makes me more powerful, more deadly, and way more handsome!"

Having been the only one to see the whale before, Sir Nathan was the only one that knew what the villain was talking about. He took a moment to study the villain's walking contraption and realized it was indeed considerably different than the one he had been using when he had smashed his way into the Royal Palace.

While impressive, the first walking contraption was crude compared to what the whale was now using. The new device was made entirely of black iron, rough and dangerous looking. Sir Nathan could see countless interlocking gears, pistons, chains, and pulleys, glistening wetly with lubricating oil. Tightly wound springs stretched down the massive, multi-jointed legs and each limb ended in sharp metal claws, like the feet of a dragon.

It was clear the whale's new walking doohickey was a big, dangerous improvement over the old one.

"As you can see, I am improving my inventions every day!" boomed the whale. "Nobody can accomplish what I can, not even with magic! With my new mechanical walking suit, I am just like a deadly spider and no one will be able to stop me! I am a genius!"

"Excuse me," Grace called out in a puzzled tone. "Your contraption there only has seven legs.

Spiders have eight."

"What?!" The whale looked flustered. He tried to crane his neck around to count just exactly how many legs the walking device actually had, but quickly remembered being a whale meant he really didn't have much of a neck in the first place. He gave up in frustration just as Tupolev said, "Yeah, you're right. Spiders have eight legs and that gizmo only has seven."

"No they don't!" yelled the whale.

"Um, I'm pretty sure —"

"Shut up! None of that matters! You're all going to die soon, so just shut up!"

The whale spun about, faster than anyone would have thought possible for such a large creature. The front set of claws on his mechanical suit reached out and grabbed hold of a group of pipes jutting out from the wall. In a flash, he was climbing up towards the ceiling just like a massive seven-legged spider. The whale's laugh drifted down to them, filled with craziness. The villain was so excited, his huge tail wagged back and forth just like a puppy's.

"Seven legs or not," said the horse in a depressed tone, "I think he's right about us all dying soon."

"Oh, be quiet, Tupolev!," snapped Grace as she tightened her grip on her soup ladle. "That's not helping."

\* \* \* \* \*

"Tupolev! Help!"

Grace was hanging by one hand, high off the

floor. Her fingers started to slip one by one as they struggled to hold on to an oily pipe sticking out from the wall. In her other hand, she held her soup ladle, which she used to fend off attack after attack from Kale the Whale.

They were halfway up one of the walls in the massive room in which they had found the villain's terrible Sea Slurping System and Grace could barely remember the details of the fight that had caused her to be in such a dangerous position.

The evil whale clung to the wall with six of his mechanical legs while he lashed out at Grace with the seventh. Again she knocked the blow aside. The sound of her weapon colliding with the massive, metal claw was deafening.

She tried to find a place for her feet, some little ledge or platform she could reach with her toes so she wouldn't fall, but there was nothing around her except the exposed rock of the wall, wet with a trickle of sea water.

*Clang!* She blocked another attack. The whale scuttled sideways, walking straight up the wall with ease. He tried to come at her a from a different angle so he could get past her defenses and smash her to the ground.

Below her, Tupolev was fending off the attacks of a half-dozen metal crabs that were each the size of a large dog. The crabs were each ridden by a smaller, living crab that controlled the contraption through a complex set of levers and dials. The horse could see clearly that the creatures were each wearing one of the whale's devious mind-control helmets, but so far he had only been successful in disabling one of them. That crab had scuttled off, muttering about having a headache and wondering how he was going to explain his absence to his wife.

The other crabs were trying to pin the horse down with heavy nets and doing a pretty good job of it. Time and again, Tupolev had barely scrambled free of a net just before the crabs could jump on top of him and tie him up.

He could hear Grace screaming his name, but his heart was heavy with a helpless sadness since he couldn't do anything to come to her aid.

Near the center of the room, the squirrel looked up at the sound of Grace's cries. The heroism flooding his tiny little body ached to rush to her aid, but he found himself torn between helping his brave companion and recovering the Sword of Power which was currently sinking out of sight into the turbulent pool of water beneath the Sea Slurping System.

"Blast!" cried the squirrel as he clung to the edge of the pool with one paw and reached for the blade with his other, which meant he was able to reach nothing further away than four inches. "For some reason I can't understand, that evil villain was able to catch me in an evil booby-trap and knock the Sword of Power from my hand! Here I am, the Hero of Mariskatania, bravest adventurer that has ever lived, stronger than the strongest man (and most of the women), and yet I fall for such a simple trap. I'm as tall as a Hootentoot Tree, or so I assume because no hero worth his pay would be caught being short, yet for some reason my arms aren't as long as I remember them being and I'm finding it difficult to reach my magical weapon before it sinks out of sight forever! What a terrible, terrible day!"

Of Sir Nathan, there was no sign.

* * * * *

"Run! Run in fear and hide!" shouted the whale at Sir Nathan as the knight bolted from the room in terror. "Your courage has been stolen and you are worthless without it! You see? You have been replaced by a tiny squirrel and it's all because of me and my genius brain!"

All this shouting had happened approximately ten minutes before the squirrel found himself stretched out at the edge of the bubbling pool, reaching for the sinking sword.

After climbing the wall in his seven-legged spider contraption, Kale the Whale hadn't flung mechanical spiders at them that shot globs of lava out of their eyes. He hadn't dropped acid bombs on them. He hadn't even dropped water balloons filled with cold water. All he had hurled at them had been insults. Lots and lots of insults, most of which were aimed at Sir Nathan and most of them calling him a chicken.

It hadn't taken long for the knight to break down in tears and run crying from the room.

After Sir Nathan had fought off the shark, Grace had thought the long days of the knight being afraid were almost over. She thought for sure he would find a new source of courage and, driven by his honor, would rise up to fight and defeat the evil whale. When instead he had run from the room, sobbing, it felt as if all hope and happiness had drained out of Grace like a bucket with a hole in the bottom leaking water.

However, as a sworn protector of Mariskatania herself, she couldn't abandon the fight and chase after Sir Nathan. The whale *had* to be stopped before the entire world was flooded forever. She had looked over at the squirrel as he stood atop a pipe, glaring at the whale clinging to the wall high above. His blue, fuzzy tail was puffed out in anger and he was chattering away in the Hobnobber Squirrel language, letting loose with what Grace was pretty sure was a long stream of naughty words.

Blue rodent or not, the squirrel was certainly *acting* like the Hero, just like Tupolev had before him and she and Abbey had done before that. Was that enough? Had they all truly been filled with Sir Nathan's bravery and courage and strength or did they just *think* they were? There was more to Sir Nathan than a lot of yelling about goodness and honor. Anyone could stand around, shouting about smiting. It took more than that to actually defeat the bad guys when they showed up. Filled with that same type of bravery and honor and courage, Grace knew how much work it was.

Unfortunately, she had no memory of the period when she had been the one holding the Sword of Power. She couldn't recall if she had actually been the Hero or was just pretending. All of Mariskatania was counting on them to put a stop to the evil whale and all his shenanigans. Pretend Hero or not, they were just going to have to make do with the blue rodent and hope things worked out.

The squirrel shot her a look. It reminded her very much of the look Sir Nathan had given right before they had battled the Duckling of Annihilation. The one, single look had said a lot and Grace had immediately known what to do. She had run left, Sir Nathan had run right, and twenty-seven seconds later the cute, fuzzy, blood-thirsty duckling was defeated.

Perhaps the squirrel really was the Hero, now that all of Sir Nathan's courage had been given to him by the Sword of Power. Grace certainly hoped so. She nodded at the squirrel and ran to the left. The squirrel nodded back and darted to the right, a streak of blue zipping under and around the pipes sticking out of the floor.

Tupolev just stood there, shouting words of encouragement at them. After all, other than the time the horse had been magically transformed into a Hobnobber Squirrel, he wasn't really good at climbing. If you were to bump into Tupolev, say at a Higgledee Piggledee Eve party, and ask him what it was like to get turned into a squirrel, he would angrily deny it had ever happened and then try to change the subject.

The whale had just watched them, a devilish grin on his broad face, as Grace quickly scaled the pipes and valves and massive gears on the wall to the left. Faster yet, the squirrel scampered up the wall to the right, not slowed down in the least despite holding the heavy Sword of Power in one paw.

"You'll pay for your mischief!" yelled Grace as

she moved swiftly upwards, unhindered by the weight of her armor.

"Your days of evil are nearing an end!" shouted the squirrel, climbing at an astonishing rate.

"I think you both are greatly mistaken!" shouted the whale in return. "In fact, I think you both are going to find yourselves a bit ... *steamed* at what's about to happen!" Kale let loose with a long, loud, deep laugh that echoed through the room.

Grace and the squirrel stopped climbing, immediately on the lookout for some sort of trap. They looked around warily, but nothing happened other than the whale's laughing grew out of control and soon he was uncontrollably caught up in guffaws so hard, tears flowed freely from his eyes and he was having a difficult time breathing.

After a long while, his laughter tapered off, quieting down to giggles and then mere chuckles. Pretty soon there was just a long, uncomfortable silence as everyone stared at him, waiting for something to happen.

"Oh, right," he said. "I should have been paying attention. That one is my fault."

With one mechanical claw, he reached out and pulled a thick lever jutting out from a tangle of pipes. A massive explosion of super-heated water shot out of the wall, hot enough to melt metal and instantly cook anyone in its path. A cloud of steam boiled off of the spray, filling the room from top to bottom in a thick fog of hot, moist air.

The whale erupted into another fit of laughter. "Ha! That foolish girl and puny squirrel were no match for my amazing smarts! I am way too intelligent to be defeated by weak-minded fools like them! Now they are destroyed and I live on, ready to drown the world in ... uh ... uh-oh."

The cloud of steam had faded enough for the whale to see Grace and the squirrel still clinging to the wall, right where they had been. They were both clearly wondering just what Kale had been shouting about.

"Oh, drat!" spat the villain once he realized the explosion of steam and water had shot out of the complete wrong wall, doing nothing more evil than partially melting one of the mechanical turtle's metal fins. Sadly enough, it was the one he did all his waving with, which hurt its feelings so much (even if he wasn't a real turtle) that he didn't cheer up for a month. "I pulled the wrong lever. You two hold still while I figure this out! Now, let's see ... was it this one?"

The whale reached out towards another lever, but before he could grab it with the mechanical claw, Grace's soup ladle came whirling through the air. It smashed into the lever with the force of all her might, snapping it off at the base. The broken bar of metal tumbled to the floor, banging and clattering on the pipes and gears decorating the wall as it fell. Bouncing off the lever as it broke, Grace's weapon bounced high up into the air and landed perfectly in her outstretched hand.

"Hey! Careful with that!" shouted Kale. "You could have really hurt someone!"

He scampered off to the side, reaching out for a pair of large, red, metal valve wheels sticking out of a massive copper pipe. Suddenly, the squirrel was there in a flash of blue. The Sword of Power rose and fell and the wheels dropped to the floor as well, severed from the pipe in a single stroke.

"Knock it off!" bellowed the villain, clearly upset and angered.

He climbed quickly to the top of the wall and then, completely upside-down, started out across the ceiling like a 50,000 pound spider. It was truly impressive to watch. Grace and the squirrel quickly followed. Up at the ceiling, the blue rodent had an easier time than Grace did, easily able to find spaces on top of all the pipes and plumbing and machinery to stand. Grace had to shove her soup-ladle into its loop on her belt and swing herself hand-over-hand. Looking down, she felt momentarily dizzy at the long, dangerous drop below her feet.

"Get back here, you ... you ... you *stupid* whale!" she shouted in frustration. She simply could not move as fast as the evil creature could with all seven legs of his mechanical suit. Even the squirrel couldn't move as quickly, having to pause after each jump to find a new place to leap to. Kale could simply grab whatever was sticking out of the ceiling in his mechanical claws and move along almost as quickly as he could on the ground.

Grace was so intent on chasing the whale, she wasn't paying attention to where she was headed. Suddenly she found herself right next to the twirling corkscrew at the top of the Sea Slurping System. Up close, the noise and the power of the shooting water was unbelievable. Grace truly believed that if she were to reach out and stick her hand in the water's flow, her fingers would be plucked from her body by the force of the water as easily as Mitzy plucking a flower.

Hanging from a greasy metal bar, she looked around. She was surprised to see the whale was suddenly nowhere in sight. She twisted her neck to look behind her as best she could, but couldn't even see the squirrel. She felt her fingers slipping on the bar and quickly pulled herself over to a cleaner copper pipe that wasn't so slippery. Unfortunately, the pipe was very hot to the touch and she quickly had to swing herself over to a thick beam.

That was when the whale got her.

Unseen, he had adjusted one of the thousands of valves and levers covering the surfaces of the room. A redirected jet of water squirted out of the spinning vortex and caught her in the face. The force of the water stung her skin like a slap across the cheek. She let out a yelp of pain and twisted away.

Hanging on to the beam with one hand, she plucked her soup-ladle out of her belt with the other. However, the whale made another adjustment and a super-narrow squirt of water shot out of the vortex. It hit her hand with the force of a hammer's blow, knocking her ladle loose from her fingers. A scream of outrage tore from her lips as she watched her prized weapon fall to the floor below.

She reached up and grabbed the beam with her empty hand, spinning quickly in place and flying like a monkey across a set of thin, glass pipes. Jets of water chased after her, each just missing. Around the vortex she went, quickly swinging from one hand hold to the next, not caring whether or not the pipes were intensely hot or bitingly cold to the touch. Halfway around, she spotted the whale. He was hanging upside-down, frantically working a bank of dials as he tried to blast her off the ceiling.

Weapon or no weapon, she was Amazing Grace and she was going to put a stop to the whale and his evil ways once and for all. With a look that promised plenty of smiting, she swung towards the whale. With one final vault, she flew through the air like a bird in flight, aimed perfectly for the whale's face.

But it was all a trick.

A solid blast of water shot out of the open end of the wide pipe and knocked her out of the air. She realized the whale really was the genius he claimed he was. She had done exactly what he had wanted and put herself in exactly the spot he had planned so he could knock her out of the air like a swatted bug.

Amazing Grace flew backwards in a detonation of water, realizing that Kale the Whale was too much of a genius for her to defeat alone.

She had been smashed by the blast so hard, she had flown all the way back to the wall behind her where she hit with a crash that knocked the air from her lungs and the senses from her head.

\* \* \* \* \*

Now, it was all Grace could do to block the whale's attacks. The villain was plucking jagged chunks of metal and stone off the wall in his powerful claws and throwing them at her. They came in so fast, she could barely block them in time.

After getting caught in the villain's trap, she had lost consciousness when she had struck the wall. Fortunately, her body had gotten tangled in a messy cluster of pipes which had prevented her from falling all the way to the distant ground below. Smashing into the wall had hurt enough.

By the time she had realized where she was and remembered what she was doing, Kale the Whale was clawing his way across the ceiling, ready to finish her off. She figured her only hope was to climb down before he could get to her, but before she could start she had heard the most beautiful sound in the world.

It was Tupolev, her soup-ladle clenched in his teeth, galloping across the floor beneath her. "Grashe!" he had yelled. "Grashe! It ish me, Tupolev! I have shomething shiny you might find intereshting!" With a toss of his head he hurled the ladle with perfect aim. Up, up, up it flew, slowing as it climbed into the air. It reached the top of its arc and started to fall back to the ground, right beside where Grace was clinging to the wall.

She plucked it out of the air and turned in time to deflect a thrown chunk of rock that would have hit her in the head had it not been blocked.

Again and again, the whale had whipped large, dangerous projectiles at her, and Grace had avoided or deflected every one. But she was sore and tired and her head was still spinning from getting smashed into the wall. The whale was stalking closer and closer and she didn't think she could fend him off much longer.

She risked a quick look down at the squirrel, but

it was obvious the Sword was too far away for him to reach. Tupolev was doing his best to pick his way across the cluttered floor to help the rodent, but it didn't look like he could make it to the squirrel's side before the blade sunk out of sight forever.

It was at that very moment that Grace was hit with the realization they would lose the battle. She knew Mariskatania would be flooded forever! The thought smacked her in the brain harder than any thrown projectile could, hitting her more painfully than any attack the whale could ever spring on her.

She had never felt such sadness before in her life, even when her parents wouldn't let her quit the Preening and Cleaning Crew to become a knight.

A voice suddenly cut through the air, deep and bold. At first Grace thought it was the whale, gloating over his victory. But Kale looked as equally surprised as she was. They looked down to the center of the room, both of them surprised to see Sir Nathan standing beside the Sea Slurping System, holding the Sword of Power.

Later, Grace would tell everyone she talked to that a dazzling, golden light shone out of the magical blade at that very moment as Sir Nathan held it over his head. Neither Tupolev, the squirrel, nor Sir Nathan himself would say they had seen such a light and would suggest Grace had just imagined it. But she knew they were wrong. She knew she was seeing Sir Nathan's honor and bravery and courage shining out for all those who had need of a Hero.

"Surrender now, oh evil creature! Surrender to the forces of good, for you shall never succeed so long as happiness and honor is around to save the day!" shouted Sir Nathan. "Climb down from that wall and turn off this devious machinery or I'll turn you into a plate of fish fry!"

Kale the Whale gave a little yelp of surprise.

"I told you crazy people, I'm not a fish!" he yelled, then turned and scrambled away, fleeing through a secret, whale-sized panel in the wall.

Grace climbed down the wall as fast as she could and joined Tupolev as he picked his way across the cluttered floor. They hurried over to the Hero as he handed the Sword of Power back to the squirrel. "Here," he said. "You've been doing such a good job, you should keep it."

The fuzzy rodent accepted the weapon gratefully, then bowed low to Sir Nathan. Straightening, he saluted the knight with the massive blade, then scampered off to chase after the whale.

Grace touched Sir Nathan gently on the arm. "You gave up your sword," she said softly. "But, what about your courage?" Even though Sir Nathan had handled the magical weapon, she was surprised to see the same uncertain look on the knight's face he had worn earlier. She had been sure that once Sir Nathan had taken his weapon back in his hand, all his stolen courage and bravery would flood back into him and he'd be like his old, loud self that liked to charge out of the room first and ask what the mission was later.

Somehow, none of that had happened. Later on, the squirrel would tell her there had been no mysterious spark, no strong smell of a thunderstorm. Sir Nathan had just appeared at the squirrel's side as the weapon was about to sink out of sight forever and plunged his hand into the boiling waters. The knight grabbed the sword and lifted it as easily as he always had, but nothing special happened when he did. He had simply turned, gave the squirrel a sad little smile, and yelled up at the whale before the villain could finish Grace off.

"My courage?" asked Sir Nathan. He looked up to see the squirrel scampering back up one wall, shouting something about smiting and whale-burgers. "I don't think courage comes from a magical sword. It doesn't come from special armor or from having a dragon for a mount or even from mind-controlling helmets. It all comes from inside, deep in here somewhere." He tapped his chest lightly.

"When I ran away, terrified at the mean things the whale was saying to me, I found a dark corner and hid. I was ready to hide there forever, ashamed, and never come out, not even for a Smooshelberry milkshake. But I could still hear the battle raging on. I could hear the whale laughing and all the noise as he clambered around using that mechanical walking contraption of his. That's when I realized that being brave doesn't mean having no fear and charging into danger whenever you can. Being brave means charging into danger, even when you're afraid. It means doing the things that need doing, especially when no one else can. It means ... it means helping your friends when they're in trouble, even though you're terribly afraid of getting eaten by a whale."

Tupolev looked away, mumbling about getting something in his eye as he tried to hide his tears. On the other hand, Grace had no problems showing her emotions and wrapped the Hero in a hug so tight, he could feel the squeeze through his armor.

"Okay, okay," said Sir Nathan, embarrassed. "Let's go help our squirrel friend before he wins the battle all by himself."

"But ... you gave away the Sword of Power. What will you use for a weapon?"

"Well, it just so happens that a good friend of mine does a terrific amount of smiting, using nothing but a soup-ladle. Perhaps she can recommend something?"

Grace grinned and blushed. "Well, I don't have a spare ladle, but will this do?"

Reaching behind her, she pulled something off her belt. It was an experimental weapon she had the Royal Chief Master of Arms make for her. It was dangerous looking. It seemed ready to burst with power. It looked ready to walk off on its own and smite the nearest rock troll it could find, just for something to do.

It was a ball of chocolate pudding.

Sir Nathan took the blob from Grace's hand. It was no bigger than the smallest Wobble Melon fruit, about eight inches across. The surface was perfectly smooth and a glistening dark brown in color. Sir Nathan could see his distorted reflection in its surface.

"I know, I know," Grace was saying, "you're thinking I could have come up with something a little bit more ... weapon-ish. A month or two ago, the Chief Master of Arms and I went through dozens of different sorts of weapons, all the time trying to find something that was just the perfect sort of thing for bonking someone truly evil on the head. I was trying to figure out if there was something a bit more knightly than, you know ... a soup ladle. But we just couldn't come up with the perfect thing."

"Then one day we were taking a break in the palace kitchens. We were eating some of Huggo's delicious Exploding Death Plumb tarts and listening to him explain how tough it was to work with some of the more dangerous foods he kept in the kitchen. He showed us a special spatula he uses whenever he's making his recipe for Pinky Pancakes of Power."

"Are those the ones that everyone thinks are okay to eat with their fingers, but ..."

"... but really the pancakes bite their fingers off," finished Grace. "Yes, those are the ones. It was while Huggo was showing us his reinforced spatula that the Chief Master of Arms and I were both struck with the same idea at the same time."

"Uh ... you both thought of a blob of pudding?"

"No! We thought we could learn something about powerful weapons from Huggo and some of his more ... *adventurous* recipes. Besides, that's not just *any* pudding. It started out as one of Huggo's special batches of chocolate syrup. You know ... that stuff he keeps in a steel safe so it doesn't escape again. After that, the Chief Master of Arms took it and worked on it, day and night, for ten straight days without pausing to sleep or eat!"

"And ... all he got out of it was a blob of pudding?"

"It's more than that, you dolt! Watch!" snapped Grace. She grabbed the dark sphere from Sir Nathan and, holding it firmly in her left hand, she plunged her right hand deep into the blob. Then, holding it carefully away from her body, she gave her wrist an odd sort of twirl and a flick and the pudding uncoiled itself like an attacking snake. Faster than Sir Nathan could follow, the pudding had formed itself into the shape of a long, narrow sword.

"That's impressive!" gasped the knight. "But ..."

"Yes?!" asked Grace impatiently.

"It's ... still just a sword made from a blob of pudding."

"Oh, yeah? Could regular pudding do this?" She swung at a nearby set of pipes and the weapon cut through them as easily as if they were made of paper and glue. And that wasn't all, not by a long shot. Grace did another odd little twist and twirl with her wrist, and the pudding reformed into the shape of a battle axe. Again and again, she was able to reform the blob of pudding into many different weapons, each as dark and deadly as the last.

"And, that's not all!" cried Grace in excitement, clearly pleased with herself. She reformed the pudding into a dark ball and held it on the palm of her hand. She swiped the index finger of her other hand across its surface and licked it clean. "It's also delicious!"

For the first time in a very long while, with a somewhat naughty smile on his face, Sir Nathan was starting to feel like a Hero again.

* * * * *

The massively huge room deep inside Kale the Whale's fortress was a disaster and looked like an epic battle had been fought within its walls.

Which is exactly what had happened.

Pipes, valves, and various bits of machinery were smashed and broken. Jagged metal hung from the walls and ceiling, and the floor was littered with piles of destroyed equipment.

In the center of the room, the Sea Slurping System was quiet. The pool beneath it was still, the flow of water silenced. A horse-shaped hole was punched clean through its innards and Tupolev was already complaining about how bruised he was feeling.

In the only somewhat clear space in the room, Kale the Whale lay on his back. Tears flowed steadily from his eyes and the sheer loudness of his crying made any sobbing Sir Nathan had done seem puny in comparison. The whale's walking contraption was gone, smashed to bits and bent beyond recognition. Lying on the floor around him, all suffering aches and pains and bruises beyond counting, were Sir Nathan, Amazing Grace, Sir Tupolev, and a fluffy, blue squirrel holding a very large sword.

Though they had won the battle, the party of four was still feeling a bit too mangled to feel very victorious. Maybe they would feel better about what they had accomplished when they had healed from their wounds, say in a month or two.

"What am I going to do?!" sobbed the whale. "I am nothing without my inventions!"

Grace sighed. They had gone through this before. *Seven times* before, to be exact. "Look, I told you ... it's just like Sir Nathan taught me. Who you are and what you are worth comes from inside yourself, not from the tools in your hand. No one can give you honor by strapping a walking device to your belly."

"Nor by shoving a sword in your hand," added the Hero with a smile.

"But what am I going to do with myself?" The whale's tears slowed a bit, but he still sniffled continuously, which is quite a thing to see on a whale. "I was so caught up in my evil plan, I don't know what else there is to do."

"Well, I'll bet Queen Gobbledeegook would be delighted if you were to put some of your contraption-building skills to work and invent something to help clean up all the flooded lands."

The whale seemed to think about this for a long minute. "Do you think so? Because I'd really like to – uh-oh!"

Sir Nathan looked to where Kale was pointing with one massive flipper. Up on the ceiling, a long seam of metal had ripped apart, weakened from the battle. Sea water flooded into the room at an alarming rate. Simultaneously, several more leaks opened up around the room, the water flowing in through broken pipes and shattered valves.

In no time at all, the floor was covered in several feet of water, which continued to rise.

"You've got to get out of here, before the whole thing collapses!" shouted Kale.

"We're not leaving you behind!" yelled Sir Nathan. "Tupolev, Grace! Get over there and start pushing the whale onto his belly. Squirrel, come help me pull from the other side!"

"No, there's no time! Leave me here and get out before it's too late! It's flooding too fast!"

"Nonsense!" shouted the Hero. "Goodness and honor will never abandon the innocent to die, not so long as there is a puff of breath in honor's lungs and the strength to fight in ... uh ... goodness' arms, or something."

Grace shot him a dark look and the Hero thought it might be better to practice his heroic proclamations a bit before getting back into all of his shouting and hollering.

\* \* \* \* \*

Deep, deep down, on the floor of the Sea of Silliness, there was a massive stone mountain of rock. It was covered with mechanical statues of mermaids, each holding a spear, or trident, or both.

For the past several weeks, a violent whirlpool had risen up out of the peak of the mountain. Suddenly, the whirlpool died, leaving the waters of the sea calm once more. After that, bubbles started to leak out of the massive stone, rising up out of countless nooks and crevices in the rock.

Kale the Whale's fortress was leaking, destroyed beyond repair. Water was gushing into the empty spaces inside. Anyone trapped within was doomed to drown.

A massive burst of bubbles, bigger than the biggest house, broke out of the top of the mountain. A small tremor shook the sea floor all around. In a dark silence found only deep beneath the waves of the deepest seas, the mountain fortress collapsed in on itself. A wash of mud and silt, stirred up from the sea floor by the catastrophe, hid the disaster in a cloak of blackness.

At the sea's surface, the water was calm after the violent twisting of the whirlpool had ceased. The water spout that had risen up out of the waters had collapsed and the dark cloud hovering above, deprived of its source of energy, drifted away on the winds and dissolved into the air.

Now, another bout of violent activity disturbed the waves as the massive bubbles from the collapsing fortress rose to the surface. The water churned and boiled. But soon, the bubbles were gone, leaving behind only peace and quiet.

For a long while, there was nothing but the rise and fall of the waves and the push and pull of the wind.

Then, right where the whirlpool had once spun and churned, the surface of the sea erupted upwards in a fine spray, glistening in the sunlight. A massive whale, gray and muscular, leaped out of the depths of the sea and high into the air. Free of the waters, he flipped a graceful somersault, then landed with a mighty splash.

As the frothy water around him calmed, the whale swam along the surface, slowly and cautiously, as if he were looking to see if there was any danger. He had escaped whatever odd catastrophe had occurred deep below. A creature as large and mighty as he was could survive by holding his breath long enough to get to the surface and safety.

Anyone else stuck down deep below wouldn't have been so lucky.

The whale swam silently along the surface. A fisherman sailing past grew depressed after seeing the miserable look on Kale's face as the whale thought about all the trouble and disaster he had caused. The massive creature's tears flowed freely into the sea.

The fisherman quickly turned his boat around, figuring it was better to not linger and see what was upsetting such a big creature.

If the fisherman had stuck around for a bit, he would have heard a voice coming from the whale. The voice would have sounded very muffled, as it said, "Phew! What did this beast eat for his last meal?! It stinks!"

Another muffled voice would have been heard answering the first, "And who taught him to brush his teeth? I can see several potential cavities right from where I'm sitting."

After a long pause, a tiny voice would have been heard squeakily asking, "Hey, I'm sitting right on his tongue. I wonder what I taste like."

The fisherman would have seen the whale roll his eyes and then most likely taken his own temperature as he sailed for home, figuring he was feverish and starting to hear things.

The whale answered the squeaky question as

best he could, considering he had a mouthful of two humans, a horse, and a squirrel, also while trying to prevent a flood of sea water rushing into his mouth and washing them right down his throat. "Okay you guysh, shettle down in there. And shomeone shay shomething to that shquirrel about not shwinging that shword around. I'm shcared he ish going to shlice off my tonshilsh."

"Fear not!" came a tiny, muffled, high-pitched reply. "The Hero of Mariskatania *never* drops his sword! He is – oops!"

The whale yelped in pain, knocking the riders in his mouth around violently and accidentally letting in a couple of thousand gallons of water.

"Sorry," said the high-pitched voice. "I keep forgetting I'm not actually the Hero. Here, Sir Nathan, you can have your sword back."

"You don't want it any more?" asked the knight.

"Nah. I'm thinking something a little bit more Huckle Nut-ish would be more my style. Besides, did you ever notice that that blade is so big, it's always dragging on the floor?"

There was a long awkward silence.

The knight's voice finally said, "Well, sure, for *you* it would. You're tiny and short. I'm the Hero of Mariskatania, brave and bold! Someone as courageous and heroic as me must be super tall! Uh ... right?"

There was another long, uncomfortable silence before the other three broke into a conversation about the best way to go about cleaning the flooded land of Mariskatania.

"Guys?" asked Sir Nathan, a note of concern in

his voice. "I am tall, right? Guys? Hello?"

Kale the Whale just chuckled as the others ignored the knight. With his massive tail driving him steadily along, the whale pointed himself at the shores of the Sea of Silliness and the lands of Mariskatania beyond. He softly hummed a tune and thought about a multi-legged contraption he could build, powered by FlibbertyJibbits and capable of draining away all the flood waters drowning Mariskatania. He just needed to get his flippers on one hundred and three sponges, nine buckets, a couple of bales of hay, and a sack full of cat litter.

Off in the distance, a colorful sailboat drifted lazily along on the light breeze. It was stuffed to overflowing with ogres, half of which were frantically bailing water out of the boat while the other half were frantically bailing water *into* the boat in the firm belief the best way not to sink and drown in the Sea of Silliness was to completely empty it of water.

\* \* \* \* \*

# ABOUT THE AUTHOR

Mark Smith lives in a small town in the Midwest and has enjoyed the creative outlet of writing since a young age. The author's first book, Sir Nathan and the Quest for Queen Gobbledeegook, was originally written as a silly romp through a land of adventure for the author's young nieces and nephews. Now it has been rewritten and edited for a general release, aimed at other children like the author's 10 year old son and for those young at heart.

The author's second book, Sir Nathan and the Troublesome Task, continues the adventure of the Hero of Mariskatania. It seems like someone is always getting kidnapped and this time, Sir Nathan has to put up with help that he does not want.

Sir Nathan must ride to the rescue of Mariskatania again in the third book, Sir Nathan and the Clammy Calamity, but has a bit of a difficult time doing his job when he finds himself suffering from dampened derring-do.

The author really, really, really, really, really, really hopes you like his Somewhat Silly Stories and hopes you share them with friends and family.